RED, WHITE, AND BLUEBERRY MUFFIN MURDER

MURDER IN THE MIX 35

ADDISON MOORE

MURDER IN THE MIX

ADDISON MOORE

Red, white, and Blueberry Muffin Murder

BOOK DESCRIPTION

My name is Lottie Lemon, and I see dead people. Okay, so I rarely see dead people. Mostly I see furry creatures of the dearly departed variety, aka dead pets, who have come back from the other side to warn me of their previous owner's impending doom.

It's the Fourth of July, the festivities at Honey Lake are high, the sun is hot, and murder is afoot. Not only are Noah and Everett in dire straits with the mob, but the three of us have stumbled into a double homicide. And by the looks of it, Carlotta and Charlie's nemesis might have bitten the big one, too. Evie is making her daddy insane with worry when she sets her sights on a college boy, and my mother and her wily boyfriend are walking a tightrope when it comes to the law.

The Fourth of July in Honey Hollow is shaping up to be explosive.

Lottie Lemon has a brand new bakery to tend to, a budding romance with perhaps one too many suitors, and she has the supernatural ability to see the dead—which are always harbingers for ominous things to come. Throw in the occasional ghost of the human variety, a string of murders, and her insatiable thirst for justice, and you'll have more chaos than you know what to do with.

Living in the small town of Honey Hollow can be murder.

LOTTIE

My name is Lottie Lemon, and I see dead people. Okay, so rarely do I see dead people. Mostly I see furry creatures of the dearly departed variety who have come back from the other side to warn me of their previous owner's impending doom. But right now, the only thing I'm seeing is a plate full of hot dogs stacked on top of one another like a pyramid.

"I can't take another bite," I call out in agony after eating five in a row—bun and all.

Five.

"Sure, you can, Lot," Carlotta calls out while dancing from

side to side as she shoves another hot dog into her mouth and, God as my witness, the entire thing fits, and yes, the bun is in on the fun.

It's late afternoon on the Fourth of July, and it seems every person in Honey Hollow—heck, every person in all of Vermont—is down at Honey Lake. The weather has been hot and humid all day, as the sun spears us with its summertime rays.

The air is scented from a thousand grills going at once, and it's a little smoky because of it. An entire sea of flags and buntings is set out in every direction the eye can see. There is even a smattering of red, white, and blue top hats, and pinwheels with the pattern of the flag on them floating around in the crowd. And on the north side of the lake they're barraged with their own unique crowds as the Garage Sale at the Lake event takes place. It's basically a giant thrift shop that has descended on Honey Lake, and it's been a huge hit with everyone who comes across it.

I've already picked up a couple sets of Depression era glass goblets, an enamel mixing bowl, and a vintage Barbie for Lyla Nell. There's also an outdoor rug I had my eye on that would go perfectly on the porch. I've been trying to create a reading nook out there, and if that rug is still available next time I head that way, that beauty is mine.

Honey Lake is drop-dead gorgeous this time of year with its cobalt water, sandy banks, the lake view houses on the south end, and the woods that line the northern edge. The water is teeming with every watercraft known to man, and there are throngs of people in their bathing suits lounging along the shorelines. But it's the scent of fresh grilled hot dogs that's sending everyone's senses into overdrive as they line up to buy them from the vendor putting on the spectacle at hand.

The yearly hot dog eating competition has just gotten underway and there must be at least thirty participants. Person-ally, I would never have signed myself up for the digestion-based fun, but my birth mother, Carlotta, signed up more than a handful of people and I was one of them.

"Lemon." Everett takes a moment from his own noshing fest to look my way. He almost always calls me by my surname, and I always get a little giddy when he does just that. Although right now I'm more nauseous than I am giddy. "Don't worry. I'll do my best to secure the win. And I'll pass the prize along to you. Why don't you go down and hang out with Lyla Nell?"

Judge Essex Everett Baxter just so happens to be my husband. When we married over a year ago, it was technically just a business arrangement so he could secure his trust fund, but we never dissolved the union, and well, later on I decided we should give our romantic relationship another shot—so here we are, holy matrimony and all.

Everett has black hair, cobalt eyes, hardly ever smiles, and has been known to garner more than his fair share of female attention. He's arrestingly handsome and his body is put together in all the right ways just like the Good Lord intended.

"*I'll* win that prize for you, Lot," Noah groans as if he were on his deathbed.

And judging by the fact he's already on his second platter, I'd say that deathbed scenario isn't all that far off. Each platter contains fifteen hot dogs—buns included—and whoever can eat the most in ten minutes is crowned the Hot Dog King or Queen of Honey Hollow. Not only that, but the Hog Dog House right here in town is giving the winner a free hot dog every day for the rest of the year.

"Don't bother," I tell Noah as I contemplate my next bite. "I don't think I'll eat another hot dog ever again after today. I'll go get the baby so we can cheer the two of you on."

Detective Noah Corbin Fox happens to be the father of the baby in question. Our sweet Lyla Nell will be four months old this month. Everett is every bit as much her father as Noah is. Noah and I were pretty serious, but since we had a few rocky starts and stops I thought I'd see if there was anything left with Everett, and boy, was there ever.

Both Noah and Lyla Nell have dark hair that turns red at the tips, deep dimples, and daring green eyes. Noah, too, is a looker that women can't seem to get enough of. I'm not sure how I got so lucky to have not one but two great men in my life, but I'll be forever grateful I met the both of them.

"Lottie!" Lily, my faithful employee from the Cutie Pie Bakery and Cakery, runs up holding a wide-brimmed hat to her head. Lily Swanson is a pretty brunette who can be more than a bit pithy when she wants to. "We're running out of blueberry muffins. I'm going to ask the kitchen staff to make as many batches as the ovens can handle. Why didn't we think to frost them before?"

She takes off before I can so much as give her a thumbs-up.

I've never frosted a muffin before, but when Mayor Nash, aka my biological father, asked me to cater a few desserts for the celebration down at the lake today, he specifically requested I bring along some frosted blueberry muffins. He said his mother used to make them with white vanilla frosting. So in honor of the grandmother I never met, I did just that. Actually, I took it a step further by adding some red and blue sprinkles to each one. And I have to admit, they look adorably festive.

Speaking of grandmothers, a week ago, my Grandma Nell's ghost came back from the other side and showed me a vision that set both my teeth and my very soul on edge. I saw Noah and Everett arguing, then a gunshot went off and Everett took three bullets to the chest. I saw his ghost lift right out of his body. Not only was that disconcerting in every way, but then Nell told me that I had the power to stop it.

When I asked Nell when this horrific vision was set to take place, she told me it would happen within the next month—and here we are, standing in that horrific window of time.

A shiver runs through me because I can feel the clock ticking away as we draw near to that fateful moment.

I look over at my handsome husband as he chugs a quick drink from his water bottle.

"Let's have a big wedding." The words blurt out of me without warning, and both Everett and Noah stop all movement as they look my way.

"What's that?" Everett tips his ear toward me as if he couldn't make out the words.

"I said let's have a big wedding. We never had a proper wedding. I say we tell everyone we know to keep next weekend open and we'll throw something together."

Everett inches back. "A week? Throw something together?"

Noah belts out a laugh. "Way to distract him, Lottie. I have this in the bag." He clears off the hot dogs on his platter and another platter miraculously turns up in its place with fifteen new hot dogs ready to go.

Everett shoots Noah a look. "I'm in, Lemon. Whatever you want."

He gets right back to work just as Carlotta chortles to the point where I think she might be choking.

"Way to go, Lot Lot!" she calls out from the other side of Noah. "You just cost Sexy and Foxy thirty seconds on the clock. Why don't you go down the line and propose to all the men here? That might give us girls the advantage. There are only three of us, and there's never been a Hot Dog Queen of Honey Hollow before."

I make a face at her. "Well, I won't be the queen. I'm out. It's up to you and Evie."

Evie lets out a hard groan from the other side of Carlotta before knocking the platter right off the table, thus disqualifying herself in the process.

"I hate everything!" Evie howls. "I'm never looking at a hot dog again as long as I live!"

The crowd lets out a few whoops and hollers at her declaration. It's mostly the teen scene that has gathered around to watch the spectacle.

Evie, *Everly*, Baxter is Everett's sixteen-year-old daughter that I adopted as my own last year. Her biological mother is a socialite who hid Evie from the world, more specifically from Everett, but thankfully, we found out about Evie, tracked her down, and now we're one big happy family.

Carlotta finishes chomping down another hot dog. "Don't just stand there, Lot. The men are gaining ground. Get to proposing, take off your top, offer everyone a free donut for a year as an incentive to quit! Do something. I want this win, Lot Lot."

"Don't listen to her. She's a nutjob," a female voice calls out from below and I spot my newly minted sister Carlotta, *Charlie*, Sawyer. Charlie and I are just about twins in every way with the same wavy caramel locks—hers is a touch darker—same hazel eyes, and the same ability to see right through to the other side.

Carlotta, our shared birth mother, is basically an older version of the two of us with a smattering of gray hair and wrinkles.

The three of us are actually something called transmundane, which is further classified as supersensual. There are many supernatural abilities that fall under the transmundane umbrella, but ours is the only one that can see the dead.

Charlie just came into my life a few months back, and as it turns out, she's my full-blooded sister, another product of the affair Carlotta had with Mayor Nash at the time.

Carlotta just so happened to name both Charlie and me after herself. My adoptive mother, Miranda Lemon, decided to call me Lottie, and that's all I've ever been known as. But when it was time to name my own daughter, I decided to name her Carlotta as well.

Call it delirium, altruistic thinking, or serendipity, but I unwittingly pulled my poor sweet daughter right into the Carlotta cult I was a part of. Although, just like me, no one will call my baby girl Carlotta. She'll go by the nickname I gave her, Lyla Nell.

I hold up the red paddle in front of me, formally disqualifying myself before making my way off the makeshift stage and taking a look at the contestants participating in the madness.

Aside from Everett, Noah, and Carlotta, I recognize Mayor Nash, Evie's old boyfriends, Conner and Kyle—yes, she had two, and at the very same time, although she's currently single, unless you count that college hunk she's been eyeing. And then there's Forest (my brother-in-law), Alex (Noah's brother), and Rooster Puddin' aka Carlotta's ex-boyfriend slash nemesis. Other than that, it's a sea of unrecognizable faces, all moaning and groaning as they shove one last hot dog into their mouths as an oversized clock counts down the last thirty seconds.

My eyes flit back to Rooster for a moment. He's the one that stole those briefcases that belonged to Noah and Everett—or technically to the mob bosses they had agreed to work with in exchange for protection from the hits they had on them.

Rooster waltzed into Honey Hollow last month after finishing a stint in prison. Apparently, he tricked Carlotta and Charlie into robbing a liquor store after hours while he supervised. He was essentially able to convince them that he owned the liquor store in question. Anyway, Carlotta and Charlie were furious and lied on the stand at his trial and landed him a nice stay at the Iron City Inn, Carlotta's words, not mine. And well, as fate would have it, he's come looking for revenge.

My sisters, Lainey and Meg, pop up—and in Meg's arms is the sweetest little four-month-old baby girl I ever did see.

"This is so exciting!" Lainey trills.

"Says you," Meg groans.

Meg has black hair and pale blue eyes and looks like a Goth princess with fishnet stockings paired with shorts. And Lainey pretty much shares my caramel-colored hair and hazel eyes despite the fact we're not blood-related.

These happen to be the sisters I was raised with. I came into a few more sisters and a brother when I found out that Mayor Nash was my father. It's been fun and interesting to watch my family expand in unconventional ways over the years.

Lyla Nell coos over at me in Meg's arms and I scoop her right up and plant a kiss on her forehead. She's wearing a frilly dress with red, white, and blue flowers printed all over it just for the occasion and looks every bit the pint-sized American beauty queen.

And bouncing in Lainey's arms is her little girl Josie, a blonde, amber-eyed cutie who was the first to crown my mother Glam Glam, her chosen moniker for her newly minted matriarchal position in life.

"Lyla Nell, have you been playing with your cousin Josie?" I lean over and land a kiss to the tip of Josie's nose and she breaks out into a giggle fit, causing Lyla Nell to do the same. "I can't believe she's going to be one next month!" I say and the glee melts right off my sister's face.

"Did you have to remind me?" Lainey makes a face at the thought. "It's all moving way too fast. First, she turns one, then she turns *twenty*-one and brings home a biker named Bruno. And the next thing you know, she'll be moving to Antarctica to study the effects greenhouse gasses have on the weather." A wailing sound emits from her. "I need another blueberry muffin." She stalks off just as the buzzer goes off and we look up to see an entire row of contestants who look more than a little green around the gills.

The tall blond man next to Carlotta is quickly crowned the Hot Dog King of Honey Hollow and rock music begins to blare over the nearby speakers as the festivities for the evening officially kick off.

"Look at that," Meg says, rocking her hip to mine. "That Clark guy won."

"What Clark guy?" I ask, squinting over at him as Mayor Nash places a large gold paper crown over the man's head. "Should I know who he is?"

Meg clucks her tongue. "You know him. He's the one who had that horrible home invasion break-in a few years back. It was the same year I left for Vegas."

Meg used to work the female wrestling circuit in Las Vegas as Madge the Badge. Now she works at the Honey Pot Diner, right next door to my bakery—in addition to working down at a gentlemen's club in Leeds, teaching exotic dancers their dicey moves. The pay is decent, and I think she likes the dicey setting, too.

"Oh, that's right," I say, bouncing Lyla Nell in my arms. "I think I remember something about that. It was pretty terrible."

Noah and Everett head our way, along with the winner and another man with dark curly hair.

"Lemon"—Everett pulls me in—"I'd love to introduce you to Bridger Douglas." He slaps the dark curly haired man on his back. The man looks classically handsome and stands a few inches shorter than Everett. "Bridger and I used to hang out back in the day."

Bridger laughs as he ticks his head back. "By *hang out*, he means barhop. I watched Everett pick up more women than should ever be legal. It was like watching a master at work. I was in awe. I could only hope to be so proficient in the female anatomy as this one."

Noah leans my way. "Precisely why you should dump him, Lot."

I laugh it off. "Nice to meet you, Bridger. I'm Lottie Lemon, Everett's wife."

The man's mouth rounds out. "I'm sorry, I had no idea." He

smacks Everett's arm. "You've finally been reeled in, huh? I'd say I was sorry to hear it, but it looks as if you caught a good one."

Noah nods. "She's smart as a whip and she bakes." He pats the winner on the back. "Congratulations, Clark. It's been a long time. Lottie, this is Clark Willoughby. He's the one responsible for the garage sale madness taking place at the lake."

Clark, the blond king, gives a jovial laugh. He's about the same age as Noah and Everett. I'm guessing mid-thirties. He has a kind look about him and a calm demeanor despite his ability to pack away an entire hog's worth of hot dogs.

"It's been a long time indeed, Noah. And yes, I've got a license to host the Garage Sale at the Lake event for the entire month of July. If it's a hit, I might extend the event through August. This character right here is helping me out."

Bridger nods. "That's right. I'm his partner in crime." He winks over at Clark. "I manage the Willoughby Antique and Thrift Shops. He's got three in the neighboring towns."

"Ooh, I love antiques and thrift shops," I say. "I'll have a brand new home to furnish soon. I might just stop by."

It's true. Last October, my house burned down, along with Everett's, and since we were next-door neighbors, we're building one big mega house over both properties. And I'm happy to say construction is about halfway finished.

Clark pats his belly as he looks to Noah. "And if I remember correctly, it's your girlfriend who owns the bakery."

"That's right," Noah says, wrapping an arm around my waist. "Lottie owns and runs the Cutie Pie Bakery and Cakery. And this is our daughter, Lyla Nell."

I nod. "I have a booth set up right behind me. If you can squeeze anything else into your stomach, you should try one of my patriotic blueberry muffins. They're turning out to be quite the hit."

Clark laughs as his crown sits askew. "I sure can, and I'm off to do that right this minute." He takes off and I note Everett's friend, Bridger, is looking at Noah and me with a look of morbid confusion. I'm guessing that confusion has to do with that whole wife-girlfriend thing. Believe me, it confuses me, too.

"You know"—Bridger lifts a finger—"I'm in the mood for a muffin myself." He zips off with a wild look in his eyes.

I'm about to suggest we join them just as Carlotta and Mayor Nash join *us*.

"Good show, gentlemen." Mayor Nash gives a mock bow our way before looking at me. "The Garage Sale at the Lake looks as if it's going to be a great hit. Just so you know, your bakery is welcome to keep the booth open for the rest of the month and sell those blueberry muffins if you'd like."

Mayor Nash has light hair, mostly gray, light eyes, and a mischievous smile he wears nonstop. Now that he's officially divorced from his wife, he and Carlotta have had a thing. It's sort of an open relationship that for some reason works for the two of them. It's a little strange knowing my biological parents are essentially together now—even if it does involve a third party on occasion.

"Thank you," I tell him. "The booth at the lake was such a hit last month, I don't mind taking you up on it." Last month, Honey Hollow underwent a beautification project that essentially shut down all of Main Street for thirty painful days and caused a financial pickle for almost every one of the businesses on it, including mine. But Mayor Nash allowed us to set up booths at Honey Lake, and that more than helped take the financial sting off. Having both my bakery *and* a booth at the lake would be a win. I don't think the staff will mind since it's temporary.

Mayor Nash nods to Noah. "Detective, there hasn't been a homicide in weeks here in Honey Hollow. Any hope of keeping things that way for the foreseeable future?"

Noah winces. "I'll do my part, but I can't control the world."

"So what keeps you busy down at the precinct when business is slow?" Mayor Nash says the word *business* with air quotes.

"There has been a string of ATM robberies all around Vermont for the past six months. It's very strange. The security footage always seems to malfunction when this person steps up to the plate. He or she is heavily disguised, baseball cap, dark jacket, nothing that isn't worn by every third customer. We can't seem to catch them. But we've been marking bills as of late, and hopefully we'll make some headway soon enough."

I consider this a moment. "Noah, those bills are destined to get back into circulation. How are you going to trace them?"

"When they make their way back to the banks. It's been hard for the banks to log the numbers, but at this point it's a necessary evil."

"Well"—Mayor Nash flashes his pearly whites—"I'd better go mingle." He winks. "I love it when all of my constituents are in one place. After an hour or two of power schmoozing, I can take the rest of the month off." He dissipates into the crowd just as a large spotted cat leaps from behind Carlotta and lands on Everett's shoulder.

A wild yelp shrills from me as I quickly give Lyla Nell to Carlotta.

"Get her to safety!" I shout as I give Everett a few smacks on the chest, trying to scare the spotted beast away. It's at least twice the size of my own cats, a couple of sweet Himalayan brothers named Pancake and Waffles, and it looks ten times as ornery as they could ever be.

"Lemon?" Everett twists his head as he offers a curious look my way.

"Don't stop, Lot," Noah says. "I'll join in on the beating if you want."

"Please do!" I howl as I give Everett a hard shove to the arm, trying to knock that prehistoric looking feline off of him. Everett is playing it way too cool if you ask me, but then, that's Everett's modus operandi in life—he's cool as a cucumber no matter what the circumstances. "Go *away*!" I shout at the steely beast with hard yellow eyes. "My word, you probably have rabies!"

"*Lemon?*" Everett's brows furrow as he examines me.

Noah laughs so hard he's in stitches. "I don't know what you did to tick her off, but keep up the good work, Everett. Don't worry, Lot. I've got a great divorce lawyer who can untangle this knot he's roped you into."

I spot a shovel leaning up against the stage that was built posthaste over the weekend, snatch it up, and swing it at Everett. He narrowly ducks out of the way in time to evade a decapitation, but I come at him again and knock him right over the top of the head this time.

"*Oops*, sorry!" I shout as Noah breaks out into a spontaneous applause.

"Don't be afraid to aim below the belt, Lot."

"Judas Priest," Everett says as he comes up from his fancy duck and evade maneuver. He grabs the neck of the shovel, so I drop it and try to grab the cat with both hands, but it disappears into thin air, and I end up inadvertently strangling Everett instead.

Noah shakes his head. "I take it the big wedding is off, too."

"Lemon?" Everett grabs ahold of my wrists and kisses each of my hands. "Are you having an allergic reaction to something you ate?"

"No, I was trying to get the cat off your shoulder. It about scared the living daylights out of me."

"What cat?" Everett asks, glancing behind him.

A horrible moan evicts from my throat. "You didn't see it either, did you, Noah?"

He shakes his head.

"That can only mean one thing," I pant as I look out at the murky crowd. "Murder is afoot."

LOTTIE

*T*he sun sears us one last time as it begins to sink behind the evergreens in the distance.

I dust off poor Everett and haul him back to my booth where I've procured an icepack for his head.

Noah just finished telling Lily and Suze, his mother, all about my shovel swatting ways. Of course, he left out the tidbit about the long deceased cat. Not many people know about my ability to pry into the afterlife, and I'd like to keep it that way.

For as long as I can remember, I've been seeing the dead—mostly tiny furry creatures that have come back to help their old owners. They used to be a sign that nothing more than a sprained ankle would befall the person who cherished them, but for the last couple of years it almost always means death. And now, either the ghost of an animal or a person comes back to help me solve the murder of someone who loved them very much.

Suze shakes her head at Everett after hearing of the flat nose travesty.

"You should run, Essex," she tells him.

Everett typically goes by his middle name because he's more comfortable with it, but the women he's bedded have taken to calling him by his first name as if it were a door prize. Although Suze doesn't qualify for that door prize herself, it's never stopped her from utilizing his proper moniker.

He should run?

I shake my head at her not-so sage advice.

Suffice it to say, Suze Fox has never been a member of the Lottie Lemon Fan Club. Suze is a larger woman with short blond hair that swoops low over her eyes. She's been helping me out at the bakery and, along with Lily, she's become a star employee.

Suze is also transmundane, although she's loath to admit it. She's what's called a beguiler, a person who can entice both the elements and people into doing her bidding—albeit she has no interest in utilizing her powers. Either that or she's not very good at it. Probably both.

"You should run, too, Noah," she tells him despite the fact he's happily bouncing Lyla Nell in his arms. Coincidentally, Suze has about as much interest in her granddaughter as she does with me. "It's just a matter of time before she clobbers you both in your sleep. And then she'll hire that fancy lawyer that spared you a prison sentence, Essex, and she'll get away with *murder*. It's her specialty, you know."

"She's got your number, Lot," Carlotta says, poking around at the bevy of desserts I've brought along for today's festivities. Mayor Nash is picking up the tab, so everything is free to the general public while they last. Mostly I've brought chocolate chip cookies, brownies, and those frosted blueberry muffins. There's a huge vinyl banner hanging above the booth that reads *Cutie Pie Bakery and Cakery, best cakes and cookies in town!* I just had the banner made last month after Mayor Nash had the sidewalks on Main Street dug up and nearly buried my finances.

"I haven't gotten away with murder." I roll my eyes. Okay, so to the untrained eye, it might seem as if I've done just that. I've run into a rather large number of corpses over the last two years, and suspiciously each one happened to have one of my desserts on or near their person.

Carlotta snorts. "And not only will Lot off Foxy and Sexy, she'll stuff one of these blueberry muffins into their pie holes."

Lily and Suze laugh it up.

Suze leans toward Carlotta. "She's not only a master serial killer, she's a master at marketing her bakery as well. I believe they refer to that as killer marketing skills."

The three of them share another set of wild cackles. I'm about to say something when I spot the hot dog king himself arguing with that man I met earlier, Bridger Douglas, the manager of his shops.

Noah and Everett step my way as they look in the same direction.

Everett nods to Noah. "Do you think we should head over and break things up?"

Noah blows out a breath. "I'd hate to see a fistfight break out."

"That's right," Carlotta says. "If it's not you and Sexy exchanging blows, then it's not all that entertaining."

Lyla Nell slaps Noah on the cheeks with both hands and I laugh at the sight.

"Easy, you," I say, pulling one of her tiny hands my way and kissing it.

"On second thought"—Carlotta says as she narrows a mean stare at someone or something over my shoulder—"I might be moved to kill myself."

I glance back just as Charlie and Rooster pop into our midst.

"You are a liar and a thief!" Charlie shouts right into his face. "Go on and head to the police. See if I care. But let the record show, I will find a way to put you six feet under if you so much as try to take me down. Carlotta and I are starting a new life in Honey Hollow. Why don't you find a cliff to swan dive off? We don't need you hanging around and making noise."

Rooster chuckles, and it only seems to infuriate my sister all the more.

Shelby Hardy Tuttle, aka Rooster Puddin', is tall, barrel-chested, has salt and pepper hair, a maniacal look in his eyes, and he also has one of those pointed, twirly mustaches that gives him a classic villain appeal. Somehow he's gotten into bed with Manny Moretti of the Moretti crime family.

The Morettis hail from New Jersey, and they've been poking around Vermont, causing trouble for the two crime families we already have to put up with here, the Canellis and the Lazzaris.

Fun fact: Carlotta is intimately familiar with both heads of those families, Jimmy Canelli and Luke Lazzari.

What can I say? The woman gets around.

"Call me every name in the book." Rooster rocks back on his heels and laughs.

"I'll call ya heartless," Carlotta shouts over at him. "You're a monster."

Rooster has donned a black and white striped suit and has on a pair of patent leather shoes to go along with it. He reeks of new money from head to toe, which doesn't surprise me seeing that he stole a briefcase full of money just a week ago.

Apparently, when Everett went to Luke Lazzari for protection from the hit Jimmy Canelli took out on him, Luke wanted him to wash a suitcase full of money as a litmus test of some sort. They've already given him a few terms. And Everett has already said he'd think about going easy on any mobsters who passed through his courthouse. But knowing Everett the way I do, he isn't going to go easy on anyone.

Rooster points down at a platter of my sweet treats and looks at Suze. "Box up one of everything for me, Sweet Cheeks." He pulls a hundred dollar bill out of his pocket and hands it to her.

Suze scoffs. "You don't have to pay. Everything is f—"

"For *sale*," Lily says as she takes his money and proceeds to box up a bevy of cookies and muffins for him.

I'm not saying a word. That briefcase of Everett's that Rooster stole just so happened to be laden with one hundred dollar bills like the one he produced.

Last month when I found out that Noah and Everett were not only flirting with the mob but about ready to be indoctrinated into their crooked club by way of those nefarious briefcases, I was furious that they had kept things from me for as long as they did. So I stole their briefcases and locked them in the yacht Everett has parked in the marina.

But unbeknownst to me, Carlotta had given Rooster a copy of the key to the boat and he had been spending the night on *The Lucky Lemon*. Yes, as fate would have it, that's the name of the luxury yacht.

Anyway, not only did Rooster swipe Everett's briefcase full of cash, he stole the one that Noah had full of coke—as in cocaine. I guess Jimmy Canelli wanted Noah to make a delivery to one of his men. Noah knew moving drugs was enough ammo for Jimmy to blackmail him into doing his bidding forever so he never did the deed. And Everett never washed the money for Luke Lazzari either.

Once Rooster got ahold of both briefcases, he took off for his new pal, Manny Moretti, and I'm not entirely sure what happened after that.

Manny was arrested and made bail just as fast, and he didn't have the briefcases when the cops came looking. It's all sort of murky from there.

One thing that's clear as a bell is that the hits are back on for Noah and Everett unless they can get the mob bosses their pricey loot back—or meet the terms as far as the washing and the delivery go. Things could get very ugly if one of those two things doesn't happen.

Hey? I bet that's how Everett ends up taking three bullets to the chest at some point this month.

Suddenly, the vision Nell gave me makes perfect sense.

Rooster sheds a greasy smile my way. "Don't you worry, missy. Your sister and your mama aren't gonna hurt a hair on my chinny chin chin. They'll both be too busy getting processed by the Ashford County Sheriff's Department." He crows out a laugh that sounds suspiciously like the animal whose moniker he's borrowing.

"I'm not doing any time," Carlotta bellows at him. "In fact, I'll do time over your dead body."

"You'll be serving *life* when I get through with you," he shouts right back. "You're a mean witch, Carlotta. Sorry, Charlie." He winks over at my sister. "But you're both going to pay in spades for what you've done to me."

"Done to you?" Carlotta's face turns tomato red. "You mean what you've done to *us*. Get out of this town, you two-bit moron. I *hate* you, Rooster. And I hope you die!"

He laughs in her face. "I'll be headed down to speak to the sheriff myself come morning." He winks over at Carlotta and Charlie just to add kindling to the fire. "Have a great time tonight, little darlings. It's gonna be your last night of freedom. Your sins have come home to roost, ya hear?" he shouts over at them before taking the box of my sweet treats that Lily gives him, and I watch as he heads right over to where my mother, the saint who raised me, and her boyfriend Wiley stand.

Wiley just so happens to be Noah's look-alike of a father.

How I wish he were as law-abiding as Noah.

The three of them get right into a conversation before taking turns to look back this way while shaking their heads in dismay.

Noah groans, "I wish my father weren't such a magnet for trouble."

Carlotta lets out a hoot of a laugh. "Are you gonna just stand there, Lot, and let him bad talk your mama like that? Come to think of it, Miranda Lemon's middle name is trouble. That's why she sold the inn to those two ditzes and gave all the money to Wiley."

Any trace of a smile melts off my face. It's true. Mom sold her B&B to a couple of ditzes, but I managed to get back one half of it by way of humiliating myself for one of the ditzes in question. That would be Cressida Bentley, Evie's bio mother.

Cressida thought having me do a paternity reveal on a sleazy talk show was a fair exchange for her piece of the B &B, and lucky for my mother, she was right. The other half belongs to an airhead named Cormack Featherby—and oddly enough, it's Cormack who is now hosting that sleazy talk show.

"Cormack," Noah says as she crops up with her blonde hair freshly blown out, a tiny red dress on and matching heels.

"Where is Big Boss?" She gives a wild look around. "Where's that hunk of burning love that I'm gonna set the night on fire with?"

Carlotta shakes her head at the woman. "Cormack, your screws are loose. You're looking Foxy right in the eye."

For as long as I've been with Everett, Cormack has been crushing hard on Noah. She's practically obsessed, but as of late she's been pushing her affections on another poor unfortunate soul.

"I'm talking about Rooster," Cormack says as she cranes her neck past me. "There he is, talking to Lolita's mother." She zips off in their direction.

Cormack can't seem to get my name straight no matter how

many years I've known her. I'm still not sure if it's a tactic to get under my skin or if she's genuinely that ditzy.

We watch as she sashays her way over and wraps her arms around Rooster's new suit. She's partial to money, and now that he has oodles of it, she's more than interested in keeping company with him.

"No loss there," Noah says as he dots a kiss to Lyla Nell's cheek. "It's going to get dark soon, Lot."

"You're right. I'd better feed her before Keelie takes her back to the house." My best friend Keelie offered to watch Lyla Nell for me this evening so I could stay and monitor the bakery stand and catch the fireworks show as well. Keelie has a baby boy that's about to turn one, and Lyla Nell just loves little Bear to pieces.

I take the baby from Noah, toss a small blanket over my shoulder, and begin to nurse. I spot Everett looking sternly at someone just past me and I follow his gaze.

"What's going on?" I ask just as Noah looks that way as well and we see the hot dog king arguing with a lanky brunette. She's fit and trim, as evidenced by those short shorts she's got on, and she's wearing a white beaded beach cover-up that shimmers in the evening light.

Noah sucks in a quick breath through his teeth. "That's Clark and his wife, Sammy."

"Sammy Willoughby," Everett says it low like a whisper. "Once in a while when I think I hear a noise outside the house, my mind drifts right back to that violent break-in they had."

"It was terrible," Noah says. "The intruder knifed them up pretty bad. They're both lucky to be alive."

We watch as she shakes her head at him and shoots him a lethal look before taking off.

"That didn't end well," I say.

"They're estranged," Everett offers. "I know for a fact she tried to retain Fiona as counsel a few months ago. For what, I don't know."

Fiona Dagmeyer was Everett's defense attorney who helped him out of a legal tussle a few months back.

Both Noah and Everett were arrested for stealing Florenza Canelli's body from the morgue. It was Flo's idea. She came back as the ghost to solve her own murder investigation and got uppity when she saw the coffin her family picked out was the wrong color, not to mention what they were about to do to her hair, and that horrid dress they wanted her to spend eternity in. She threatened us until we complied, and, well, things ended badly.

"Maybe there's an impending divorce?" I ask with mild curiosity.

A loud yowl of a cat comes from behind and I jump as I turn. And there he or she is, that ghostly spotted Bengal cat slinks by, pausing to wink my way before traipsing right off into the lake.

"Oh dear," my voice warbles as I say it. "I saw that ghost of a cat again. Something very bad is about to happen."

Noah tips his head back. "Everett, please stay with Lottie. I'm going to call for backup. It's a busy night. No one will bat an eye." He takes off just as my mother and Wiley pop up with a blonde woman between them.

"Lottie, Everett," Mom sings my name and her blonde curls bounce loose over her shoulders. My mother is gorgeous and sweet and has evidently forgotten to age. "I was talking to my good friend Betsy here, and she says she knows Everett from the courthouse."

"Hello, Betsy." Everett offers her a gentle nod. "How are you doing tonight?"

"I'm great." The young blonde bites down on her lower lip as she looks his way. She looks pretty taken by him, and truthfully, I can't blame her.

"Lemon, this is Betsy Monroe, one of the stenographers down at the courthouse."

"Nice to meet you," I say, holding out my hand as best I can while hiding the baby.

Everett nods her way. "Betsy used to work closely with one of my colleagues at the courthouse, Judge Gorman. How's he doing, anyway?" He poses the question her way.

Betsy swallows hard, her cheeks flooding with color. "I don't know." She clears her throat. "I haven't spoken with him since he moved to Europe." She gives a stiff sniff, and I can tell there's more to this story than meets the eye. I bet they had a thing, or a *fling*. And I bet the rat broke her heart, too.

Mom gives a short applause. "Oh, that's wonderful. It's such a small world, isn't it? Betsy's mother is a very good friend of mine, Lottie. Henrietta and I go way back. She's in charge of the bowling league I used to belong to." Her mouth falls open as she looks to Wiley. "We should take up bowling."

Wiley's dimples dig in deep and he looks exactly like Noah in the process.

"You know I've got a lot on my plate," he tells her as he looks our way. "We're organizing our fall book festival. There are a lot of details to work out. You wouldn't believe the logistics involved."

Mom smiles. "We're hosting a very big to-do at the B&B this September. Stay tuned for details." She smiles over at Betsy. "I bet a smart girl like you just loves to read. I've got a couple of my romances in the back of my car. I'll go get a few copies for you and you can pass them around the courthouse. I'll be right back." She takes off and Wiley hikes a brow our way. "I'd better have a few words with Rooster while the little woman is away. I'll see you folks later for the fireworks show."

Everett growls and catches him by the arm. "You have no business with Rooster. You'll stay away, if you know what's good for you."

"The hell I will." Wiley breaks free and disappears into the crowd.

"Wow," Betsy marvels as she feasts her eyes on Everett. "You're just as tough outside of the courthouse as you are in it."

A dry laugh pumps from Everett. "I'd like to think I'm fair in both scenarios."

The sound of two men shouting steals our attention as we look to our right. There stands the hot dog king once again with a medium-build man with dark hair and a light windbreaker on. He's saying something to Clark and shaking his finger at him. They don't look nearly as angry as Clark did with his soon-to-be ex-wife, but they look serious and their voices are hiking above the noise. That says something right there.

"There he goes again." Betsy shivers as she says it. "Clark can't go ten steps these days without upsetting someone." Her eyes harden over the man as if he's upset her as well. "Excuse me, those frosted muffins are calling my name. It was nice meeting you, Lottie. You're a very lucky woman. I know for a fact you're the one who stole Judge Baxter's heart. The rest of my colleagues aren't very happy with you."

We share a warm laugh as she takes off to pick up one of my desserts, and I spot that celestial cat again as he walks right over the platters laden with my cookies and brownies.

"Everett, that cat is practically taunting me," I say just as Lyla Nell falls asleep on my chest.

"Don't worry," he says, wrapping an arm around me. "I'll be with you during every moment tonight."

"Thank you. I just wish we could circumvent this."

"Me too."

Keelie shows up, along with her husband, Bear, and I get Lyla Nell's things together and put her in their car. Keelie and I've been closer than sisters since preschool.

"Hey, Bear," Everett says. "Are you ready to do that thing we talked about?"

"Got it set for tomorrow. Are you ready?"

"We'll be there." He nods.

Keelie promises to watch over my peanut as if she were her own and they take off just as darkness settles around us.

"Everett, can I ask what thing you and Bear will be doing tomorrow?"

"You can ask." A smile twitches on the corners of his lips as he wraps his arms around me and holds me tight. "But I can't tell you a thing. You'll have to be there with everyone else to see it." He lands a kiss to my lips.

"*Ooh*, a surprise. I like that."

Everett and I get to the shoreline, along with the rest of the crowd, as the fireworks begin.

Noah finds us and wraps an arm around my shoulders while Everett holds me at the waist. We watch as one spectacular firework after the other explodes high above Honey Lake.

Patriotic music blares from the speakers as the black sky ignites in bursts of red, white, and blue fireworks that bloom like fiery flowers against the velvet night.

The show goes on for what feels like hours, but in truth it's only been about thirty minutes.

"I wish this would last forever," I say as the three of us tip our heads to the sky and watch our world transform with magical flares in every shape and size.

The grand finale hits and the ground shakes as the fireworks detonate like bombs overhead. It's one boom after another, so loud and deep, the sound ricochets through your chest as the sky lights up as bright as noonday with the majestic display. And then in a whisper it's over and a wild applause takes over from one end of the lake to the other.

"That was wonderful," I cheer along with the rest of the crowd. "I can't wait until Lyla Nell gets to watch this with us. Speaking of daughters, has either of you seen Evie?" I give a quick look around, to no avail.

"She's with the teen scene, Lot," Carlotta shouts from a little farther down on the sand. "Don't you remember how you spent your Fourth of Julys as a teenager?"

"I spent them alone because Bear was out cheating on me," I tell her. It's true. I dated Keelie's hubby way back when, and he was pretty much a cheat through and through. He's since changed his ways and married my bestie. I'm about to tell Noah and Everett that I much prefer these days to those when I see that spotted giant cat traipsing past me, glowing a strange shade of pale blue, looking every bit the ghost he is.

"It's here again, the cat," I say as I follow along, bringing Noah and Everett with me.

Noah steps in close. "Do you have Ethel with you?"

"No. I have you and Everett with me—not to mention I knew I'd be with Lyla Nell all day." Ethel is the pet name I gave to the Glock handgun Noah and Everett teamed up to buy me a while back so that I could protect myself while in those homicidal predicaments I keep landing in. I hardly bring her anywhere anymore because of the baby. Babies and handguns just don't mix, nor do I care to make them.

We head toward the north end of the lake where it's markedly darker, notably colder as well, right into the area where the garage sale tents have been sealed up for the night. I run up ahead of the two of them, trying not to lose that sneaky specter, and trip over an old towel or something equally as soft. I fall onto the sand and roll right into the water.

"Gah!" I crawl on all fours until Everett helps me up. "I lost it," I say as I crane my neck every which way, trying to spot the spooky cat. "What is that, anyway?" I head over and attempt to pluck up the towel, but it's not a towel at all.

Instead, a body rolls over and a familiar sandy face looks up at the sky with a vacant stare. Stuffed in his mouth is one of my blueberry muffins, and judging by the large crimson stain over his heart, he's not going to get a chance to finish it.

Clark Willoughby is dead.

A scream gets locked in my throat.

"That's him," I pant. "That's the hot dog king," I say, staggering backward until I trip over a rock and land on my rear, sitting on a log of some sort.

"Lottie," Noah pants, helping me up before giving the ground a double take. "Is that a shoe?"

I look down, and sure enough, a man's shoe is sitting straight up in the sand, and that was no log I was sitting on—that was his *leg*.

"Lemon, stand back," Everett says as he dashes over and pulls the man out of the water by his feet and we look down to see yet another body lying motionless in the night.

Noah checks for a pulse and shakes his head.

"Oh my goodness," I whisper.

"It's him, isn't it?" Noah pants out the words.

"That's right," Everett says. "It looks as if Rooster bit the big one, too."

LOTTIE

$\mathcal{M}$y chest bucks as I try my best not to let a shrill scream rip from my throat, but no sooner do I have the thought than a cry of terror goes off behind us.

We turn to find Sammy Willoughby visibly shaken as she looks down in horror at her husband.

"Clark?" The thin brunette looks our way as the whites of her eyes shine like shards, and that beaded cover-up she's wearing glitters like a thousand fallen stars. "That's Clark, isn't it?" She drops to her knees in front of him and another cry rips from her, this time alerting the rest of the lake to the tragedy.

Noah nods to Everett. "I'm calling this in. Take care of her."

Everett and I head toward the woman and do our best to calm her down.

"Who did this?" Sammy howls at the two of us. "Did you do this? Did he owe you money?"

"What? No," Everett says. "We stumbled upon the scene ourselves. Let's get you away from here. We could take you home if you like."

"That's my husband," she riots in his face. "I'm not going anywhere." She pushes past us, and to our horror she dives right onto Clark Willoughby's body and begins to wail.

"Geez," Noah shouts as both he and Everett do their best to wrestle her off.

The woman screams at the top of her lungs, her white beach cover-up now splotched with the blood of her husband.

"Let go of me." She elbows Noah in the gut and hauls off and clocks Everett with a right hook on the jaw.

Both men retreat as she falls over her husband's body once again.

"Clark! My dear Clark," she says his name over and over again and Noah plucks her off once more with what looks to be all his strength.

"You are contaminating evidence," he shouts right at her as he does his best to restrain her hands. "Now do you want me to cuff you? Because so help me God I will. You may not touch that man until the coroner gives you clearance. Do you understand me?"

A flood of sheriff's deputies race this way as red and blue flashing lights cut through the darkness.

Sammy gives a quick nod and takes a moment to glare over at the corpse. Gone is the blinding grief, replaced with what looks like outright hatred for the man.

"I'll leave him alone," she pants. "I promise."

A swarm of deputies covers the grounds, and soon both Clark and Rooster are surrounded.

"What's happening?" a female voice cuts above the chaos as Cormack enters our midst.

I look to Everett a moment.

Cormack was all over Rooster this last week. Seeing the man lifeless might be a real shock to her.

Mom and Wiley run up on her heels and Wiley lets out a hard groan as he takes a look in Rooster's direction.

"What the hell is going on?" he barks as he heads that way and we follow along with him. "Ah shoot." He gives Rooster's shoe a kick, much to the horror of the deputies in the vicinity.

"*Dad*," Noah barks as he gives his father a shove. "Don't touch the guy. He's dead, okay?"

"He's right." Mom pulls Wiley to the side. "Didn't Rooster say he was staying at the Evergreen Manor?"

"What?" I ask as I tug at her elbow. The Evergreen Manor is the king-size version of my mother's humble B&B and they're not too far from one another. It used to be that my mother would get the overflow from the Evergreen Manor as far as guests go, but once word got out my mother's B&B was amply haunted— and it is by way of four very friendly ghosts—well, as of late, the Evergreen Manor now gets my mother's overflow. "Why do you care where Rooster was staying?"

Her eyes linger over Wiley's a moment too long. "Lottie, I'm in the B&B business. If something happened to one of my guests, I'd like to be notified right away." She tucks a quick kiss to my cheek. "We'll talk soon."

A blonde steps up and Mom's mouth opens at the sight of her.

"Betsy." Mom pulls her in. "I'm so sorry. It's Clark, he's been killed. Along with this man who was a friend of my boyfriend's. Do you need any assistance? Would you like to stay at the B&B for the night?"

"No." The woman looks mildly confused—most likely because she has no idea why my mother is suddenly offering up lodging. "I'll be fine. What a tragedy, though." Her gaze darts to where

Clark lies and then a few feet over to where Sammy is holding herself while speaking to a deputy. "I'll be just fine, in fact." She sheds an eerie grin before it slides right off her face. "I'll see you at the courthouse, Judge Baxter." She nods to the rest of us before taking off into the night.

"That was weird," I whisper to my mother. "Did she have some connection to Clark?"

Mom nods. "She mentioned they were friends. We'll see you all later."

Wiley grabs her by the hand and the two of them zip right out of here.

A rustling sound garners our attention and we find Cormack on her knees with her hand deep in Rooster's pockets.

"*Hey*," Noah shouts as he quickly pulls her way. "What the heck has gotten into everyone tonight? What are you doing? What's in your hand, Cormack?"

"*Nothing.*" She bites the air between them as she gives Noah a hard shove to the chest, and it's enough to make both Everett and me inch back with surprise.

Cormack typically venerates Noah as if he were a deity, so to see her try to rough him up is a sharp U-turn as far as her affection goes.

Way back when in high school, Wiley was married to Everett's mother, Eliza, making Noah and Everett stepbrothers for the duration of that short matrimonial mishap. Wiley basically pilfered Everett's wealthy mama and then proceeded to fake his own death.

Cataclysmically for us, he managed to perform the second resurrection known to mankind when he resurfaced in Honey Hollow and conned *my* mother into selling her B&B and giving him all her money. It sounds so ridiculous it's hardly believable, but it's true as gospel.

Anyway, back in high school, Cormack was dating Everett

when Noah thought he might want Cormack for himself, and Noah's been paying for it ever since—or so he believes.

Noah is still convinced that the only reason Everett stepped into the picture with me romantically was as a form of revenge.

I don't believe it in the least.

Everett leans her way. "Cormack," he grumbles her name. "You were looking for something. What was it?"

"Fine." Her brows dip as she frowns at the two of them. "Rooster said he was going to propose. He said he bought a diamond the size of my head, and I thought he was going to drop to one knee tonight."

"*Eww*," I say out loud without meaning to. Rooster and Cormack have at least thirty years between them. Not only that, but Rooster was the human equivalent of pond scum according to Carlotta and Charlie. "All right, so did you find the ring?"

"No," she snips my way. "Are you satisfied, Lorena? You get two happy endings and I get none." She growls before taking off.

I watch as she nearly trips over a rock before howling at the moon and dissolving into the shadows. I'm about to turn back to Noah and Everett when I spot Sammy huddled near the woods speaking to a man with a familiar looking face. He's holding her now, rubbing her back, whispering into her ear, and I can't help but think it looks intimate.

"Hey," I say. "That man who's talking to Mrs. Willoughby, I saw him having an exchange with Clark earlier. He was shaking his finger at him. It didn't look friendly."

"Good to know." Noah pulls out his phone and taps into it. "Just made a note. I'd better go over and introduce myself."

"Good," Everett says. "I'll head over to the Evergreen."

"What for?" Noah doesn't sound pleased with the idea.

I'm not too thrilled with it either.

Everett glances over his shoulder before leaning in and whispering, "That's where Rooster was staying. Don't make me do the math for you, Noah. For all we know, Naomi could be packing up his things right now. And we both know when Manny's place was searched last week it came up empty. Rooster's got those briefcases. And do you know what those briefcases have? Your prints, mine, and Lemon's. I need to get over there and make sure they don't end up in the wrong hands. And by *wrong hands*, I'm talking about the sheriff's department."

"I am the sheriff's department," Noah says, giving Everett a quick shove to the chest.

Everett growls as if he's about to draw blood. "And that means you and probably Ivy, and Lord knows who else, have to get a warrant before you can enter to look for clues if that man's death turns out to be a homicide. We both know it will. Do you think Ivy and the rest of the boys in blue are going to be fine with you popping two of Rooster's briefcases in the back of your truck? I don't think so either. Now if you'll excuse me, I need to commit a little breaking and entering to get us out of this never-ending pit you've landed us in."

Noah's eyes close a minute and he certainly doesn't contest the fact.

In Everett's mind, it all boils down to the fact I let Noah dictate whether or not we stole Florenza Canelli's body from the morgue. Everett was against the idea from the get-go. And well, now Noah blames himself for the endless amount of trouble we've drifted into as well.

"I'll go," Noah says as he gives a quick look around. "Ivy just got here. I'll let her handle things. Everett, why don't you take Lottie home? I'll tell Ivy there's an emergency with Lyla Nell or that Lottie needs me." He blows out a breath before pointing a finger at Everett. "You will let me handle this. I work for the sheriff's department. It makes sense. Besides, I don't want to see you get kicked off the bench again. Don't make me do the math for you," he says that last part mockingly as he repeats Everett's words back to him. "Now get out of here."

We're about to do just that when a tall redhead in a long navy jacket steps up.

"Well, well, the gang's all here." She flashes a short-lived smile my way.

"Detective," I say, offering my own brief curve of the lips.

Detective Ivy Fairbanks is Noah's partner down at the homicide division in Ashford. She's as brilliant as she is stunning, and I've suspected for some time that she's got the hots for Noah. Recently, I was proven right. Not that I want to be right about something like that. She was after Noah back when Noah and I were still together, and for that reason alone I don't care for her.

"I saw the blueberry muffin jammed in one of the victim's mouths." She nods to where Rooster is lying. "What did you do to that guy?"

"Nothing," I tell her. "I didn't touch either of them—well, at least not until after they were dead."

She sighs my way. "Why do I have a feeling we have different definitions of the word *dead*?"

The coroner gets our attention and calls Noah and Ivy over to where Rooster lies with his eyes wide open to the sky. His face is pale, washed blue from the moonlight and most likely his lack of blood flow. It's an unnerving sight.

"Check this out." The coroner casts his flashlight over a couple small red protrusions on the side of Rooster's arm. "Snake bite."

"Snake bite?" I look to Noah and he looks stumped by the revelation.

"It looks as if we'll have to run toxicology."

The sounds of footfalls speed in this direction, and both Carlotta and Charlie nearly trip right over Rooster as they come up panting.

"It's true, Mama," Charlie pants through a laugh. "He's dead," she sings, and the relief in her voice is palpable.

"He ain't dead." Carlotta walks over and gives Rooster a swift kick to the cookies and both Noah and Everett make a guttural noise as they cinch their knees a notch.

"*Carlotta*," Noah says it sharp, and yet there's a note of defeat in his voice because corpse-kicking season seems to have come a little early this year.

Carlotta pulls her foot back and does it again—twice as hard —and this time the coroner looks as if he's about to be sick himself, but Rooster doesn't move an inch.

Carlotta harrumphs. "Well, I still don't believe it. Shelby Hardy Tuttle aka Rooster Puddin' is pure evil. And Lord knows it takes a heck of a lot more than death to kill this kind of wickedness." She pulls Charlie close. "Come on, Cha Cha. I'll buy the whiskey. Good work, Lot. We'll toast to your gallant effort in trying to off him."

My mouth opens as I look to my sister. "Does that mean you'll drop the lawsuit?"

Charlie served me papers last week letting me know she was suing for half of everything Grandma Nell left me in her will.

Charlie's chest thumps. "My dreams might be coming true tonight, but yours are on ice until Mr. Sexy turns up the charm. I guess you can't have everything. Isn't that right, Noah?" She winks his way as the two of them take off.

Noah lowers his chin as he glares at Everett a moment. "Goodnight, Lottie," he says as he gives me a quick peck to the cheek. "Kiss Lyla Nell for me, would you?"

I nod as Everett and I say goodnight to both Noah and Ivy before heading home, and I text Noah regarding the faux emergency before we ever hit the driveway.

I'll be right there. Noah texts back.

And we know exactly where he'll be—the Evergreen Manor.

NOAH

The Evergreen Manor is set against a hillside with pine trees surrounding it like a fortress.

It more or less looks like Miranda's B&B but triple the size, and I'm sorry to say, an upscale version of it. In Miranda's defense, she was going for the cozy appeal right until Cormack and Cressida dug their gilded claws into that place and turned it into a bubblegum pink wonder. And whereas the B&B looks like a large mansion, the Evergreen Manor looks like an enormous prep school with its white Roman columns and the ivy crawling along the walls as if trying to hide its secrets. Inside, it's covered in dark wood paneling and smells like expensive perfume.

I spot Naomi Sawyer at the reception counter. That's Keelie's twin sister, same face, but Naomi is a brunette to Keelie's blonde. From what Lottie has told me, Naomi has never cared too much for her due to the fact Keelie loved Lottie so much. I can understand the jealousy to an extent, but now that everyone is older, and you would hope wiser, you'd think Naomi would be a little nicer to Lottie, but that's just not the case.

She's talking to someone, a woman with wavy hair, and when she turns to laugh, I see it's Charlie who has already beaten me to the punch.

What the heck is Charlie doing here?

She's not here to swipe those briefcases, is she?

She's a smart cookie. I wouldn't put it past her. But she's also smart enough to know those briefcases are trouble. And she's also friends with Naomi, so here's hoping she's here for a genuine gab session.

I clutch my hand tightly around the oversized duffle bag that I made the trip home to retrieve. The point of this operation is to get in and out with little to no one noticing me. And if they do, I don't want them to remember me as the man with two briefcases. I dug up the biggest gym bag I could find, and I'm pretty sure they'll both fit inside nicely.

I'm about to head toward the entry when a familiar looking couple steps out of the foyer, and I jump behind a large backlit sign as they pass by.

Holy smokes.

I close my eyes a moment. It's Dad and Miranda.

What the hell are they doing here?

Miranda adjusts her skirt and fiddles with the buttons on her blouse, and suddenly I have an inkling of what they could be doing. I don't get it, though. They live together at her B&B.

Variety is the spice of life?

"I just feel so dirty," she says, and I wince because I don't want any part of a private conversation—especially not a dirty one that concerns my father.

"Don't feel dirty," my father says. "We're just getting what's ours."

They take off toward the parking lot with a spring in their step and I shake my head at them. Fine, I envy the guy. I wish I were getting what's mine with Lottie tonight.

I step into the lobby and then quickly duck behind a large silk plant. I've donned a baseball cap and a jacket I don't typically wear, in the event Ivy and I need to review any footage. I want all my bases covered. I know the Evergreen only has security cameras in the lobby because I've done my fair share of investigations concerning this place. I'll be fine once I get upstairs. I also have access to the guest register database because of those numerous investigations, so I've already gleaned the fact Rooster was staying in room 203.

Naomi laughs at something Charlie tells her, and I use the opportunity to inch my way toward the stairs. The elevator is smack in front of the reception desk, so that's out, but the stairs are slightly to the right of where they're standing and I should be able to run up unnoticed. But since I need to ensure this fact, I decide to hold out for a few minutes in hopes that a crowd will walk through those doors. Heck, I'd take a single person, a dog would do nicely. Anything to distract from me.

"I just hated everyone in high school." Naomi glances at her nails.

"Did you hate Lottie?" Charlie asks as if she were rooting for it.

"Who could I hate more?"

The two of them break out into a deep belly laugh and I shake my head at it. Lottie has been nothing but kind to both of them. Naomi is still holding grudges, and Charlie is suing her.

A family of six walks in through the door—mom, dad, and four tired looking kids in stair step heights, two boys and two girls. The young girl in her father's arms is already asleep. Her hair is dark crimson and she reminds me of Lyla Nell the way her mouth hangs open limp as she blissfully snoozes.

My heart warms at the sight. That could be Lottie and me one day with our brood. It should be Lottie and me one day. We're already a kid down, three to go. But I've got Everett mucking up the waters.

The family passes by me. Mom heads for the reception counter, dad heads for the elevator, and three of the kids decide to race up the stairs—and I join them.

My heart lets out a few hard wallops as I make it to the second floor, just enough heavy thumps to assure me I'm out of shape.

The carpet is a green mosaic pattern and the walls are covered with red damask wallpaper, both of which are overloading my senses.

It's late, and I'm tired. I've got two homicide cases staring me in the face, and despite the fact I ate nearly thirty hot dogs, I'm miraculously hungry.

Room 203 comes up on my left, so I pull the trinket out of my pocket that can pick the lock on just about anything. I insert the pick into the lock when a sickly sweet perfume surrounds me and a pair of cool hands covers my eyes.

"Geez," I grunt, turning around and I let out a little howl. "Cormack," I hiss. "What are you doing here?"

The grin glides off her face. "I can ask you the same thing."

"I'm here—as a part of my investigation."

She cocks a brow. "Got a warrant that fast, Detective?"

I take a breath. "I don't need a warrant. As you pointed out, I'm a detective—the lead detective in the case." The truth is buried loosely in that jumble of lies.

She plucks something out of her purse and flashes it my way —her own detective badge. I'd like to say she got it out of a Cracker Jack box, but she didn't.

43

A few months back, Cormack decided to give Lottie a run for her investigative money and struck out on her own in the PI game. She had her wealthy father buy her that badge she's bearing. Cormack never did any of the fieldwork required to hone her chops. She's essentially a danger to herself and others at this stage of the investigative game. Lucky for her and any prospective clients, she's not open for business per se. She simply uses that shiny badge as an excuse to meddle in my cases.

"Featherby Sleuths Investigative Services, ready and willing to meet your demands." She runs her tongue along her lips. "Both in and out of the bedroom."

"Aren't you supposed to be grieving the man you love?"

"Hard to do when the man I love is standing right here." Her fingers walk up my tie.

"Sorry, Mack." A heavy sigh expels from me because Cormack is a vibrant woman who deserves to find happiness. I need to cut her loose gently once and for all. "You're not getting lucky. Not tonight, not ever. I'm afraid I'm too emotionally tethered to Lottie. You don't want to waste your time with me. It's never going to happen."

A couple of female voices carry this way just as Naomi and the mother that walked into the manor head toward us.

I can't let her see me.

Reflexively, I pull Cormack into a tight embrace and land my face to hers as if we were in the throes of passion. I've given Cormack an inch, and she's not one to merely take a mile—she goes for the gold, jamming her lips to mine and moaning as if she's in the heat of passion. And knowing Cormack's obsession with me, she's just that.

Naomi lets the woman into her room, then heads back down the stairs, and I pull Cormack off me as easy as plucking a suction cup off a window.

"Oh, Noah," Cormack says it in a breathy whisper as her eyes speedily drink me in. "I had forgotten what it felt like to be close enough to have your magical lips on mine."

"I don't have time for this now. I'm sorry, Cormack. I'm going to have to ask you to leave." I try to insert my pick into the lock and she slaps my hand way.

"Would you stop with that? I left my best pair of panties in there last night. I've got a key." She inserts the keycard and the door glides open.

She lets herself in before I can stop her and we find the lights still on.

The room is disheveled, bed unmade, curtains askew, a couple of drawers left opened. I can't be sure, but this mess may have been my father's doing or Miranda's.

For their sakes, I hope they gloved up.

"Ta-da!" Cormack produces a pink pair of underwear off the floor that looks like cotton candy. "Hey, why let a good room go to waste? I only had these on for fifteen minutes. I could put them back—"

"No," I say, pulling her close. "Listen to me, Cormack. You can't tell anyone that I was here with you. And you have to leave right now. You're right. I don't have the warrant yet. But I need to get a leg up on the investigation, so it's not unheard of that I would do something like this."

She narrows her eyes over mine. "I'll keep your secret. But under one condition."

"Anything," I tell her, even though I only vaguely mean it.

"I get to tell all of Honey Hollow that we're back together."

I take a deep breath. "Sure, go ahead."

I don't see why not. She's been living in her delusions for so long, I don't see the harm in letting the town celebrate them with her.

A high-pitched squeal comes from her as she shakes her fists victoriously.

"You won't be sorry, Big Boss. You know that whole thing

with Rooster was just a ruse. You're the one my heart truly belongs to." She pecks a kiss to my cheek before I can stop her. "Could you ever forgive me?"

"Believe me, I'm not offended that you were with Rooster," I say, navigating her to the door and walking her right out.

"I just can't believe we're back together. I can't—"

"We'll talk." I shut the door, pull on my gloves, and promptly get to work.

I do a quick scan under the bed, in the drawers, the bathtub, then finally the closet, and *bingo*. There they are, practically right out in the open. Two dark briefcases calling my name.

I scoop them both up at once, and one feels markedly lighter than the other. I toss them both into my duffle bag, opening each one just enough to peer inside. The brown bricks of cocaine are still neatly compartmentalized in the briefcase Jimmy Canelli gave me. Thank goodness for illegal mercies.

I crack open the briefcase Luke Lazzari gave to Everett and see enough green to satisfy me, so I shut them both, stuff them into my duffle bag, and zip it tight. I leave the light on just the way we found it and hightail it out the door. No sooner do I hit the stairs than Cormack accosts me.

"There you are, Big Boss." Her hands snake their way behind my neck and I inadvertently drag her down the stairwell with me. I can't think straight with the contraband in my hand, and I'm not talking about Cormack. The front desk is barren and I breathe a sigh of relief as I navigate Cormack straight out the front door.

The night air is balmy and heavily perfumed with a scent I've come to associate with this hour. My breathing picks up as I spot my truck not too far off.

It's almost over.

"Cormack?" a woman calls out. "Noah? Is that you?"

Every muscle in my body freezes as I glance to my left and spot Naomi barreling in this direction.

"Well, well, what have we got here?" Naomi gives us the once-over with her hands tucked into her hips. She's got on a long black dress, and her hair is bobbling on top of her head in a loose bun.

"Big Boss and I are back together," Cormack announces as she tightens her grip on my waist.

Naomi sucks in a gleeful breath. "No kidding! Does Lottie know about this?" Before either of us can answer, Naomi sucks in another quick breath. "This is something clandestine happening, isn't it? Were you up in your room with him all this time?"

"That's right," Cormack coos. "He's the one for me, and I'm the only woman for Noah Fox."

Naomi chokes on a laugh. "I knew you weren't serious about that geezer. If you ask me, Noah is a better use of the honeymoon suite." She nods down to my side. "What's in the bag?"

Cormack slaps her fingers over my mouth. "We do a little role-playing every now and again. You know, costumes, an apparatus or two, lots of kinky equipment."

Naomi's jaw goes slack. "Wow, I had no idea you were into things like that." She shakes her head my way. "In that case, it makes total sense why you'd go back to Cormack. I mean, face it, Lottie Lemon is about as vanilla as one can get. I'm sure her prissy behavior translates to the bedroom." She shrugs. "Bear grew bored of her way back when. You obviously grew bored of her. And I guess that means Mr. Sexy will soon be back in the singles scene." She bites down on her lower lip. "Guess who will be ready and waiting?" She starts to head back, and I quickly grab her by the wrist.

"Nobody can know that we were here, Naomi." I nod her way while begging her silently for her assurance.

"Of course," she says, patting me on the arm the way you would a small child. "Believe me when I say, your secret is safe with yours truly. If Lottie does find out about this little undercover foxtrot, it won't be from me."

A catcall escapes her as she heads back into the manor and I tip my head to the sky.

It couldn't be easy, could it?

I say goodnight to Cormack and drive home to the only woman for me, Lottie Lemon.

EVERETT

"*N*oah is back," I say to Lemon as I let the curtain drop. I've been stalking the window, keeping an eye out on Noah's driveway for the last half hour, with my adrenaline running full throttle. I don't think I'll get a wink of sleep tonight. Maybe ever again.

"Oh good." Lemon jumps up next to me, holding both Pancake and Waffles as they crane their necks toward the window as if they wanted a peek themselves. "Okay, let's get over there." Her own breathing has picked up and I can tell she's charged.

I much prefer her that way in the bedroom and never outside

of it. Lemon deserves to have a calm, peaceful life. And with the mob pecking around Noah and me—gunning to use us and expertly trapping us right where they want us, she may never have another calm day so long as we're in her way.

"Evie?" I turn around and find her lying horizontally on the wingback chair with her legs dangling off one side as she flicks her finger over her phone. "Would you mind watching Lyla Nell for a minute? We're going to have a quick word with Noah."

"I don't mind at all," she says, her eyes still glued to the screen. "She's sleeping, just the way I like it. And just a heads-up. My driving lessons start tomorrow at one. Don't worry. That gives me enough time to go to church and have you take me to Wicked Wok afterwards. I'm not giving up our Sunday tradition of staring at cute boys for an hour then noshing on dim sum."

Lemon laughs as she lands the cats on the couch. "It's nice to know you're getting something from it. We'll be back soon, but if Lyla Nell needs anything, I've got my phone."

I blow out a breath. "Can you move your driver's ed appointment back a notch, Evie? I've got a surprise for the two of you at one. It shouldn't take more than a half hour. An hour at best."

"Ooh, a surprise?" Evie looks up, and I suddenly have her attention. "I'll see what I can work out with Bradford."

I frown just hearing his name.

Bradford Van Horn is some college kid that's been paired with Evie to teach her to put the pedal to the metal—or more to the point, not to put the pedal to the metal.

Last month, I had the bright idea to suggest to Evie she should break things off with her steady boyfriend, a high school football player named Conner Saint. I'll admit, I was afraid the kid wasn't exactly living up to his surname. But now that the universe has thrown a college kid at her, I'm not so sure I should have campaigned so hard for her to dump the football player.

Lemon thinks we shouldn't tinker with Evie's dating life. But as her dad, I can't seem to help myself.

Evie scoffs. "Dad, you know I hate surprises. Tell me now, what is it?"

"I'd love to know, too." Lemmon shrugs with a mischievous smile tickling her lips.

"All will be known tomorrow afternoon. I'll give you a hint. It's a family affair. And it should be fun."

Evie makes a face. "Should be fun. But will it be?"

Lemon waves her off. "It will be. Like I said, call me if you need me!"

Lemon and I dart out the door into the warm night air. The heat from the day is still radiating off the sidewalks. And according to the weather report, we're due for another scorcher tomorrow.

I glance up and down the darkened street where the light from a few streetlamps offers a peachy glow. Country Cottage Road has been home ever since I moved to Honey Hollow a couple of years ago.

Lemon has always lived in Honey Hollow, but Noah made the move right before I did. In fact, he bought the cabin we're headed to at the moment. It's a Lincoln Log model with no frills, a nice yard, and the woods butt up against it at the end of the cul-de-sac.

Not long after Noah moved in, Lemon rented the place across the street from him, and I bought the home next to her rental.

Last October, both Lemon's rental and my home burned down in a freak fire, so I bought the property her rental was on and conjoined it with mine with the city's permission—not an easy feat, but you throw enough time and money at something and things eventually shift in the right direction. Now we're halfway through construction on the dream home I'll share with Lemon. And that construction site just so happens to be ground zero for the surprise I've got cooking for my family tomorrow afternoon.

Lemon gives a brisk knock over Noah's door and it glides

right open as Noah lets us in. Noah's place is rustic, with dark muted tones, wood floors, leather sofas, and no creature comforts that a woman would provide. A few empty beer bottles line the sink, and there's a stack of pizza boxes on his dining room table.

His golden retriever, Toby, greets us with a lazy romp, and both Lemon and I give him a quick scratch. I like Toby more than I care for Noah, but then that's easy to do.

Toby has a smile on his face each time I see him. Noah wears a lovesick scowl.

"Where are they?" I ask, quickly surveying his living room. "Is everything still intact?"

"I just got back and tossed the duffle bag on my bed," he says. "Let's check it out."

We head into Noah's bedroom, and sure enough, a large navy duffle bag sits in the middle of his unmade bed.

"You're not just going to leave it out in the open like this, are you?" I growl his way. I can't help it. Noah's slovenliness has seeped into my life and almost took down my career a few months back.

"Relax, *Nancy*. Like I said, I just got home. I'm pretty sure the briefcases will fit in my attic. I'll buy a safe in the morning and have it shipped out."

Lemon blows out a breath. "That's going to have to be a big safe. It'll be expensive, too."

"Only if he gets a good one," I say. "I'll pay for it. Clear a space in your garage."

"*I'll* pay for it." He frowns over at me. "It'll be the best money can buy. Only top quality will do to store your contraband, princess."

"*Noah*." A nervous laugh streams from Lemon. "Will both of you please calm down? It's going to be okay. Wait a minute—why don't you just return the briefcases to their wicked owners and be rid of them? Besides, just a thought of a large safe in your garage, Noah, sets me on edge. I have enough things to worry about, and I don't need to add Lyla Nell getting stuck in your new safe to the list." She shrugs. "I'm a new mom, and my hormones are on fire. All sorts of disturbing things run through my brain."

I twitch my lips her way. "I hate to say it, but I have a feeling Jimmy and Luke won't want anything to do with these just yet. But we'll get rid of them as soon as we can."

Noah nods. "I'll clean the prints off them tonight and shove them in my attic. Don't worry, man." He slaps me on the back. "We're not going to hell in a handbasket just yet."

Noah regales us with an odd story of running into Cormack at the manor as he unzips the duffle bag. I'll admit, a swell of relief hits me when I see those dark briefcases sitting there like a couple of leather-bound demons. At least I have the comfort of knowing they're not floating around out there waiting to fall into the hands of the Ashford County Sheriff's Department by way of some ATF agent. Our prints are covering them both, and I refuse to let the mob take us down. A bullet to my chest would be easier for me to live with—despite the fact I wouldn't be alive to appreciate it.

Noah springs open the latches on the first briefcase and pulls the lid back, exposing us to rows of cocaine bricks wrapped in brown packaging. He opens the next one, and as soon as he pulls the lid back my heart sinks.

"Crap." I close my eyes a moment.

I used to be the lucky one. The one that got all the big breaks, the green lights—Yes, I worked hard to get where I am, but doors have always opened for me. And as of late, it seems all of my luck has been turned on its ear. Coincidentally, I see a parallel with the fact Noah has stepped back into the picture.

"Oh, Everett." Lemon wraps her arms around my waist. "More than half the money is missing."

"Two-thirds," I tell her. "All right. Get this mess cleaned up and in the attic before anyone finds out about it."

The sound of footsteps comes from behind and we turn to find Carlotta with her hair mussed, poking her head over Lemon's shoulder.

A laugh gravels from her. "What do a judge, a cop, a baker, a briefcase full of drugs, and a whole lot of money have in common?"

"We are indeed going to hell in a handbasket," I say as I look at the illegal loot spread out over Noah's bed.

Lemon does her best to shove Carlotta out of the room, but it's too late. The damage has been done.

"Carlotta, what are you doing here?" she asks as they nearly get into a scuffle.

"Little Yippy was going off like a fire alarm earlier and I couldn't sleep, so I used that spare key we've got lying around to Foxy's place and holed up in his guest bedroom." She cranes her neck to look at Noah. "So what happened after you made out with Cormack?" she asks.

Noah looks less than thrilled with the way she's framed her question—an honest one at that.

"None of your business."

"Fine, Foxy. Have your secrets. But you've still got flannel sheets on the mattress in the guest room, and now I'm soaking with sweat. Order up some of those bamboo sheets, would ya? I hear they keep you nice and cool."

"I'll get right on it," Noah says while glaring at her.

Lemon and Carlotta drift to the living room while Noah and I sanitize every inch of these briefcases in an effort to remove any trace of our DNA. We look for hairs, fibers, anything that could potentially incriminate us, and all the while glaring at one another.

We've pulled ourselves into blunders before, and each time we seem to outdo the last, yet we've always managed to bring ourselves back to safety.

But this feels as if it's the biggest blunder of them all.

Something tells me there will be no coming back from this one.

We're going to pay. I can feel it in my bones.

Here's hoping we don't pay with our lives.

THE NEXT MORNING, Sunday, Lemon makes me breakfast in bed —eggs, bacon, and a stack of waffles to the ceiling—as if it were my last day on earth.

Church goes off without a hitch, and Lemon and I take Evie and Lyla Nell to Wicked Wok for lunch, then reconvene with everyone at the construction site of the new house, right next door to where we reside now. As much as I like the convenience of it, the banging and shouting all day from Bear's construction crew makes me regret our choices. Moving even a block or two away would have given us a little more peace and left Noah to enjoy all the bumping, thumping benefits.

"What's going on, Sexy?" Carlotta asks as she stands next to Mayor Harry Nash. Lemon's mother and sisters are here— Lainey, Meg, and I guess Charlie falls into that equation, too. Wiley has joined the brigade. Noah is here, and oddly, Cormack, who followed him home from church, Evie, and, of course, Bear, his wife Keelie, and their bruiser of a baby boy.

Our new property is spread over an acre and a half, and we're building the house set off from the street to secure a little more privacy. The backyard will be an ample size as it butts up to the woods. I'll fence it in so the cats can roam free, or in the event Lemon wants to add a dog to the mix or any other creature. I'll build a barn if she wants me to.

I glance up at the structure that will one day soon be our

forever home. It's still in its skeletal phase, nothing but wood framing it and concrete footings. The plumbing has already been laid out, and that includes the pipes for front yard landscaping.

I asked Bear to let me know when he'd put in the foundation for the walkway, and that's the exact reason we're standing here today. There's a small cement mixer not too far off, and Bear has already poured a square along the path that will lead to the wrap-around porch.

"First, I want to thank you all for coming out in the heat," I tell everyone. "As you know, just shy of four months ago, Lemon gave our family the gift of Lyla Nell. And as a token of my love for Lemon, Lyla Nell, and Evie, I wanted to commemorate our family in a special way."

Keelie gasps. "This is Lottie's push present, isn't it?"

"That's right," I tell her.

Carlotta looks to Mayor Nash. "Foxy put a tree in front of his house for Little Yippy."

"And it'll have a swing hanging from it soon," Noah chimes. "Just as soon as I get it to grow a bit more."

Wiley slaps his son on the shoulder. "I'll help you fertilize the thing. We can't have her waiting to swing. She'll be in college before you know it."

Carlotta nods. "If she's anything like her mama, she'll be swinging long after college, too."

"Oh, stop it," Lemon reprimands her. "That doesn't even make sense."

"She's right," Evie tells her. "Uncle Noah's not married."

"And I'm not fooling around with him," Lemon tells her.

Evie rolls her eyes. "Come on, Mom. It was just last night you and Dad snuck off across the street, and when you came back you said so yourself the three of you were just having a little fun."

"That's not what I meant," Lemon says, clutching Lyla Nell tight.

"That's not what happened," I say it sternly in the event anyone wants to question the fact.

Evie shrugs. "Suit yourself. But it was you, Dad, who was hovering at the window for an hour straight just waiting to see when Uncle Noah pulled into the driveway. You seemed the most excited to get over there."

"Stood at the window for an hour?" Meg, Lemon's no-nonsense sister, laughs at the thought. "Sounds as if Judge Baxter here likes to watch things happen."

Soon, everyone joins in on the laughter, the loudest of which is little Lyla Nell.

"All right, back to business." I pull Lemon in close and look deep into her honey-colored eyes. "Lemon, I love you. And although I could never repay you enough for bringing Lyla Nell into our lives—"

Carlotta raises a hand. "You may not be able to pay her back, but you might want to think about giving Foxy a tip."

Lainey nods. "That's true. Without Noah, we wouldn't be standing here today."

"To Noah!" Wiley breaks out into a full-fledged applause and the others follow weakly.

I take a moment to cut him a glance. "Fine. Thank you." I nod back to Lemon. "I'd like you to know that though it might seem my push present has been a bit delinquent, it was thought out well before the baby was born. But since it was dependent upon a certain level of fabrication around here, it wasn't possible until today. I asked Bear to prepare a wet slab of cement where we could put our handprints to commemorate our family forever, right here on the grounds where our family will continue to grow and bloom."

The women in the crowd coo in concert.

Lemon's eyes fill with tears as she nods my way.

"This is the most beautiful thing you could have done for me, Everett. It's perfect."

"It is perfect," Keelie cries out as she dabs her eyes with a tissue.

"Hey," Cormack barks. "Noah is giving the kid a swing on a tree he bought in her honor. I think that's downright perfect in my eyes." She wraps her arms around him and gives him a squeeze.

"I'm not competing with Noah," I tell them. "In fact, I'm inviting you, Noah, to leave your handprint along with ours. As Lyla Nell's father, you're a permanent member of this family."

Lemon sucks in a breath. And that look of wonder and love in her eyes assures me that including Noah was the right thing to do.

It was.

Keelie tilts her head at the wet slab before us. "Do it in the shape of a sunflower and leave some space between your hands so we can make room for all the new babies coming this way. We can add them in with paint or something."

Lemon presses a hand to her chest. "That's a great idea! We should start adding to our family right away." She shoots me an odd look I can't quite read.

Noah steps in as if he was breaking up a fight. "Don't you want to wait until Lyla Nell is a little older? Like sixty?"

Lemon laughs as she pushes past him. "No. Everett needs this. And we're going to have a big wedding right away, too."

Charlie smirks. "I bet it'll be the biggest shindig to end all shindigs. At the ritziest locale imaginable."

Miranda moans, "All the best locations are booked three years in advance."

"We don't have three years," Lemon says in haste. "We have to act fast. We can get married right here, on our own land asap."

"Asap?" I cock my head to the side, trying to figure out what's going on. Come to think of it, after that king-size breakfast she gave me this morning, she gave me a deep tissue massage and kept whispering how much she loves me, and how much Lyla Nell and Evie needed me.

A sinking feeling hits me in the gut.

Could this be another facet of those hormones she's got brewing? Something is cooking, that's for sure.

I want all those things with Lemon, too, but her sense of urgency has me more than a little curious.

Bear helps us out as we get ready to do the deed and Keelie guides us until our sunflower is complete. In addition to Lyla Nell's handprint, Keelie and Lemon include her tiny feet in on the fun and leave a track of baby footsteps trailing along the bottom of it. Keelie takes a stick and draws a stalk to the sunflower, adds a few leaves, then writes our names in the corner along with the date.

"It's so lovely," Miranda whimpers as she hugs Wiley's shoulder. "I'm so happy for you all."

A silver SUV comes up and stops at the base of the street before letting a few honks rip. The driver, a young man in his twenties, dark hair and dark sunglasses on, leans our way and waves.

"That's my ride." Evie gives a little hop. "Bradford said I could drive us anywhere I wanted. I think we're going to head to Starry Falls and check out the waterworks they've got going on."

"Starry Falls?" I ask a little rougher than I meant to. "That can be an hour drive depending on traffic. And you'll need to take the highway. You've never been behind the wheel before. I'm going to have to say no. And in that tank?" I shake my head at the mean machine Evie is going to have to commandeer.

"Relax, Dad." She lands a kiss to my cheek. "I'll be fine. How hard can driving be, anyhow? Besides, Bradford said anytime I want, he'll take over. He says he's going to treat me like the queen I am and make sure I have a really good time."

Carlotta chuckles. "That's funny. Those are the same words

my own driver's ed teacher said to me." She looks to Lemon. "Funny story. That driver's ed teacher was almost your father."

"Don't listen to her, Everett." Lemon gives me a squeeze. "Be careful, Evie, and don't even think about looking at your phone."

"Don't worry." Evie cinches her purse over her shoulder. "Bradford Van Horn is a consummate professional." Her lips curve with pride as she doles out the three-dollar word. "He said he's taking my phone hostage as soon as I step into his car."

I'm afraid that won't be the only thing he's going to take hostage.

"How do we know we can trust this guy?" I can feel fight-or-flight kicking in and I'm tempted to yank Bradford out of his car and fit him with a pair of cement boots.

Noah nods her way. "Remind him you're underage and that your uncle is a cop who carries a gun."

"And that your father is a judge who loves to dole out long sentences to anyone even thinking about toying with an underage girl," I add.

Evie bubbles out a laugh and she's about to skip off when she stops short as a small blue butterfly flutters past her.

"Cool! A blue butterfly." She gives me a wave. "I'll take that as a sign of good luck." She zips into the SUV and is gone before I can say another word.

It's probably for the best.

Carlotta shakes her head. "The kid must not be a fast learner. This family doesn't have *any* good luck."

"It's got a blue butterfly," Lemon says as her sisters and mother fish out their phones and begin snapping pictures of it.

"Oh my word," Lainey shouts as she chases the thing. "I think this is the Honey Hollow Blue Butterfly. They're on the endangered species list!"

Mom gasps. "Look! It's flying right over to that bush in the back of the property. Oh, there's a another one!"

Meg nods. "And it's flying right through your new house, too."

A hard groan comes from Mayor Nash. "You girls haven't sent any of those pictures to your social media accounts, have you?"

"Yup." Lainey hikes up her phone.

"Me too," Cormack says.

Miranda, Lemon, and Meg all say ditto.

"What's going on?" Noah asks the mayor, and Harry buries his face in his hand a moment.

"It's the butterfly." He sheds a depleted smile my way. "I'm afraid we're going to have to pull the plug on construction until who knows when. That Honey Hollow Blue Butterfly is a protected endangered species. And that makes this land, and your partially built home, its habitat. I'm sorry, guys, but it's going to be a long road with a lot of red tape to make this home happen for you." His phone rings in his hand, and he shakes his head at it. "And so it begins. It's the preservation society. I have to take this."

He steps off to take the call and Carlotta steps up in his place.

"Told ya this family has no good luck."

Charlie shrugs over at her sister. "I guess the golden girl doesn't get everything after all."

Lemon's lips tug as if she was about to lose it, and I'm right there with her.

"That's okay." Her voice trembles. "As long as I have my handsome husband by my side, nothing else will matter." She gives a little whimper as she and the rest of the people gathered take off to look at that bush brimming with butterflies.

Noah starts to leave and I jam my hand to his chest.

"Something is up with Lemon," I tell him.

"Yeah, she's upset about the house. I would be, too. Sorry, man. You can't seem to catch a break."

"Not that." I glance back at her as she speaks with her sisters. "She's been acting funny, wanting to speed along a wedding, kids, not to mention the things she's doing for me when we're alone."

Noah tips his head back as his chest expands.

"Not that," I tell him. "Look, I know Lemon enough to realize something has her rattled. I asked her if something was wrong this morning and she clammed up. For whatever reason, she's not talking to me about it. That's where you come in. Get to the bottom of this. If something is bothering my wife, it's bothering me."

"If she's not talking to you, how am I supposed to get her to open up to me?"

"I don't know. Think of something. Wine her, dine her"—I pause a moment to offer up a quick smile—"I'll do the rest."

He glowers at me. "I bet you will." He starts to take off. "Don't blame me if she falls right back in love with yours truly. Not that she's ever fallen out of it." He turns around and winks. "Who knows? This little quest of yours might just turn into a reversal of fortune for us both."

He takes off and I glance back at the small crowd of family as a blue butterfly spirals in the air above them.

I'm suffering a reversal of fortune, all right.

Let's pray Lemon and I aren't the latest casualty.

*E*verett is going to die.

Nell says I have the power to stop it, but I've never felt so helpless in all my life.

It's obvious the mob is going to gun him down. And poor Noah. No thanks to Wiley he's got a hit on him.

That terrible vision comes back to me. Everett and Noah in the woods. Everett pushing Noah away just as a loud bang goes off, then Everett taking three bullets to the chest.

A sickly moan comes from me as I stare out at my bakery. It's perfectly cozy with its butter yellow walls, pastel furniture, and a walkway that leads into the Honey Pot Diner. That's the restaurant Grandma Nell left me along with a million other real estate holdings—all of which Charlie is suing me for. There's a resin oak tree smack in the middle of the Honey Pot Diner, and its branches extend over the ceiling and into the café of the bakery. Each one is meticulously wrapped with twinkle lights, and it makes both this place and that look like a fairytale come true.

It's Monday, Everett is at work—safe at the courthouse.

Hey? There's a thought. If Everett stays at the courthouse that vision will never get a chance to manifest itself. And Noah should stay away from Everett in general.

A thought hits me and my fingers dance across the screen of my phone.

Stay away from Noah! I send the text to Everett and instantly regret it.

Good grief, that was an ominous message if ever there was one.

Everett texts right back. **What's going on with Noah? Did he say something to you?**

Goodness, here I was trying to make things better, and I've only made them worse.

Never mind. I don't know what I was thinking. I hit send again. **Have a great day!**

Perfect. Everett is going to think I'm psychotic if he doesn't already.

It won't be wonderful until I'm home with you.

"Aww," Carlotta coos from over my shoulder.

"Would you stop sneaking up on me like that!"

"It's not my fault, Lot. You're standing in the middle of the bakery, that's fair game. If you wanted privacy, you should have snuck off to your office or to the freezer. With Sexy messaging you sweet nothings you might need to cool off."

I make a face as I take a look around the bakery. The temperatures might be rising outside, but it's definitely cool in here. That, coupled with the fact the scent of my blueberry muffins is wafting down the street, explains why it's standing room only at the moment.

My mother has already sent two of her Haunted Honey Hollow Tours my way. After Mom found a way to capitalize off the ghosts that have taken up residence at her B&B, she decided to share the wealth by sending them my way for what she's dubbed as The Last Thing They Ate Tour. Sadly, it showcases the dessert that was quasi-involved in the latest homicide. I'm not sure how or why, but one of my desserts always seems to find its way to the scene of the crime. And on occasion, it's used as a modality to the murder itself.

Not with Clark Willoughby, though. He wasn't killed by way of one of my blueberry muffins. He clearly sustained a gunshot wound to his upper torso—a shot to the heart. Just like the one Everett is about to take on.

I bite hard on my lower lip just as Suze waves me to the counter.

"What is it?" I ask as I come upon her and Lily.

"I'll be working the kiosk down at the lake." Suze sheds a sarcastic smile, and for the life of me I can't read between the lines.

"Thank you," I tell her.

"It's going to be hot," she growls. "I'll need to stay hydrated, you know, and drink lots of water. The bathroom is a ten-minute walk."

"Wear a diaper." Lily shrugs. And oddly enough, it seems less of a snarky remark and more of an honest suggestion. "Don't women your age wear diapers, anyway?"

Suze averts her eyes at the thought.

Fun fact: after you've had a child, your bladder decides to have a mind of its own—more to the point, a *timeline* of its own. I can't laugh or sneeze without wishing I were wearing a diaper myself.

"I'm not wearing a diaper," Suze grouses and ten customers scuttle away from the counter.

Carlotta lifts a brow. "No shame in your diaper game, Suze. All the cool kids are doing it. Actually, Lot's boobs wear a diaper."

She's not wrong, but still.

"Would you ladies keep it down." I nod to Suze. "What are you trying to get at? If you don't want to work the kiosk, just say so. I can send Lily."

"No way," Lily is quick to protest. "The humidity turns my hair into a mop. My tresses require some serious climate control."

"I don't mind the heat," Suze says.

"Good thing." Carlotta lifts her chin. "It's going to be real hot at your last rest stop, Suzie Q."

Suze takes a moment to glare at Carlotta. "I was thinking I could get paid time and a half. I've looked into it, and it's not uncommon to pay your workers a little more if there's a hazard on the job."

"Hazard pay?" Lily looks suddenly interested in subjecting her curls to the extremes of summertime madness. "I think maybe I should work the lake." She huffs over at Suze, "After all, I have superiority around here."

I'm pretty sure she meant *seniority*, but then again, knowing Lily she meant what she said.

"Fine," I say to Lily. "But I'm not paying time and a half. Just close down the booth when you think you're about to melt."

"Fair enough." She snatches up a box of gloves and napkins. "I've already got the bakery van packed and ready to go. I'll see you ladies tomorrow."

She takes off and Suze titters to herself.

"Hey," I say, tipping my head her way. "You just played Lily like a fiddle, didn't you?"

Carlotta jerks. "You beguiled her! And here I never thought I'd live to see you use your powers."

Suze waves Carlotta off. "It was nothing more than good old-fashioned manipulation. I shine where others go dim. Ask my ex. I even manipulated him into leaving me." She gives a cheeky wink before heading over to help out a line of customers.

"Too bad my mother couldn't figure out a way to do that." I sigh at the thought of my poor mom getting sucked dry by Noah's shyster of a father.

"Your mama's manipulating that man into staying," Carlotta points out—and she's probably not wrong.

"Well, she's got Lyla Nell for the afternoon, so I'm sure Wiley has made himself scarce."

"What's on the agenda, Lot? You're not gonna fritter away all your free time baking cookies and sending naughty texts to Sexy, are ya? There's a whole world out there to seek, kill, and destroy."

"Funny you should say that, I was just thinking about paying a visit to someone who I think could crack this case wide open."

The bell on the door chimes and in walks Charlie eliciting a gasp from both Carlotta and me, but it's not Charlie we're gasping at. It's the large spotted cat with big yellow eyes perched over her shoulder like an exotic parrot.

"Who's your friend?" I ask, taking up Charlie's hand and leading her behind the counter and in the corner farthest from the registers.

"You're a mighty cool cat," Carlotta says, giving its tail a quick pluck. "I bet they named you something goofy like Hairball or Dingo Dottie."

"You're a dingo." I make a face at Carlotta before looking at the wondrous creature. "My name is Lottie, and I'm so glad to meet you. I'm going to help you track down Clark Willoughby's killer. What's your name?"

It lashes its tail between us before smacking Carlotta on the head with it. "I'm neither Hairball nor that Dingo Ditty you tried to curse me with. My name is Leo." His voice is deep and his confidence is high. He has the rapt attention of all three of the women before him, and he reminds me a little of Everett because of it.

"Nice to meet you, Leo. I'm sorry about Clark."

"A true tragedy," he roars out the words and tiny silver stars appear around his whiskers. "I'm angry with whoever did this. Not only did they send Clark to paradise, they hauled me out of there. I'm not sure which is the bigger crime. But I am sure you'll figure this out sooner than later. Charlie here is late for work." He bats her over the nose with his furry plume. "Let's make tracks as they say. Chop chop."

"What?" I say, extracting the furry cutie off Charlie's shoulder and into my arms. "You can't go to work with her." Not only should he be spending time with me, specifically solving this case, but Charlie works at a seedy strip club. It's a long, sordid story, one I'm hoping ends quickly. "You have to come to work with *me*. We're working on a case, remember?"

A low growl comes from Leo. "All right, fine. But make it snappy, would you? Charlie works at that club Clark used to frequent. He'd come home and tell me all about it. So may pussy-cats to behold, I can't possibly bear being apart from them another minute."

I frown over at my look-alike sister. "It's pussycat galore, all right. But they have nothing to do with the felines in general. Red Satin is a gentlemen's club."

Carlotta nods. "Sounds as if Clark was tossing dollars to the scantily clad among us."

"That might explain the separation from his wife," I say.

"Is the battle-axe still around?" Leo jerks his spotted little head my way, and I can't help but bite down on a smile. His question came out so genuine.

"If you're talking about Sammy, then yes," I say. "I take it you knew her?"

"Oh yes, I was around up until just a few years ago. I suppose I would have been around a bit longer, but Sammy let me out of the house one night and I got into a tussle with a coyote. I had already taken down three of his ornery kind, but alas, he got the best of me. Clark liked to keep me inside. He told Sammy I was to be strictly an indoor cat. But if I mewled loud enough, or dragged my claws over Sammy's favorite sofa, she'd boot me outside as a punishment. That's where the real fun began for me. Clark used to say Red Satin was his playground. Well, the woods behind the Willoughbys' lakefront home were mine."

Charlie plucks him right out of my arms. "I'm actually not on the schedule tonight, Leo. But you're welcome to come down to work with me as soon as my mean ol' big sister is through with you. I'm on again tomorrow night." She tucks her mouth next to his ear. "I'll let you in on a little secret. Lottie is a battle-axe, too."

"I am not." I quickly swipe a fudge brownie from the bakery shelf and feed it to the flirty feline.

A moan comes from him. "Now this is living. You don't have this in tuna, do you?"

"No, but stick with me and I'll make it in any flavor you like."

The dead weren't always capable of noshing on my sweet treats, but as my abilities grew, so did theirs. I seem to hold a sphere of influence among the dead and I don't know why, but I suppose since they're here to help me, it makes sense in a way. Once the case is solved, the ghosts usually pop right back to paradise, although those ghosts haunting the halls of my mother's B&B seem to have an extended day pass.

"So where are we headed, Lot Lot?" Carlotta demands. "We gotta move before Little Yippy sends Miranda to the funny farm, and you end up back on diaper duty. Besides that, you and I both know your boobs are on a timer. If you don't want them to turn into bowling balls, we'll have to act fast."

She's not wrong. If I go too long without nursing, my boobs turn to stone—and worse yet, they begin to weep, with milk, of course. Thus, the boob diapers Carlotta brought up earlier.

"I don't know," I say, pulling out my phone and fiddling with it. "It doesn't look like Sammy Willoughby has any social media sites, or at least none that she keeps up regularly enough to rat out her location."

My phone buzzes in my hand and it's text from Noah.

Are you free for a hot date?

Both Charlie and Carlotta inspect my phone and proceed to make catcalls.

"Stop," I say as I let Noah know I've got a suspect to track down. At least I'm being honest about it this time.

He texts back. **If Sammy Willoughby is on your hit list, then it's your lucky day. I'm headed up to her couple's massage class and need someone to couple with.**

"You bet," I say as I text him those exact same words. "Well, Leo, it looks as if we're in business."

My phone bleats again.

"Wear a bathing suit. I'll pick you up at the house in twenty minutes," I read. "A bathing suit? Regardless, we're going to have a great time, Leo. With Noah and me both grilling Sammy, we might make huge strides when it comes to the killer."

Leo twitches his head toward Charlie. "Should I go with her?"

She shrugs his way. "I guess so."

His little mouth falls open. "But you said I couldn't trust her."

"What?" I say, poking my sister in the arm.

Leo nods. "She told me all about the property you stole right from under her. She said you're holding back her inheritance like a miser. Are you a miser, Lottie Lemon?"

I make a face at the two of them. "I'm no miser."

"Then give me half of what Grandma Nell left you," Charlie doesn't miss a miserly beat.

"No," I snip it out harsher than intended just as Suze passes by us.

"You sound awful miserly to me," she sings.

"Never mind that right now. Stick with me, Leo. You're about to be reunited with Sammy Willoughby."

Carlotta nods while tapping into her phone. "And I'm about to do a little couple's massage with Harry." She sheds an ear-to-ear grin my way. "A killer good time will be had by all."

"Emphasis on *killer*," I say.

And that's exactly where my emphasis will be.

LOTTIE

I t turns out, this couple's massage class is a traveling troupe. And today's locale of choice is a nearby stream known as the Trickle. It's tucked away in the woods just above the Honey Hollow Public Library, the exact place where my sister, Lainey, works as the head librarian. And I bet if she wanted, she could see us parading around up here in our bathing suits.

At least thirteen couples have shown up for the occasion. The women have predominantly donned one-piece bathing suits, but a couple of the twenty-somethings have opted for skimpy dental floss masquerading as two-pieces. And don't for a minute think I didn't fire a silent threat to Noah should he choose to do a visual inspection. Most of the men here have already given them the once-over, but Noah's wisdom and fear of me has led him to think better of it.

I'm firmly in the one-piece division. It's a swimsuit I bought recently and have worn a handful of times since having Lyla Nell. I may be bursting at the seams, but I'm just thrilled I was able to squeeze myself into it. I may have had the baby, but my body seems to be holding onto the baby weight. Stuffing my face with crullers every morning isn't exactly helping the situation either.

Noah takes off his shirt and tosses it onto a nearby rock. I can't help but notice that he looks lean and mean and perfectly sculpted.

"My eyes are up here, sweetheart," he teases.

I make a face at him. "I was just thinking you look just as fit as ever. No fair seeing that we both had a baby. You were just as hungry as I was half the time."

His dimples dig in deep. "You're right. No offense to Mother Nature, but I didn't think any of that was fair. I wish I could have done it all for you." He wraps his arms around me and touches his nose to mine. "Next time we're having a baby, I'll make sure to eat twice as many fried pickles as you do."

"Sounds fair to me."

His brows arch. "You're giving me hope. I like that."

"Stop," I tease, swatting him away.

"Hello, Lottie," Leo mewls, perched on a boulder not too far away. With his caramel-colored coat and those dark spots and stripes, he looks like a miniature cheetah in the wild.

The woods are dense, but there's a clearing here next to the stream, which really is more of a slow moving trickle. The air is heated, but since the evergreens offer an ample amount of shade it feels pleasant. And the scent of the pines, mixed with damp earth, makes me feel grounded with nature.

"Hey, Leo," I whisper his way. "Do you see Sammy?" I take up

Noah's hand so he can hear Leo, too. I learned a while back that I act as a supernatural conduit, and those that just so happen to be touching me can hear the dead as well.

"I see her." He whips his tail back and forth while giving a mean look to Sammy Willoughby standing up stream a bit, helping couples take a seat in the water.

It looks so refreshing and I can't wait to get in. The stream is clear, only about a foot and a half deep at most, and the bottom is covered with large smooth stones.

"She hasn't changed a bit," Leo says. "I'm assuming you know she's guilty."

"What?" Noah and I whisper his way in unison.

"Oh yes, she's been threatening to murder him for years. It was an everyday phrase around the house."

"That's probably all it was," I whisper. "I can't imagine her murdering her husband, estranged or not."

Noah ticks his head. "She is teaching a class less than forty-eight hours after his demise. She's either strong as steel or couldn't care less."

"It's the latter," Leo says as he stands on his hind legs and stretches his front paws as he elongates his frame. "If you don't mind, I'd like to roam. I smell a raccoon sleeping nearby. I think I'll have a little fun with it." He twitches his tail back and forth before leaping off the rock like a cougar.

"And he's off," I say.

"I bet he's a cool looking cat," Noah says. "I thought of getting a Bengal myself."

"How did you know he was a Bengal?"

"You described him perfectly."

"So what stopped you from picking one up?"

"The price tag. The breeder wanted more than I paid for my first truck. They're great cats, a little wild, and yet they have dog-like tendencies. So I opted for the dog."

"Toby was an excellent choice."

A bell goes off a few feet away and we look to find Sammy Willoughby with a chime in her hand. Her thin body looks that much more elongated with her black one-piece on. Her skin is heavily tanned and her arms and legs are well toned. Her dark hair is pulled back into a low ponytail and I can't help but notice that she looks well rested. Her eyes aren't puffy in the least.

"All right, I see we have a few new students here. Welcome one and all." She nods our way. "Detective Fox, I'm glad to see you took me up on my offer. It's a pleasure to have you."

"Don't start!" a familiar voice chirps from a distance and we look back to see Carlotta and Mayor Nash doing a little bowlegged side-to-side shuffle as they scoot their way over. Mayor Nash has on a pair of swimming trunks that travel past his knees and he's paired it with a white tank top—oh wait, I think those are his tan lines.

Oh dear Lord.

Carlotta's no better with her itsy-bitsy pink polka dot bikini, but thankfully, she has a neon green inner tube around her waist, sparing us from seeing too much flesh.

"We're here! We made it!" she shouts as they land beside Noah and me. "As you were."

I give a little wave to Mayor Nash before reverting my attention back to Sammy.

"As most of you know, this isn't just a massage class," Sammy says above the hum of nature. "This is a spiritual adventure that brings healing to your body, your mind, and your relationship. Though each of you has issues that vary in severity, the one commonality you share is that you are here to work to make yourself better together." She claps her hands. "Now get into that water and sit facing one another, knee to knee, holding hands, and we'll get started with our first exercise as we enter into our affirmations to one another."

Noah and I get right into the water and it feels icy cold, and yet the sensation is a welcome reprieve from the sweltering heat.

Noah lets out a hearty groan as we sink into the water together.

"*Whoo!*" I let out a quick cry and Carlotta lets one rip twice as loud.

"My tush is gonna freeze off," Carlotta bleats.

Mayor Nash laughs. "Yeah, and the rest of you will melt. It's a scorcher today. We had thirteen people faint at the lake. It's panning out to be a real natural disaster. Speaking of which…" He grimaces my way. "The preservation society made it official. The construction of your new home is frozen from here on out."

"Until?" I hold my breath as I wait for an answer.

He grimaces. "Well, until the butterfly has had ample time to replenish its species in the wild."

"Oh, is that all? I counted at least eight cocoons nestled up in that bush. I'm sure they'll morph into butterflies soon enough. Maybe a week or two?"

"Oh no." He shakes his head emphatically. "It'll take a good fifteen seasons or so for the preservation society to be satisfied. We've been through this before with the three-toed frog. It's a long, arduous process, but it's a good feeling to know you're doing your part for nature."

"That's me," I say as I shoot Noah a look. "Just doing my part for nature." I lean his way. "You didn't plant those butterflies, did you?"

A dark laugh strums through him. "No, but if I did, I would have tossed in a few in Everett's boxers. I wouldn't mind if he was a no-fly zone for fifteen seasons." He scoots in another notch. "Speaking of Everett—"

A wail-like cry comes from behind.

"Wait for *me!*" That last word stretches out in a melodic warble and we turn to see a bleach blonde in a skimpy two-piece bouncing those beach balls in her bikini top all the way over.

"For the love of all things good." I give Noah a little kick in the rear. "Why does your stalker have to be so proficient?" I ask as Cormack plops right next to him.

"Big Boss." She smothers his cheek with kisses as her hands rake up and down his body. "I didn't realize you needed me for a stakeout." She gives his face a brisk slap and Noah blinks over at me.

"That's what you get." I shrug over at him.

He inches back from his assaulter. "How'd you find me?"

"I talked to Ivy when I couldn't reach you. I was half afraid you were in danger. She told me exactly where you were headed. Why would you bring Essex's wife when you could have brought me?"

There's a genuine look of hurt in her eyes, and a part of me feels sorry for her.

"Did you forget about our little agreement?" She tries to peck another kiss to his cheek and Noah expertly evades the effort.

"No, I didn't," he says it flat and somewhat angry.

"What agreement?" I whisper to him as if she magically couldn't hear me, and a part of me thinks that's true with Cormack.

She turns a shoulder up my way. "None of your business, Lima."

The class starts and Sammy directs us into various stretching exercises that require some serious pulling and tugging between Noah and me. For the most part, Cormack seems content rubbing his belly and trying to press her body as close to his side as possible.

I'm about three seconds from stoning the witch. And maybe Noah, too, for tolerating it.

"Now"—Sammy calls out—"we're going to head into the deep tissue massages. Men first. Ladies, I'll give you a brief demonstration of today's techniques." She comes our way and looks to Noah and me. "Would the two of you mind demonstrating for the rest of us?"

"Not at all," I say as I sit up and adjust my top. Now that I'll have a broader audience, I want to ensure my bits and pieces stay within the bounds of my bathing suit seeing they've been known to escape on occasion.

Cormack lifts a finger. "But it's not just the two of them. It's the three of us."

"What?" I hiss over at her in shock, but oddly enough, Noah seems to be taking it all in stride.

Sammy shakes her fist in the air and gives a little cheer.

"Let's welcome our first throuple!"

Carlotta chuckles. "Maybe yours, Toots, but not hers. That's Lot Lot's specialty."

I glower a moment at the woman who bore me.

"I am not in a throuple with Cormack," I hiss her way.

Sammy comes over and has Noah sit facing the other direction while Cormack and I sit on either side of him and offer Noah our best massaging efforts.

Sammy shows us how to knead our elbows into his back.

"Now do your best to lie over him, come on, side by side, you'll have to make room." She flicks her fingers for us to hurry. Noah lies forward and rests his head on a rock with his nose just above water.

Carlotta hacks out a laugh. "Hear that, Lot? You'll have to make room." She smacks Sammy on the thigh. "You'll have to excuse her. She's not that good at sharing her men. Lot is more used to having two men lying over *her* back. That's why the paternity of Little Yippy was such a mystery for nine long months. But Foxy's swimmers took the gold."

"All right," I snip at her. "We get it." I motion for Sammy to continue because I'm not sure how much longer the left side of my body can take being pressed up to Cormack like this. I've held Noah like this plenty of times, but having Cormack encroach in our personal space makes me more than a little twitchy. It makes me want to slap both Cormack and Noah—

and maybe myself for getting involved in yet another throuple.

We get on with the massage as a class, then move on to changing positions, and we do just that.

"Noah," Sammy calls out. "You'll have to work twice as hard to make sure both of your partners are satisfied. But I have a feeling you're already well experienced in that department."

I shoot a dirty look Noah's way that says *don't you dare*.

Noah starts in on my shoulders, and I let out a little cry.

"Oh, right there," I say, tapping the spot next to my neck. "I've got a horrible knot. I stayed up all night nursing the baby, and I tried to sleep in the rocking chair."

"Don't worry, Foxy," Carlotta calls out. "I'll get it all on tape for you so you can play it back later."

"Don't you—" I'm about to reprimand Carlotta, but Noah and his magic hands are at it again and I'm right back to moaning and groaning at the top of my lungs.

"A-*hem*." Cormack shoots Noah a threatening look, and soon she's moaning right alongside me.

We howl up a storm as Noah brings us both to a rather satisfying conclusion and every kink in my back has been successfully dissolved.

"Oh wow!" Cormack shouts. "Oh yes! Yes! Yes! *Yes!*" Cormack wiggles and pants until she flops herself up onto the embankment and clutches the grass.

Noah is good. I'll give him that.

A maniacal laugh strums from Carlotta. "The Trickle Tickle strikes again. That's enough footage for one day." She chucks her phone to the side. "Get cookin', Harry. I've got a kinky side, too, you know," she says, pointing to the top of her shoulders.

He gets to work just as I tap Noah's chest with my foot and hitch my head toward Sammy.

Noah catches my foot and kisses the top of my big toe as a forlorn look crosses his face.

"I miss making you glow like that." He touches his finger to my nose.

"Who do you think put that glow on my face?" I ask, standing up and taking him with me. "Come on. Sammy is all by herself over there. Let's go shake her down."

We get out of the water and the heated air dries us off almost instantly.

Noah picks up his phone and wags it my way.

"In case I need to take notes." It buzzes in his hand, and I can see it's a text from Everett with the words **I'm going to kill you**.

"I'm going to kill you?" I lift a brow his way.

He winces at the screen. "I take it he's seen the video."

"Wonderful." I glance back at Carlotta, who's splashing around as if she was trying not to drown.

Noah and I make our way over to Sammy, and the first thing I notice is a long scar running up the side of her right leg. The flesh around it is sunken in and swollen, a shade lighter than the rest of her skin along the pale thick line.

"I see you looking at it," she says with a light laugh as she tosses a beach towel into a bag. "I got it that night." She offers a complacent smile to Noah. "Of the break-in." She looks my way. "A few years back, Clark and I had a couple of masked men break into our home. They wanted jewelry and money. They roughed us up quite a bit. I got the bloodier end of the stick, you might say. They carved my leg, my arm." She touches another less prevalent scar on her forearm. "They gashed my stomach open, too. Clark was knocked out, but when he came to, they were gone so he called for help. I was almost dead on the floor by then." She shivers a moment. "It was a long time ago, but it feels like yesterday. And now Clark is gone." She shakes her head. "It's all so hard to believe."

"I'm sorry," I tell her. "What do you think happened? Did someone have a vendetta against him?"

"I wouldn't know." She pulls on a beaded cover-up over her

bathing suit, and it's the same style as the one she had on the other night with the exception that this one is baby blue—and has far less blood on it. "We haven't been close in years. We were pretty much keeping to ourselves, just waiting to see if we could work things out, I guess."

Noah turns his head, his eyes still latched to hers. "But you lived in the same house, isn't that right?"

"That's right." She ticks her head to the side. "We were two perfect strangers living under the same roof. Can you believe it? I can hardly believe it myself. I don't have any kids. But Clark had two daughters—both grown and married. One lives in Maine and the other in Florida. They're both coming out for the memorial service. The older, Lydia, has already tried me in the court of public opinion and hung me for her father's murder." She glances to the sky as if it were absurd. "I didn't do it. You both saw me come upon the scene. I was in shock seeing him like that."

Someone calls her name from across the way and she motions for them to wait.

"Sammy"—I lean in before she trots off—"do you have any idea who could have done this to him?"

Her lips move from side to side just as a spray of silver stars appears above her head like a halo and Leo lands over her shoulder. His tail whips her in the face every few seconds as he licks his paw as if it were the most natural thing in the world.

I take up Noah's hand so he can hear Leo, too.

"Has she confessed yet?" Leo inspects Sammy at close range.

I shake my head his way.

"She will," Leo assures me. "She swore to me that one day she'd confess to all her crimes."

What's that supposed to mean?

Sammy nods. "If anyone has the answer, it's Bridger Douglas. That is, if he didn't do the deed himself. Sure, they were friends, but they worked together closely, too. And if I know anything about Clark Willoughby, it's that people could only take him in small doses. He's kind and harmless as a kitten from a distance, but when you dig down deep he's as caustic as that Bengal cat he used to have. Boy, that thing was all piss and vinegar." She leans our way. "I finally fed that thing to coyotes." She winks as she takes off.

Leo lets out a hearty roar. "She's pure evil, Lottie. Don't believe a word she says, except perhaps that last part." He leaps through Noah's chest and disappears.

Noah sways for a moment. "Whoa. I think the heat's getting to me. Let's get home to Lyla Nell. What do you want to do for dinner?"

"I don't know about you, but I'm hungry for another suspect."

"Bridger Douglas?"

I nod. "And I know exactly who can put him on the menu."

LOTTIE

"$\mathcal{N}$oah is going to die," Everett says with a look of rage in his eyes as he glares at the soon-to-be deceased. But I'm not going to let that happen. I'm not going to let Everett die either.

"Everett, stop," I say, not daring to get too close to the action.

It's evening, the sun has set, the air is as warm as a furnace, and the scent of night jasmine and fresh oven baked pizza lights up our senses.

The three of us are standing right outside of Mangias, looking spiffy enough for me to call this a date night of sorts.

As soon as I asked Everett if we could meet with Bridger for dinner, he made arrangements and Bridger agreed to meet us here at seven-thirty. That gave me plenty of time to hang out with Lyla Nell and nurse her. Noah hung out with us, too, and it's been a nice day overall right up until Everett got out of his SUV about a minute ago and pinned Noah to the wall by way of his fists balled up in Noah's shirt.

"I gave you one inch and you had to take a mile," Everett grits it through his teeth.

Noah's hands fly up. "It was perfectly innocent."

"The hell it was." Everett lets go of Noah with a shove. "It's never innocent with you. Not when it comes to Lemon."

"It was innocent," I say as I pull Everett to me. "And what did you mean by you gave him an inch?"

Everett shoots Noah a dark look.

"Nothing." Everett lands a calm kiss to my lips as if the shoving match hadn't even happened.

If I've learned anything between the two of them, it's that once in a while a good shoving match is all that's needed to reduce their urge to kill.

"So"—I iron Everett's shirt with my hands—"how was the court-house?" I bite down on my lip as I examine my handsome husband. The scruff on his cheek is darkened by the night shadows, and it only makes his eyes siren out like twin blue beacons all the more. My heart thumps each time I look at him. And his anger is only giving him the bad boy appeal that drives women batty—me included.

"It was fine. No one was sentenced today. All I had to do was sit back and listen. Not a bad day at the office." His jaw redefines itself as he looks to Noah, and a part of me wonders if they're speaking in code.

Noah's phone goes off and he glances to the screen.

"Okay"—Noah blows out a breath—"this is what I was afraid of. Toxicology came back and Rooster was indeed poisoned with snake venom."

"Well, that's good, right?" I nod. "His demise was natural. That means the mob didn't suddenly start making good on those lethal promises. Maybe they have a heart after all?"

A heart that will hopefully choose not to kill Noah and Everett.

"No, they don't have a heart," Noah says. "The venom in Rooster's blood was from a Russell's viper. The Russell's viper isn't indigenous to Vermont or anywhere else in the United States. Not only that, Rooster had almost twice the venom a viper could dispense at a time. That bite mark on his arm was meant to throw us. They found an injection site on his arm."

Everett nods. "They got him. But don't think for a minute they didn't know you and your men would figure this out. It's a warning. They can make it look like an accident if they want, and I'm guessing when they go after a cop and a judge, they'll do just that. For as dirty as they are, they do like to keep their noses clean."

My entire body comes alive with fear for the two of them.

"Everett," I moan. "I won't let that happen. I promise."

"Hey ho, the gang's all here," a deep voice calls from behind and we spot Bridger Douglas with a grin on his face. His dark curly hair looks as if it has a blue cast in this dim light, and he quickly slaps both Noah and Everett with a manly handshake before offering me a much more civil version. "So let's catch up. I came hungry. And this is my treat. I won't hear of anything different."

We share a warm laugh as we head on in. Mangias is the best —even if it is the only—Italian restaurant in Honey Hollow. It's been our go-to place for as long as I can remember. If we're not here, we're picking up takeout at least four times a week.

It's dimly lit, the floors and furniture are comprised of dark wood, and the scent of garlic and perfectly stewed marinara sauce calls us to attention. An Italian version of soft rock music is playing, and for the first time, I spot bodies congregating near the back where there seems to be a makeshift dance floor.

"Hey!" Sergio, a partial owner here, is the first to greet us. He's tall, with dark hair, and always has a smile at the ready.

"Hi, Sergio," I say. "Is the dancing thing new?"

He shrugs. "A couple of women insisted we clear a space. They said they needed men and they were going to fish in the pond they were standing in. You know I can't deny a beautiful woman anything." He winks my way and nods as if I should know what that means. "Just four tonight?"

"Just four," Noah says, and I shoot him a look.

"Are you sure your stalker isn't going to join us?" I ask. "Maybe we should save Sergio the trouble and make it five?"

Noah's brows hook together. "Are you trying to jinx me, Lot? Sergio, we're sticking to four."

Everett's chest rumbles with a silent laugh. "If that video Carlotta sent me this afternoon is any indication, Cormack will want more of that action sooner than later."

Noah groans, "Dude, don't say her name. The last thing I want is for us to conjure her up."

Bridger laughs at Noah's expense as Sergio lands us at a table near those gyrating bodies.

"Everett, you've certainly had your fair share of sticky women," Bridger points his way as he says it. "I'm sure you could give Noah a few tips on how to cut the cord."

Everett's lips curve. "This woman has a chain, not a cord. And my hot tip for Noah would be go for it." He sheds a short-lived smile and you can practically see the sarcasm dripping off of him. "You're single. She's single. I don't see the problem here."

Noah's expression hardens.

I look to poor Bridger, who is going to feel clueless despite the fact he'll very much feel the tension.

"Noah and I used to date," I tell him. "We share a daughter—

the baby that was with me at the lake that day. And as I mentioned at the lake, Everett and I are married."

"It's a technicality," Noah says without missing a beat. "Everett wanted to sink his claws into his daddy's trust fund and needed a wife to complete the transaction. Lottie has a good heart, so she volunteered to do the deed. She was my girlfriend first. We were married ourselves a short time before Everett hired a bunch of legal eagles to dismantle that union."

Bridger's head ticks back a notch. "Whoa. I got a little dizzy when you zigged and zagged."

"Don't worry," Everett tells him. "I can't keep up either."

I look to Bridger and laugh. "And Everett's the smartest one in the room."

"*Hey*," Noah says my way.

"Ooh, sorry." I tap my lips with my fingers in an effort from doing any more damage with them.

I'm about to ensure Noah of his cerebral prowess when a sprinkle of silver stars appears to my right and Leo materializes in his full Bengal cat glory.

Leo's nose twitches in Bridger's direction as if he were sniffing the man out.

"Oh, it's him," Leo growls, and I quickly pick up both Noah's and Everett's hands so they can listen in on the celestial conversation. "Clark liked the guy. They were a little too chummy, Sammy used to say. She didn't trust him. But I'll tell you who I didn't trust—Sammy. The woman is wicked. Ask Bridger. I take it he didn't care much for her either."

Bridger squints as he looks down at our conjoined hands.

"I can see you still hold Noah in high regard." A nervous smile swims on his lips as he looks my way. "To each his own," he mutters that last part under his breath.

We order up a couple of pizzas, and they seem to be delivered just as quick.

We're about to dig in when a murmur erupts around us and

we note people looking over at the dance floor and covering their mouths as if holding back a laugh.

I glance that way momentarily before doing a double take.

"Oh Mylanta." I close my eyes in hopes when I open them that it would have all been a bad dream but nope—there they are, Carlotta and Charlie doing some weird thumb hitching, foot jerking moves, drawing unnecessary attention to themselves as if it were their lot in life. And I'll bet dollars to donuts it is.

"Excuse me," I say as I cut through the crowd, risking my reputation as I land in front of them.

Leo leaps onto my shoulder and I can feel his heft when he lands. It always amazes me that the dead have the power to feel as solid in every capacity as they choose.

"Carlotta, *Charlie,*" I hiss and they both momentarily cease all movement despite the fact the song marches on. "What in the heck is happening to the two of you? Are you having some sort of mother-daughter seizure? Because if not, you're scaring the customers—me included."

Charlie lifts a finger and Leo jumps onto her shoulder, caressing her neck with his tail as if they've been a team all along.

"It's called having a good time," Charlie snips my way. "Something I see you're allergic to. Carlotta was right about you."

"Enough about me, what's with the scary moves?"

Carlotta nods to Charlie. "Didn't I tell ya those moves were too powerful? Now the entire place is going to want in on our secret."

"What secret?" I ask.

Carlotta huffs, "May as well tell her, Cha Cha. She is family, after all."

Charlie gives a bored glance to the ceiling. "This is our we-need-a-man dance. Whenever we put out these moves, it sends a signal to the universe and men come crawling out of the wood-work, trying to make off with us and make us their own."

I don't even know where to begin with this one.

"Charlie"—I decide to address the slightly more lucid of the two—"you're trying to tell me this is your mating dance?" I ask and she nods. "Honey, those men weren't crawling out of the woodwork. They were stumbling over from the bar from which they inebriated themselves. And the reason they were trying to make off with you is because they wanted to take you to bed. They weren't looking for a long-term relationship. All they wanted was some wham, bam, thank you, Cha Cha."

Carlotta nudges Charlie in the ribs. "Told you she was a slow learner."

Charlie thumps out a laugh. "So you cracked the code, now scat." She stomps her foot in front of me. "You're cramping our style. I had three prospects before you showed up."

"Fine." I reach over and yank Leo back into my arms. "But I'm taking my cat with me."

I head back to the table just as the three of them share a quick laugh.

Bridger gives a wistful tick of the head. "I was just telling Noah an old story about your husband. I'd repeat it, but I don't believe in sharing stories like that around ladies. I hope you don't mind."

"Not at all." In fact, I'd rather not hear it. I completely understand that Everett had a wild past. But I'd like to keep the past where it belongs—in the rearview mirror.

Leo bounces out of my arms and sits at the edge of one of the pizzas they've already dived into. His tan fur and dark stripes and spots give him the appeal of a much more dangerous cat—one I wouldn't fight with over a slice of pizza or anything else for that matter.

I take up a slice and start in myself—as does Leo. Here's hoping Bridger doesn't care that a slice of pizza is slowly evaporating into thin air.

Noah lowers his chin as he looks to Bridger. "Not to darken the subject, but the night Clark died we lost another man, too."

"That's right." Bridger dabs his mouth with his napkin. "I saw there were two bodies on the shore. For the life of me I don't know what that was about."

"How could you?" Everett shakes his head. "The odds of two men dying within feet apart is unbelievable. But then, Honey Hollow has had a run of bad luck for a while now."

I know Everett doesn't believe in luck, bad or good. And I also know he's trying his best to help Noah pump his old friend for info.

Bridger looks to Noah. "But he died from natural causes, right?"

I shrug over at him. "It could have been a double murder, or even a serial killer."

Bridger turns his head, his eyes still pinned on mine. "Serial killer? I bet that's what it is. A serial killer right here in Honey Hollow. Who was the other man that passed away?" He directs the question to Noah.

"A man by the name of Rooster. He was poisoned, injected with a toxin," Noah says. "So I guess I do have two homicides on my hands to investigate."

"And don't forget the ATM robberies," I tell him. "You'll need to clone yourself to get it all done." And since he can't, he should be thrilled that he has me to help him. Although Noah is seldom thrilled by the fact.

Noah shakes his head. "I might have to bow out of the task force." He looks to Bridger. "I'd like to say there's a big bust coming down the pike for the robbers out there cleaning out ATM machines left and right, but I think I have a better chance of solving this double homicide than that happening."

"Double homicide." Bridger fumbles for words. "I don't know what to say. I guess that's pretty incredible." He tips his head back and nods. "And—I bet you're right. There might be a serial killer on the loose."

I know neither Noah nor Everett believes that. I certainly

don't. One was a mob hit and the other—well, Clark's death is more of your run-of-the-mill homicide. That is, if a homicide can ever fall under that classification.

Leo twitches his head my way, and his yellow eyes glow like ambers. "So where is his ghost?"

"His ghost?" I ask lower than a whisper while trying to make heads or tails of Leo's question, then it hits me.

Where is his ghost...

Rooster would be the subject in this equation.

Huh, that's strange. Where *is* the ghost that should be helping me solve Rooster's case?

On second thought, after getting to know Rooster, maybe he didn't really love anyone at all, furry or human. I mean, that is the criteria. The one who the murder victim cared for the most—typically a pet, shows up to help nail down the killer. I guess Rooster's death will have to remain a mystery. Either that or the Ashford Sheriff's Department will have to kick into high gear and solve it. Lord knows I can't be bothered with it. Unless...

Oh my word, what if whoever snuffed the life out of Rooster is the same person who is about to fill my beautiful husband's body with bullets?

Good grief. Now I'm practically obligated to hunt down Rooster's killer.

There you go. I've just doubled my pleasure, doubled my fun.

But I'm not going to bother to say anything to Noah or Everett. They'll just try to double up their efforts to stop me.

Noah's chest expands a moment. "Bridger, I know that Clark must have been on the dark side of the lake securing the site of his garage sale. Can I ask where you were? Did you see anything at all that might help out?"

Bridger tips his head back and forth.

"Careful," Leo says. "A rock is liable to fall out of his ear. Sammy always said Bridger's head was full of them."

A tiny laugh lives and dies in my chest. Leo is a riot even

though he's not trying to be. I really appreciate his dry wit. If you ask me, that's the best kind of humor.

Bridger sniffs. "I was on the south side myself enjoying the fireworks with everyone else. But I knew Clark would be securing the site, so as soon as the show ended I headed that way. I'm sorry, I didn't..." He stops mid-sentence and takes a deep breath. "Wait a minute. Just as the show was starting, Sammy flagged me down. She asked where Clark was. I thought it was strange at the time. I mean, they never exchanged two words, not in years anyway. But I did tell her where she could find him."

Noah nods. "And she was the first person on the scene."

Everett shakes his head. "If she did it, I doubt she'd be the first person on the scene. She's a smart woman. I think she'd steer clear, at least in the beginning."

Bridger purses his lips at Everett as he contemplates this. "You always were the smart one, Everett. You're right. Honestly, Noah, if you really want to kick-start your case, I'd talk to Betsy Monroe."

"Betsy?" Everett inches back as if he couldn't see the connection.

"You must know her." Bridger nods. "She works down at the courthouse, court reporter. She used to moonlight at one of the antique shops Clark owns. I don't know what was going on, but one night I caught the two of them going at it. All I know is she must have done something very wrong because she pleaded with him not to call the sheriff's department on her. It sounded serious. He told her to never darken his doorway again. And that was the last I ever saw of her at the antique shop. But I did see her at Honey Lake the night of the murder."

Everett takes a deep breath. "She was there. I spoke with her."

"Thank you, Bridger," Noah says. "I'll be sure to speak with her. Maybe I can get her to open up and tell me what that was about."

We finish up dinner and Bridger takes off, citing the fact he needs to be at the lake at the crack of dawn to start the massive garage sale still going strong. He anted up at the register, so we're free to leave, too.

A couple of men seated a few tables away garner my attention. They're both dressed in suits, matching goatees, matching serious expressions, and they don't hide the fact they're glaring in our direction.

"Do either of you see those men?" I ask, hitching my head casually their way.

Everett nods. "They sat down five minutes after we did."

Noah glances their way. "I saw them, too. They've been making me twitch all night. I guess we need to get those briefcases back where they belong."

"You get yours back," Everett tells him. "Mine is missing a few hundred thousand dollars. I'm pretty sure Luke isn't interested in the luggage alone."

Noah's mouth opens and he pauses.

"What is it?" Everett grouses. "Don't make me shake it out of you."

Noah gives a long blink. "I forgot to mention that the night I went to Evergreen, I saw my dad and Miranda leaving the manor."

"What?" I shake my head. "What did they say?"

"Nothing. I didn't confront them. Your mom was buttoning her blouse. They looked a little wrecked. I'd like to think they were merely having a tryst."

Everett growls hard. "As opposed to cleaning out the loot from my briefcase? Noah, you should have taken care of this the very first night."

"It's only been a few days," I point out. "That is, if Wiley took the money. And believe me, my mother is clueless. He probably had his way with her in some dark corridor, took off and did the deed on his own, and she was none the wiser. My mother is an innocent lamb—at the slaughter."

Noah's dimples dig in. "I'd like to think my father has nothing to do with this."

Everett's chest bucks. "Your father is the reason you have a bullseye on your forehead—and so do Miranda, Lemon, and Lyla Nell by proxy."

"I'll talk to him tomorrow." Noah shoots a look to those mobsters that says he, too, is ready to kill.

Sergio comes over. "Sorry, guys." He glances to the men in suits. "But I don't want any trouble. I think maybe for your own safety and the rest of the customers, you should leave."

Sergio seems to be in the know enough to sense a potential massacre in our midst.

We take off, and no sooner do we get outside than Carlotta and Charlie stumble out the door after us.

"I saw 'em," Charlie says as she struggles to catch her breath. And I have no doubt her breathlessness has more to do with those jerky, twerky dance moves than her jaunt over. "Those men, they belong to Manny Moretti."

She should know. She dated Manny just a few months ago. From what I understand, Manny would have offered Everett protection once again against Jimmy's hit, but as a payment he wanted Everett to get Charlie to date him. It was a no-go.

Noah and Everett exchange a look. No doubt that news threw them for a loop.

"Come on, Cha Cha." Carlotta yanks Charlie over to her as she navigates her toward the parking lot. "We can't hang around with this crowd out in the open. They've got the Grim Reaper on his toes. It was nice knowing ya, Foxy and Sexy."

"What about me?" I ask.

"What about you?" Carlotta juts her chin out. "There you go again. Always trying to make it about yourself."

"And I want my cat," Charlie snips, and Leo leaps from the middle of my chest and wraps himself around her shoulders like a stole.

"Geez," I say as I press a hand to the spot he just materialized from. "I will never get used to that."

"I don't plan on getting used to a lot of things either," Noah says. "Starting with this Moretti business. I need to talk to Jimmy."

"I'll go with you," I volunteer.

"No," Everett bites the word out.

"But I can help," I offer.

"You can make things worse"—Everett doesn't miss a beat and our eyes lock with a fury—"for yourself, for Lyla Nell, for Evie—by getting yourself killed."

Noah steps in close to Everett. "Mind how you speak to her."

Everett grabs ahold of Noah's shirt again. "This is all your damn fault."

Charlie snickers. "I knew if we left too soon we'd miss the show."

"He's right, Lot," Noah says as he attempts to shield me with his body, but I don't take my eyes off Everett.

"I'm going with him," I say. "Jimmy responds to me in a positive way."

"You are not going with him. Do you hear me?" Everett is unrelenting with his harsh tone, and his heated emotions are palpable.

That vision Nell shared with me over a week ago flits through my mind and my own fury burns anew.

"You don't tell me what to do," I seethe. "You don't know what I know."

Everett ticks his head back a notch. "What do you know, Lemon?"

My mouth opens and closes. I cast a threatening glance to the peanut gallery in the event Carlotta or my sister decides to have a sudden case of loose-lips-itis.

"That I love you," I tell Everett. "I love you both, and I'll do anything to protect you. Just you try to stop me."

Noah's phone goes off in his pocket, and he pulls it out and groans hard as he looks at the screen.

"What is it?" I ask in a panic. This entire night has me on edge.

"It's Rooster," he says. "He's—*alive*."

Both Carlotta and Charlie let out a horrific howl.

"I told you he was wicked," Carlotta says, yanking Charlie off toward the parking lot. "Come on, Cha Cha. We'd best stock up on holy water while we still can." She turns back our way. "You can't kill evil."

Noah, Everett, and I exchange a look because in this case, Carlotta just might be right.

LOTTIE

The next afternoon Noah and I make tracks to my
mother's B&B.

Noah dropped Lyla Nell and me off at the bakery this
morning while he ran to the sheriff's station down in Ashford to
look into what was going on with Rooster a little more in depth.
And then he came back and picked us up.

"He just woke up?" I ask as we pull into the parking lot of the
Rendezvous Luxury Resort and Razzle Dazzle Day Spa, formerly
the humble Honey Hollow Bed and Breakfast.

"That's what happened." Noah looks just as baffled as I am as
we glide into a spot up front. "Apparently, the coroner was

getting set to carve him up like a Thanksgiving Day turkey and he noticed some movement in his chest. Sure enough, he was breathing—barely breathing but still."

"And now he's in a coma at Honey Hollow General."

"Yup. And you can bet as soon as he so much as blinks, I'll be there to question him. You can come if you like." He sheds a dimpled grin my way.

"Why, Noah Corbin Fox, I do think you're trying to get on my good side."

"I don't have to. Every side is your good side."

"Smooth, Fox. Smooth."

Noah scoops up Lyla Nell, and I sling the baby bag over my shoulder as we head into the hot pink monstrosity. Back before Cormack and her socialite counterpart, Cressida, attacked the place with a glitter gun—by way of a hired hand, of course—the mansion-like structure with its Roman columns and decorative wrought iron railings was a humble hue of alabaster as opposed to the hot pink monstrosity before us.

Inside the foyer hang two expectantly tall oil paintings, one of my mother and one of Cormack. Both of which have been glammed up and their decollates boosted and made to look more ample. Before I won back my mother's half of her old haunt, there was a picture of Cressida that hung next to Cormack.

Speaking of haunts, I can't wait to see the ghosts who reside at the B&B. And seeing that I'm terrified to ask my mother if she has anything to do with that missing money, I'd much rather talk to the dead while I'm here than the living.

The mahogany paneled walls inside the B&B are thankfully untouched, but the floors are pink in areas, and everywhere you look there's something glittery or gilded, neither of which was a part of my mother's cozy décor pre-hijacking of her home.

A roar of laughter comes from the direction of the conservatory and we head that way. The conservatory is a glass structure that was tacked on a couple years back by none other than Bear Fisher.

One might think the woods behind my mother's B&B would have been a great place for the Honey Hollow Blue Butterfly to repopulate the species—and if it did, the conservatory wouldn't be here, and theoretically all of the people who have met their demise in that glass casket would still be roaming the earth.

It's true. My mother's B&B, or the Rendezvous Luxury Resort and Razzle Dazzle Day Spa as it's now unfortunately called, has had more than its fair share of homicides on the grounds.

We step into the conservatory, and it's breathtaking to see the evergreens right outside these glassy walls toward the back. The roof is made of sloping glass as well, and it lends an airy light to the cavernous space. The conservatory is filled with bodies as groups of ten sit at dozens of round tables and in the front, commandeering a small spinning cage, are my mother and Wiley.

To my delight, on each table sits a platter of my blueberry muffins. I thought we had an unusually high order for them after I had asked Suze to deliver them to the B&B this morning, and now I know why.

"B, eleven," my mother calls out and everyone hurriedly looks down at the cards spread before them.

"Bingo," Noah says as he chuckles. "How much you want to bet your mother and my father orchestrated this to get another wad of cash into his pocket?"

"Let's hope that's the only cash he's stuffing it with," I say while Lyla Nell vocalizes and kicks her legs and arms as she looks out at the room.

"I'm mad about it, too," I say, giving her a little kiss over the nose. "Oh look, there are Carlotta and Charlie—and Cormack, Naomi, and Greer Giles."

Or more to the point, the ghost of Greer Giles.

We head in their direction and say hello, but the five of them hardly give us a quick glance as my mother calls out another number.

Mom zips over. "There's my princess," she sings as she scoops the baby from my arms. "You just look like the yummiest little cream puff, and Glam Glam is going to yum you right up." She dots a row of kisses over the baby's cheek, and Lyla Nell squawks and laughs as she grabs onto my mother's earrings with a death grip.

"Oh no, no, no," I say. "Glam Glam doesn't need another hole in her head. Or any of the holes in her head to get any bigger." Her brain is liable to fall out. "What's with the bingo?"

"It's game night," Mom says as she untangles her earrings from Lyla Nell's beastly strong clutches. "But we have to host it in the middle of the afternoon. Cormack said it would get in the way of the dance parties."

"That makes perfect sense." Noah frowns as his father calls out another number.

Greer abandons her card and floats my way.

Greer Giles was about my age, late twenties, when she died a couple years back. She has long dark hair, perfectly sculpted features, and eyes that give off an eerie glow. She's still wearing that white ruched gown she had on the night she was gunned down, and that crimson gunshot wound over her chest almost looks like a necrotic corsage.

"Lottie, she's getting so big." She attempts to take the baby from my mother and Mom holds Lyla Nell a little tighter.

"Whoa." Mom shakes her head. "Lyla Nell, you almost jumped right out of my arms. Now don't you scare Glam Glam like that."

Lyla Nell's foot looks as if it's being pulled to the side at an unnatural angle and I'm about to reprimand the culprit when Greer beats me to it.

"*Lea*," Greer hisses at her tiny daughter. And just past the tiny menace, I see both Lea and Thirteen are up with their own bingo cards, and judging by the way those cards look, they're not doing so bad at it either.

I make a face at the sight. It's one thing to rattle a few bookshelves around here or sway a chandelier or two, but to manipulate bingo cards and markers?

"Greer, are you nuts?" I whisper as my mother steps away to show off the baby to her friends. "It's bad enough you're playing the game, but Lea and Thirteen?"

The two of them appear before me front and center when I say their names.

Little Lea—Azalea—is perennially about six. Her family was slaughtered on the grounds here, and she now roams the B&B with a machete. She has long brown stringy hair that's combed over her face, and she wears a dirty pinafore and scuffed Mary Janes. And yes, she's exactly as terrifying as she sounds. Thirteen is a black cat that once helped me solve a crime, and for whatever reason, he never had to leave. Can't explain it, don't want to.

"Lottie," Lea says my name like a reprimand and I take up Noah's hand so he can listen. "The guests love seeing me move my bingo pieces. They love being scared and I love to scare them."

Thirteen twitches his whiskers and tiny blue stars emit around them. "She's right. The woman next to her passed out twice. And the woman next to me sneezed a dozen times. Says she's allergic to cat dander." He licks a line down his ebony coat.

"Fine," I say. "Play your hearts out. I hope you win big. And don't think for a minute Wiley won't swipe the money from you." A thought comes to me. "Hey? Have any of you noticed Wiley lugging around a sack full of cash?"

The three of them nod.

"All the time," Greer says. "He does the bank runs for the B&B."

"Wonderful," Noah says. "Honey Hollow is proving to be a

fountain of funny money for the world's most notorious con man."

Wiley calls out another number, and Naomi jumps up out of her seat.

"Wingo *Bingo*—jingle all that money in my pocket!" She dances in a circle as the room begins to stir to life.

Charlie and Carlotta come this way, and Naomi and Cormack are quick to follow.

"Well, if it isn't Lottie Lemon," Naomi says with an open-mouthed smile. First time I've ever seen my bestie's twin not baring her fangs my way. "Guess you heard the good news. Cormack and Noah are back together. I saw them sneaking around the Evergreen the night of the Fourth."

"Naomi," Noah grouses.

"Oh hush." She waves him off. "This is too juicy for me not to spill. Speaking of *spill*, where's my money?" She charges to the front and Wiley antes up—a miracle in the making. Although knowing him, he's pocketing half the loot. Serves her right.

"She saw you?" I hiss over at Noah.

Cormack trots over and wraps her arms around Noah. "I guess our secret's out of the bag."

Charlie smirks. "Cormack, Noah's just toying with you."

Cormack looks mildly affronted. "I beg to differ. The Big Boss knows better than to toy with me."

"Oh yeah?" Charlie is determined to play with matches. "Then why did he take my sister out to dinner last night at Mangias?"

"Everett was there," I'm quick to add. "Not sure why I felt the need to clarify that. I couldn't care less if anyone thought Noah and I were dating again, or even if we were having a perfectly platonic dinner. He's the father of my child."

Cormack sucks in a breath. "You're dating again?"

Noah turns his ear to her. "That was the takeaway you got from that?"

Carlotta chuckles as she steps my way. "How did things end

up in the bedroom after you and Sexy took one another to the mat after dinner? Things were pretty heated. I bet they got even hotter once you closed that door last night."

She's not wrong.

Everett and I glared at one another for one hot second before his lips curved with naughty intent, and well, an inferno ignited the room.

"So you're not denying the fact you're seeing her." Cormack hauls off and slaps Noah.

A never-ending breath fills my lungs at the sight.

"Don't you dare strike Lyla Nell's father." I give Cormack a shove and she shoves me right back and soon we're pulling hair, and I think she just bit me on the neck.

"Girl fight!" Carlotta shouts, and soon every phone in the room is pointed our way while both Noah and Wiley work to pull us apart.

Cormack stumbles back as Wiley restrains her. "You haven't seen the last of me, Lomita!"

"That's exactly what I'm afraid of," I shout back.

Cormack yanks herself free and makes strides our way and Noah steps in front of me.

"Don't you dare lay a hand on her." Noah's tone is a threat in and of itself.

Cormack's face turns a frightening shade of purple before she shakes her head and lets out a rather powerful, "ARRGGHHH!" Her fists ball up at her sides. "I'm sick of this obsession you have with this, this *thing*." She points my way. "She's mousy, and plain, and she doesn't come from *money*."

"She's drop-dead gorgeous and she owns half of Vermont," Noah counters.

An exaggeration on both fronts, but who cares? Cormack is finally getting her comeuppance.

"So you're after her money?" Cormack shakes her head as if she couldn't put the pieces together.

"Something like that." Noah sighs as if it was no use, and he's right.

"Okay." Cormack gives a wild nod. "I think I can work with that. You haven't seen the last of me either, Big Boss." She stomps her way out of the room, and I give a spontaneous applause.

"And stay out," I shout, but there's a dozen conversations humming all around us, so I doubt she heard.

Noah swoops in. "Are you okay?"

Carlotta clucks her tongue. "Don't worry, Foxy. Lot Lot comes from a hearty stock. Back in Higgins Bottom, Cha Cha got in at least one fistfight a week."

"It's true," Charlie says.

Sadly, my poor sister looks proud of this violent fact.

Suze strides over and I give a hard blink.

"You're here," I say. "Is something wrong at the bakery?"

"Why would I be at the bakery? You asked me to deliver the muffins here, remember?"

"That was four hours ago. You're on the clock," I remind her.

"Your mother asked me to play a few games. I didn't want to be rude, so I agreed. And since I live here, I may as well call it a day."

"I'll let Lily know." I frown her way.

Suze has been staying here at the B&B ever since she flew into Honey Hollow on her broomstick a year or so ago. It's weird to me that she's staying just a few rooms down from where her ex-husband is holding my mother hostage and flogging her with his body.

Suze grunts, "See that look she's giving me, Noah? The woman hates me. Just yesterday she tried to kill me by way of heat, you know."

"I'll bite," Noah says.

Good thing because I don't know if I have the energy for another catfight. With Everett and me wrestling half the night, and Lyla Nell holding up the rear, I didn't get two winks of sleep.

Suze glowers at her older son. "She did! She wanted to send *me*, a woman of advance years, to the lake to peddle frosted muffins of all things."

I shake my head at Noah. "I'm not frosting them anymore. The frosting doesn't do well in the heat."

"Ah ha!" Suze wags a crooked finger at me. "She's not even trying to deny it! But I suppose you wouldn't care about that. You always seem to take her side on every matter."

Noah nods. "That's because I happen to agree with her on every matter."

Suze scoffs in Noah's face before exiting the conservatory with just as much dramatic flair that Cormack afforded.

Wiley starts to take off and Noah pulls him back.

"Not so fast. I'd like a word with you." He hauls him off a few feet and I spot my mother talking to Chrissy Nash, and just as they part ways I'm right there in her face.

"Miranda Lemon," I whisper. "What's this I hear about you sneaking around the Evergreen Manor on the night of the Fourth?"

Her eyes widen a notch before her cheeks turn a dark hue of crimson, and Lyla Nell slaps her silly and laughs right in her face while doing it.

Get a few in for me, kid, I want to say.

"Lottie," Mom brings a finger to her lips, "it's not good for business for my guests to know I've visited enemy terrain." She gives a little wink my way. "Variety is the spice of life and I need to keep things spicy, if you know what I mean."

I squint over at her.

She certainly doesn't appear to know about any cash heist.

"So that's all you and Wiley were doing at the Evergreen Manor? Fooling around? You didn't, I don't know, ransack a guest's room and rob him of all he was worth? And rumor has it he was worth a whole lot of cash money."

Her body seizes and her fingers fly to her lips.

My mouth falls open because she's all but admitted her guilt. "Mother!"

"It was role-playing, Lottie." She swats me on the arm. "Wiley rented that room. We've done it before." She waves me off with marked irritation over the fact I'm vetting her fantasies.

"You've done it before? My goodness, he was grooming you for just this occasion. What did he do with the money?"

"What money?" She looks morbidly confused and a swell of relief fills me. At least she has no idea what he was really up to. This conversation would be ten times worse if she admitted to stealing the cash with him. "Are you talking about those bundles of fake cash?" She laughs like a hyena before leaning my way. "We're siphoning them into the bank drops and pretending to *launder* them." She giggles herself into a conniption. "Don't tell me love is boring after you get over the hill."

She meanders away to show Lyla Nell off to the remnant of the guests in the room and I'm frozen solid with fear.

Noah comes over and shakes his head. "I couldn't get him to crack. My dad's a tough nut."

"He's a nut, all right. One that's going to crack both my sanity and my mother's world right down the middle."

I dish the dirty deeds that his father has roped my mother into, and now we're both seeing red.

I predict there's going to be another murder, and the victim's name just so happens to be Wiley Fox.

NOAH

"*T*ell me and tell me now, old man. What the hell do you think you're doing?"

It took less than ten seconds from the time Lottie relayed the twisted conversation she had with her mother, until I pinned my father in a dark corridor of this haunted hotel.

"Where's the money?" I grit the words through my teeth as I shake him.

"Now now. I've never been one to spill my secrets and you know it."

"You keep your dirty money, that you stole, away from the

cash drawers at the B&B. You got that? You do not get to ruin another woman. Especially not Miranda Lemon."

"No one saw me, son." Dad holds his arms up as if I was about to arrest him, and I should. It might just do him some good to serve a little time. "And if I recall correctly"—he gives a contrived shrug—"it was *you* Naomi saw that night in the parking lot. I'm afraid to say it, but it's not me who has to worry about the feds. You were there and you were seen."

"*You* were seen—by Miranda."

"She won't breathe a word. That woman is loyal to me. It's my word against yours. Now who are they gonna believe? A kind old man or some lovesick cop obsessed with another man's wife?"

"With my luck?" I give him a rattle by way of his shirt. "You."

I head back into the conservatory and tell Lottie I have to leave. Miranda offers to give Lottie and Lyla Nell a ride back home, so I give them both a kiss and take off in a fury.

But first I stop by my place and pick up one briefcase I've been dying to offload.

This never-ending nightmare only seems to be unfurling all the more, no matter how hard I try to stop it from unraveling.

Everett is right.

This is all my damn fault.

IF LOTTIE KNEW where I was headed, there would be no stopping her.

I shake my head as I walk into Red Satin Gentlemen's Club. The walls and the furniture are as red as sin, and those women dancing half-naked on that expansive stage aren't so innocent either. The scent of stale beer and cheap cologne bites my nostrils and about a half a dozen women with pasties on give me an ear-to-ear grin when they see me.

"Noah Fox," Meg calls out and gives me a friendly wave.

Her dark hair is bushy and her eyes are drawn in with black liner that matches her lipstick. She's wearing a black sack with fishnets and hiking boots, and looks every bit herself.

"You want a platter of nachos?" she offers. "I can set you up stage-side—best seat in the house. I've got a girl who is just your type hitting the stage in an hour. She looks exactly like my fun and flirty big sister."

"Charlie, I take it." I frown at the stage as I clutch the briefcase in my hand a little tighter, leather gloves and all. "I don't like the thought of Lottie's look-alike running around naked up there for all the men to see. Doesn't that bother you in the least?"

"Nope. I'm just glad she doesn't look like me. Let me guess, you're here to see Jimmy?"

I nod. "Where's the wicked villain?"

"Downstairs talking to Cormack."

"What?" I sail past her and head for the tunnels this place seems to be comprised of. Illegal gambling, loan shark central, kink club, you name it, Red Satin is a cover for it all. There's an underground lair here that seems to run under all of Vermont.

I go down a story and find myself in the whirling, twirling gambling casino with its one-armed bandits and its backgammon tables with a smattering of customers. And I spot Cormack heading in my direction.

"Big Boss!" She gives me a toothy grin. "I'm glad I ran into you. I've got a little something coming your way." She hikes up on her tiptoes and lands a kiss to my cheek. "Don't ever say I didn't do anything for you." She checks her phone. "I'm late for my show. I'll see you soon."

She runs her finger over my lips as she takes off and leaves behind the scarf of her sugary perfume. By show, she means the talk show she's managed to land herself after the old host was murdered. It's called *Getting Candid with Cormack*, and it just so happens that was the exact sleazy show Lottie was cornered into going on, to do the paternity reveal for Lyla Nell. Things swung in my favor, so I can't complain too much.

Just beyond the blackjack tables, I spot Jimmy Canelli talking to a dealer.

I'm on them in two seconds.

"Detective?" He lifts a brow. Jimmy has a head full of silver hair, mostly fit for a man his age, and he's got a determined look in his eyes that lets you know he means business. "Let's take a seat. I've got a little gift for you." He motions to the man standing with us and he disappears.

Jimmy is really good at making people disappear in general, which brings me to the point of my visit.

"I've got a gift for you, too," I say, hiking up the briefcase a notch.

"Ah, I see. Let's get to my office." We step down the hall, into a small room that can fit little more than a desk and two chairs. Jimmy lands on one side of the desk and I land on the other.

I hoist the briefcase onto his desk and pop it open before sliding it his way and spinning it around.

"Gloves?" He tosses his head to the side as he pulls the briefcase close to him. "Thinking like a cop. I like that."

"That's because I am a cop. I don't belong here. The contents of that briefcase don't belong to me."

The dealer Jimmy was speaking to just a minute ago comes in and lands four bricks of cash onto the desk before taking off like a phantom in flight.

Jimmy opens the briefcase, letting the lid slam near me.

"It's all there," I tell him.

"I don't doubt it." He takes the money and slots it in between the bricks of cocaine before shutting it closed and spinning the briefcase back my way.

"What are you doing? I don't want that cash. I don't want any of it."

"I'm giving you back what's yours."

"No, no, no. This is yours." I give it a shove in his direction. "I can't keep it. This world is full of thieves. I'd hate for you to lose it on my account."

"My men tell me you just had a nice safe delivered. I entrust it to your care. I don't want it back."

The safe was a knee-jerk reaction on my part even though Lottie told me not to do it.

"What do you mean you don't want it back?" I ask.

"You didn't deliver it." He folds his hands in a threatening manner like only a mobster can do. "I need to have your loyalty, Detective. And as long as it's in your care, you're culpable—and I can work with that. You can have my protection so long as you keep this briefcase in your possession."

"Culpable," I parrot because I know exactly what he means.

"How about I remain culpable regardless? Don't make me flush this down the toilet."

Jimmy doesn't so much as flinch. "You won't. And if you threaten to do it again, I'll be forced to send my men over routinely to check on things. I don't think Carlotta Junior or that sweet baby girl of yours would enjoy that too much. Do you?"

I glare at him a moment. "No."

"Okay then. It's nice to see we're on the same page. You take this back to your place. Your little side-piece took a loan out on your behalf. She said you were hard up for some cash." He points to the briefcase he just peppered with enough green to buy a house with.

"What? Why would she do that?"

"You didn't expect her to give you her money, did you?"

"No, I don't accept anyone's money. I've got my own money."

"Good. That means you can pay me back one day. Now, get out of here and take your filthy briefcase with you."

A beefy man with tree trunks for arms shows me to the door,

and soon I'm right back in my truck with that briefcase taking up real estate just below the passenger's seat.

How the hell did I end up here again?

That's right.

It's all my damn fault.

EVERETT

J head into the house after a long day's work, and I can hear Lemon mumbling something and grunting in the kitchen.

"I said get it in the hole before Everett gets back," she riots.

"I'm trying, Lot," Noah grunts. "The hole's too big. It keeps falling out."

It's just after six and I stopped off and picked up some Wicked Wok for dinner. I had a long day and figured Lemon did, too, but now I think I'm going to have an even longer night considering I'm going to have to bury Noah's body.

I think I'll go old school and bury him in his own backyard as an ode to this entire Florenza Canelli nightmare he's dragged us into.

"*Oh*," a hard moan comes from Lemon. "Do that again. That feels really good."

"What?" I step into the kitchen with my adrenaline pumping so hard I'm about to break Noah's neck once I spot him.

But I don't have to. They're standing right in front of me as Lemon helps steady Noah on a chair that swivels as he stands trying to land a nail into a hole that's been in the wall above the sink since we moved in. His knee is slightly over her back—thus the feel-good vibes, I'm assuming.

Strung across the length of the wall is a silver banner that reads *Happy Birthday* and my heart sinks because for the life of me I can't recall exactly whose birthday it would be. Lemon's birthday is in March and so is Lyla Nell's. Evie's is in September.

"Whose birthday is it?" I ask, setting the bag of food down now that my adrenaline surge is running in the opposite direction, and I'm feeling a little loose on my feet.

"Oh, Everett!" Lemon darts over and sends Noah toppling to the wall before hopping down to safety. "It's *your* birthday."

"Mine?" My eyes grow in size as she wraps her arms around me and I sink a kiss to her lips before pulling back. "But my birthday is—"

"In November." She takes a breath. "I know, I know. But I thought, who cares? What's to stop me from celebrating my wonderful husband *today*? I made you a triple fudge cake and an entire platter of brownies to go along with it." She waggles her brows because she knows her brownies are nothing short of an aphrodisiac to me. "I just want you to know that *you*, Essex Everett Baxter, are a ray of sunshine in our lives."

I grimace at the thought involuntarily. "I'm pretty sure no one has ever referenced me that way before. I hate to break it to you, but I'm no ray of sunshine."

"You are to me." Her eyes travel south a moment, she's right back to waggling her brows, and I'm tempted to steal her away to the bedroom.

Noah pops up behind her and shakes his head at me, mouthing the word *no*, and I frown over at him just as that birthday banner sails to the floor on one side like a streak of lightning.

Lemon lands another kiss to my lips. "I'll call Evie and Carlotta and let them know you brought dinner. Perfect timing. I was just about to call the Wicked Wok myself!" She scoops up Pancake and Waffles off the floor on her way out as she calls for everyone to come to the kitchen.

"What the heck is going on with her?" I ask Noah, just low enough for his ears only. "I told you she was acting strangely." And I mean that in the best way. But I can't stand back and pretend I'm not concerned.

"I don't know. I didn't get a chance to focus my full attention on you today, sunshine." He gives a wry smile. "I went to the B&B and spoke to my dad."

"What did he say?"

"Nothing until Lottie broke Miranda wide open like a piñata." He closes his eyes a moment. "Miranda seems to think breaking into Rooster's room—a room she says my father rented for his own ploy—was nothing more than a role-playing activity. She said he pretended to have a bag full of money."

"I'm a little surprised she fell for it, but I'm glad for her sake. Where's the cash?"

"That's where it gets tricky. Miranda said they're siphoning it into the bank drops and pretending to launder it."

"She's going to role-play her way right into a prison sentence if she hangs out with your father another minute. Now I see why you're so dangerous. You have his destructive genes running through your body."

"I'd watch what you say about my body. Lyla Nell just so happens to be derived from it."

"She's mostly derived from Lemon. The scant bit your DNA has infiltrated should be well deterred by having me around as an influence." I nod. "Go on. Did you get the money from him?"

"No. I was about to put him through a wall so I left. I tried to take my briefcase back to Jimmy, but he said he couldn't take what was mine." He tips his head. "He stuffed it full of cash and handed it back to me. He said he likes the way it makes me culpable. I can have his protection from Luke so long as I keep that briefcase in my possession."

"What's with the cash?"

"Cormack figured the way to my heart was through money. She didn't want to part with any of her own, so she took a loan out from Jimmy."

"The laws of mobster attraction are just swimming in your direction. If you crawled into a cave, you'd come out with a hit on you. You can't stay out of trouble, can you?"

"I'm not touching the cash or anything else in that briefcase. I put it back in the attic. I think maybe the safe I had delivered is too obvious."

My stomach sours just hearing every last detail. "All right. I'll take care of Wiley."

"I'll do it with you."

I shake my head at him, but before I can say another word, Evie hops into the kitchen and jumps all over me.

"Happy birthday, Dad!"

All four of them, Evie, Carlotta, Lemon, and Lyla Nell, have a party hat on.

Carlotta blows a party horn in my ear and nearly blows out an eardrum, and Lyla Nell laughs herself silly.

"All right." I take her from Lemon and land a kiss to the tip of her nose. "Let's have a party."

"*Dada!*" Lyla Nell slaps my face, and I nod because I probably deserve that, and then some.

"Hey, Mom?" Evie's eyes spin in a way that can only mean

trouble. "You fought Cormack like a boss—I saw the footage. So you're cool with me getting into fistfights at school, right?"

"It's a hard no," Lemon is quick to tell her.

We start in on dinner and Evie giggles unwarranted throughout the entire meal.

Noah nods her way. "All right, what's so funny?"

Carlotta waves him off. "Don't either of you men get your panties in a twist, but our Evie Stevie is in l-o-v."

"L-o-v-*e*," Lemon corrects.

Carlotta's expression sours. "Nobody likes a know-it-all, Lot Lot."

"Are you back together with Conner?" I ask, surprised to hear this. And under no circumstances is Evie in love. She's too young to understand the concept of romantic affection as far as it intersects with genuine feelings. She's a ball of hormones. I was her age once, I should know.

"With *who*?" Evie looks confused as to who I just referenced.

"Your old boyfriend?" I ask as my blood pressure begins to rise because I'm suddenly aware that this conversation might be taking a turn in a college-bound direction.

Carlotta belches. "He's old news, Sexy. Evie is all about Van Horny these days."

"Bradford Van Horn." Evie sighs as she gazes to the wall behind me.

"What?" I glance to Lemon. "No way. Find another driver's ed instructor. It's clear this guy is a predator. I see it all the time. I refuse to fall victim to this."

"I'm not finding another driver." Evie snaps out of her lovestruck stupor and is suddenly incensed I even brought the idea up. "We've got a date tonight—as in a *driving* lesson."

"That's right." Carlotta holds up her chopsticks and toasts me with her orange chicken. "Van Horny is picking her up, for a little night drive down to Lover's Lane."

"Lover's Lane?" Noah lifts his head out of that bowl of fried rice he's inhaling.

Evie rolls her eyes. "It's just a dark hill above the library where you can look down and see all of Honey Hollow."

Lemon's mouth falls open. "Evie, that *is* Lover's Lane. That's where all the kids used to go when I was in high school to make out. Do not go there with him."

Lyla Nell shouts something from her highchair, and I happen to agree with whatever she just said. She's going to make a darn good prosecuting attorney one day. Or even a judge. She might have to work on that temper, though.

Evie scoffs. "Mom, we are *not* making out. I won't be seventeen for another two months. And Bradford is in college. Don't worry, Dad. I'm fully aware I'm jailbait."

"The legal limit is eighteen," I tell her. "And make sure he's fully aware of it, too. Besides that, your mom is right. You're not going. He's your driving instructor. This is extremely unprofessional on his part."

Noah nods. "I'll have him fired by morning."

"You'll do no such thing," Evie scolds. "He's putting himself through school. He said a little night drive would be great practice for me. And he's got a point. I'll be driving at all hours of the day, you know. Besides, he says he wants to show me something."

A throaty chuckle comes from Carlotta. "I've heard that before —about nine months before your mama was born." She tips her head back. "I'm siding with Sexy on this one. I'm sorry. You can't go, Evie. If you give Little Yippy here a friend, I'll have to move out."

Lemon shoots me a look that says *we're starting on another baby tonight*.

I take a deep breath as I look to Evie. "I trust you to make good decisions, starting with calling this man and telling him you won't be needing his services anymore. And then I want you to call Conner and tell him you're back on."

"*What?*" Everyone in the room, and I'd swear Lyla Nell was in that number, shouts at once.

"Whoa." Noah cuts his hand through the air my way. "Back off, buddy."

"That's right, Dad," Evie seethes as she jumps to her feet. "Back off, *buddy*. You don't get to boss around my love life. I get to choose who I want to spend my time with. Not you. If you think you're going to give me a dowry and get into the arranged marriage business, you're sadly mistaken because I'm not blindly going along with it. That's gross and inconsiderate."

A car horn goes off from outside.

"That's Bradford," she says, swiping her purse off the coffee table. "Don't worry, Dad. I'm not going to tell him my father is a lunatic who thinks he's going to pass me off to whoever he deems fit. I hope you're happy. You put me in a bad mood, and now Bradford will have to find a way to get me out of it."

Carlotta huffs, "I'm sure he'll get creative."

Evie storms off with a slam of the door, and Carlotta gets up from the table.

"Good going, Sexy," she says. "If you want Little Yippy to have a cellmate in that nursery, I suggest you keep up the good work." She takes off and Lemon shrugs.

"She's probably not wrong." She reaches over and takes up my hand. "But Evie is a smart girl. Everything will be fine. I'd better send Charlie and Meg a message. I'll pay them in cash to go and break up every private party at Lover's Lane."

"Good thinking," Noah says. "I'll double it."

"I'll triple it," I tell her.

"Ooh, *triple*." Lemon gives a flirtatious grin. "That reminds me. I'll be right back with something chocolaty."

Noah shakes his head at me. "You're going to have to let Evie fly a little. If you clip her wings, she might try to fly off anyway and end up hurting herself."

"Good to know. I'll relay the same message when Lyla Nell is dating a college man named Bradford Van Horny."

Noah's jaw tenses. "We're going to kill him."

Carlotta and Lemon come back into the room with a chocolate birthday cake in hand, and it just so happens to have a sparkler stabbed into it as the fiery spectacle goes off haphazardly.

The room breaks out into a cheery version of "Happy Birthday" while Lyla Nell claps like mad and cheers.

The sparks start to fizzle just before the entire stick goes up in flames.

If this is any precursor to the rest of my life, I'd better watch out.

One more spark and my entire world might just go up in flames as well.

I look to Lyla Nell and Lemon, and pray to God I don't take them with me.

And then I center my fury right where it belongs: at Noah and his dimple-faced grin.

After all, it's all his damn fault.

"Would it make me a bad person to hate a blue butterfly?" I ask no one in particular as Noah, Evie, and Carlotta sit at the counter here at the Cutie Pie Bakery and Cakery. The late afternoon crowd did a disappearing act, along with just about all of my blueberry muffins.

"Only if you try to shoot it," Noah points out while dotting his finger over Lyla Nell's nose, and she breaks out into a dainty little laugh that makes Evie giggle as well. Come to think of it, Evie has been staring moony-eyed and giggling at everything ever since she walked in.

I shake my head. "I can't believe my new house is just going to sit there like a skeleton of what it should be just because a butterfly flew past it."

"Like it or not, they're the official occupants." Suze shrugs. "I'm a part of the butterfly preservation society, you know. And well, we all voted that your home should sit uninterrupted the way it is until the Honey Hollow Blue Butterfly can replenish."

I suck in a quick breath. "Suze! You're a part of the preservation society? You can stop the carnage. Don't you want Everett and me sharing a big, beautiful house together and populating the planet with adorable little Baxters? You don't want me unhappy in my rental, now do you? Everett's working long hours, and I might be prone to wander to Noah for a shoulder to cry on. We all know where that can lead." I tick my head toward Lyla Nell.

Suze tips her head back. "So help me heaven, to tell the truth, I did try to convince them otherwise, but they were too strong-minded about it." Her upper lip twitches as she looks to Lyla Nell. "And now we'll have an entire den of Foxes on our hands." She takes off to help a trio of customers who just stepped up to the register.

"Evie, how did your driving lesson go with Bradford?" I ask as I refill her coffee.

"It was amazing," she says, holding a chocolate chip cookie in the air and staring vacantly past me. "He's taking me out again tonight at six. Driving, of course." She smirks my way.

"Of course." I slide a plate full of crullers between her and Noah.

"What about me, Lot? Don't I deserve a cruller or two after pushing you out of my *lions*?" Carlotta pounds her hand over the counter and a spray of silver stars erupts in her wake.

Within seconds, Leo appears in all his Bengal glory.

"You've summoned me?" He startles as he takes in his surroundings. "Oh look, crullers." He traipses over and begins to eat one right off the plate.

Lyla Nell screams and laughs so loud it has the power to pierce every eardrum in a ten-mile radius. She bops up and down in Noah's arms until she snatches the celestial cat by the tail.

Leo lets out a *rawr*, and Lyla Nell laughs all the louder.

Evie giggles to herself again. "It's that ghost cat, isn't it? The one Aunt Charlie says wants to follow her to work?"

Good grief, between Charlie and Carlotta, I don't know why I think my powers or theirs are a big fat secret. Luckily, Evie and most everyone Charlie and Carlotta spout off to think it's all in fun.

"I wish I could see him." Evie gives a wistful shake of the head.

"You can't have everything, Evie Stevie," Carlotta pats her on the back. "You've got brains, you've got beauty, and you've got your daddy's millions coming down the pike once he kicks the bucket." Carlotta leans her way. "I'd get a good financial advisor if I were you in the event that bucket goes airborne sooner than later."

I shoot Carlotta a dirty look for even mentioning such a thing to Evie.

Evie shrugs. "Don't worry. I'm already in with someone. Uncle Noah's brother slipped me his business card."

Noah gives a disgruntled look. "I'm sorry, Evie. I'll knock his head around for it."

"Don't be too hard on him," she says. "He was at my school a couple of months back as a guest speaker in my civics class. He gave everyone his card."

"In that case, I'll let him live." Noah taps his finger to the counter just as Suze steps over once again.

"Lily called from the lake and says she's running low on supplies, and the goods you do have left have melted into a puddle." Suze glares at me as she says it.

I think she hates sunshine just about as much as she hates me.

"I'll tell her to close down the booth," I say as I quickly text

Lily. "I'll need her to come back and help close up the shop anyway."

"Another hot date with your husband?" Suze gives me the side-eye.

I know for a fact she's rubbing my marriage into Noah's face.

"Actually, I'm headed down to the courthouse. But the fact Everett will be there is just a happy incidental. My plans revolve around someone else entirely."

Noah nods my way. "Betsy Monroe." His brows hike a notch as if to ask if he's right.

"I can't get anything past you. You'd make a great guard."

Carlotta honks out a laugh. "Foxy got a little something past the guard. That's how Little Yippy made her debut. Do you think it's too early for her to get fitted for a muzzle? Asking for a friend."

Suze breaks out into cackles, and Noah shoots her a lethal look.

Why do I get the feeling Suze is that friend?

"Oh you." Suze waves Noah off. "It was funny. I find a lot of things Carlotta says funny."

"The truth often is," Carlotta adds and only digs the hole a little deeper with me.

"Noah"—I say as I refill his plate with fresh baked chocolate chip cookies—"what brings you to the bakery so early? You don't usually get off for another hour."

His dimples dig in, no smile. "Ivy invited me to go out tonight, and once I said I was busy, I decided it was better to spend the rest of the day avoiding her. Don't worry. I've got the file for that ATM robbery case to keep me at attention."

"How's that going?" I step in close, not to miss a single detail. I always find the cases Noah works on to be fascinating.

"It's moving slowly, but it's moving. The money from the robberies has been funneling back to the bank via just about every business in this town. Yours included."

"What? You mean the robbers are coming in here enjoying my sweet treats?"

"Not necessarily. It was a nominal amount. More than likely the bait money was given as change and it trickled into your shop innocently."

Suze makes her way over. "Did I hear you mention Ivy?" Her antennae go up. "Beautiful woman. Where did she want to take you?"

"I don't know, I took off before she could sweeten the offer. But I'll head to Ashford with you, Lot. Betsy's next on my list, too."

"Perfect," I say. "I'll ask my mom to watch Lyla Nell, and maybe Everett will be able to go to dinner with us."

"Sounds like a triple header tonight," Carlotta crows, and Suze smirks her way.

"There you go, telling the truth again." Suze cuts a glance to Noah. "I remember when you used to spend your days and nights solving mysteries."

"Times are a changin', Suzie Q," Carlotta tells her. "The only mystery Foxy is trying to solve these days is how to get back in Lot Lot's pants."

Suze snorts. "That's because a thief stole his place in her bed."

Carlotta and Suze cackle up a storm and exchange a high-five.

"Don't listen to them, Evie," I tell her while shooting the two hyenas in our midst a wry look. "I'm heading down to Ashford to investigate, and Uncle Noah is helping me out."

"Lot." Noah inches back and holds up a finger my way before shaking his head. "Never mind. You're right."

Evie giggles as she pulls apart the cruller in her hand. "Bradford wants to be a private detective one day, too. Hey? If I run around solving crimes before he can figure them out, that will make us just like the two of you."

"Not true," Carlotta grouses. "You've got to find yourself a Mr. Sexy if you want to get the equation right."

Suze shrugs. "I'd simply ask Bradford if he has a stepbrother and *voila*, problem solved."

"Ignore them," I tell her. "And yes, you can solve crimes as good or better than any detective if you put your mind to it."

Her phone bleats. "It's Bradford! Thank goodness. It's been twenty-five minutes since he last texted. I thought he forgot all about me, and I was going to die alone in a house full of cats." She darts off to the other end of the bakery while tapping away at her screen.

"All right, Fox," I say, taking off my apron. "Time to make tracks and see what Betsy Monroe has to say."

"Betsy?" Leo ticks his furry face up a notch. "That name sounds familiar."

I nod his way. "All I know is that Betsy once worked for Clark Willoughby at one of his antique stores."

"Ooh." Suze digs her hand into the pocket of her apron. "That reminds me. I picked up this miniature massager when I stopped off at that big garage sale at the lake." She holds up the small square, turns it on, and it begins to vibrate and hum.

"Mom," Noah sips. "Put that thing away before a customer sees you."

"Oh, they've already seen me with it," she says, rolling it over her back and letting out a moan. "I've even given a few customers free massages with it. We should run a promo," she says my way. "Buy one cookie, get a free massage. I bet we'll get more than a few amused glances, and a few excited takers."

"My bakery isn't about exciting people in that manner. I'm with Noah." I motion for her to get rid of the thing before the health department shuts me down.

"Lottie never cares for any of my ideas," she snips to Noah.

"That's because your ideas scare the living daylights out of her," he mutters. "Stick to antiques, Mom. The garage sale might be a little too much for you to handle."

Carlotta lifts her chin. "Speaking of antiques, how about we blow this place, Suze, and see about landing us a few oldie but goodies for the night? There's a new club out in Leeds that I've been meaning to try out."

"Carlotta." I shake my head at her. "Trolling for men while you're in a committed relationship is frowned upon. One day Mayor Nash is going to have enough of your two-timing shenanigans."

"What do you think he's doing tonight?" She shoots back. "You don't have to worry about your parents breaking up, Lot. Harry and I always find our way back to one another at the end of the day."

Suze huffs my way, "Carlotta might just as easily throw your words right back at you. Trolling for men while you're in a committed relationship is frowned upon. One day Noah is going to have enough of your two-timing shenanigans."

Noah twitches his brows my way. "Not if I'm the one she's doing the two-timing with. My door is always open to you, Lot."

Lyla Nell squeals and gives Noah a wallop right over the nose.

"That was from Sexy." Carlotta nods. "You might have supplied the DNA, but he's slowly been programming her."

Noah smacks his lips. "That sounds about right."

"Any news on Rooster?" I wince as I ask because I know it's not Carlotta's favorite subject.

Carlotta huffs, "What did you have to go and ask that for, Lot? You know every time you mention someone you hate, it gives them power. And right now, that man is trying to summon all the power he can just to open up his peepers. And once he does—he's going to cause all sorts of destruction in this town. If it's one thing Rooster hates it's being cast aside. If that man burns down all of Honey Hollow, it'll all be your fault."

"Carlotta, I'm not summoning some dark force. I'm talking to Noah about a man who has essentially come back from the dead."

"Same difference," she spits out the words.

Noah shakes his head. "He's still out cold. The doctors are

baffled that he survived at all. The venom he had in his blood was enough to kill six men."

Carlotta sighs. "Sounds like a dark force to me."

Me too, now that I think about it.

"All right, Noah. Time to make tracks," I say, closing up a box of my sweet treats I've just put together. "Here's hoping Betsy Monroe can help us make headway with the case."

"Here's hoping Judge Baxter has to work late into the night." He winks my way. "I'll make sure his wife has a good time at dinner."

We take Lyla Nell and head out the door.

The Ashford County Courthouse is known for its ability to pull the truth out of a suspect or two—and Noah and I are going to make sure that's exactly what happens when we talk to Betsy.

Clark Willoughby's killer might be walking free for now, but sooner than later, justice will be served and someone will be eating a big helping of just desserts.

LOTTIE

$\mathcal{T}$he Ashford County Courthouse is a white block of a building with enormous Roman columns, limestone flooring, and mahogany walls. The air inside is crisp and cool, and holds the slight hint of justice—if justice smelled like a copy room.

Noah and I dropped Lyla Nell off at home where my mother met us. She said she was just itching to get away from the B&B because Wiley was hosting poker night for the boys.

Noah shakes his head as we step into the courthouse. "I can't believe my father. I get him out of one financial mess—okay, so

129

not really, but for the sake of the argument let's go with it—and then he stumbles right into another losing fiscal proposition."

"If it makes you feel better, my mother said he was pretty good at raking it in," I say, holding tight to that pink box full of my baked goods.

"He's pretty good at raking in trouble, too."

Noah told me all about the fact Jimmy is thrilled to have a cop in his back pocket. That he's making Noah keep that briefcase full of dirty dealings just to make sure Noah stays on the hook. And he'll gladly protect Wiley—and come to find out, anyone he's around—from that hit the Lazzaris have on him.

"Noah"—I pull him to the side and look into his evergreen eyes—"I just want you to know that I appreciate you and everything you're doing to protect my family—our family. I love you, Noah."

"I know." He brushes the hair out of my eyes and lands a kiss to my nose. "I love you, too, Lot."

"Wow," a female voice sings and we turn to find Fiona Dagmeyer with her dark hair in a tight bun and a navy blue power suit on. "Take a gander at this, Essex."

"What?" I take a full step back as Everett comes this way.

Everett looks sharp and destructively handsome in his dark suit, with his dark hair combed back, and that dark look in his eyes that threatens certain death.

"I don't need to take a gander," Everett grits as he glares at Noah. "I saw the whole thing. It's too bad I'll have to get arrested for killing a man right here on my own turf."

"Don't worry, Essex," Fiona says. "I've got you out of a legal tussle before. I can do it again." She winks Noah's way.

"Nothing happened," I say as I wrap my arms around Everett and land a kiss to his lips.

"Nothing happened?" Noah teases. "You just declared your love for me. We shared a kiss."

"You kissed her nose," Everett growls. "Like I said, I saw the whole thing."

A couple of women pass us before backtracking, and I note one of them is the exact woman I was looking to see.

"Oh good!" Betsy presses a hand to her chest. Her blonde tresses frame her face, and she's looking as professional as can be with a pencil skirt, silk blouse, and briefcase in hand.

I'm willing to bet there's not one nefarious thing in the briefcase either. I don't know if I'll ever be able to look at a briefcase the same ever again after the drama and trauma Jimmy and Luke have put us through.

Betsy steps forward. "So you're all coming, too?" She nudges Everett with her elbow. "I'm so glad you changed your mind." She looks my way. "Lonnie, you're going to love it. And you, too, Detective Fox."

"It's Lottie, but don't worry about it. We were barely introduced a week ago," I tell her as I hold out the pink bakery box. "I was just coming down to deliver some desserts from my bakery. I thought it might brighten everyone's day. Why don't you take these?"

Betsy eyes grow twice their size. "Really? Why, I guess I will. I'll take them with me and have a few in the car on the way over. And if there are any left, I'll share them with everyone else when I get there," she trills. "It's just going to be a blast. I'll see you there, too, Fiona." She waves as she steps toward her friend.

"Where are we going?" I call out, because I'm not sure I should trust Everett to tell me. I know for a fact he's not a fan of after-hour meet-ups.

"Limelight!" she calls out. "We've got an entire section reserved. It's law enforcement night. It's going to be the best. We can't wait to see you strutting your stuff, Judge Baxter!"

"Karaoke," Fiona grumbles. "But now that you're going, Essex, I'll be there with bells on." She pulls a tight smile. "Can't wait to see the three of you hit the stage." She gives Everett's tie a quick tug. "You might want to loosen those pipes." She takes off with a chortle.

Everett points hard at Noah. "I blame you for this disaster."

"Me?" Noah's chest pumps as he laughs. "It's you they can't wait to see strutting your stuff." Noah sheds an ear-to-ear smile. "Say cheese, Judge Baxter. I'm catching every moment with my camera." He nods my way. "You'd better ride with him, Lottie. I have a feeling we have a runner on our hands."

"I don't run from anything," Everett says without missing a beat.

And all the way over to Leeds, I'm sensing Everett wishes he could do just that.

"A KARAOKE OFFICE PARTY," Everett grouses as we stand in front of a tan brick building with a giant neon microphone spinning overhead. "Remind me to outlaw these come morning."

"Everett, you don't have to sing," I say, wrapping my arms around him. "I'll get you to make plenty of noise when we get back to the house." I take a quick nip out of his neck.

His lids hood dangerously low as a smile curves on his lips. "Brace yourself, Cupcake. I'll make sure you're singing my favorite song at the top of your lungs."

I bite down on a smile just as a kerfuffle heads in this direction.

"Lot Lot!" We turn to see Carlotta in a little black dress, matching fishnets, and—are those red sequin shoes? "Foxy, put out the APB. Tell me I didn't miss it. Sexy, you didn't get up on that stage yet, did you?"

"Nope." Everett's chest expands as we see Noah holding up the rear.

"Good." Carlotta's fingers dance over her phone. "Cha Cha is already in there with her friends. Evie Stevie can't make it out to see you embarrass yourself, but she said if I get a decent angle, she'll upload it to all of her social media sites. I'd better get in there. I want front row seats." She darts inside and Everett sets those death beams of his on Noah.

"Spread the word, did you, sweetheart?" Everett's jaw clenches. "Good. I'll make sure it's you on that stage."

"In your dreams, Baxter." Noah gets the door for us and waves us in with his hand. "Look out, world. A star is born," he calls out as we enter the boisterous establishment.

The walls are covered with vinyl records, the floors are made up of a dizzying checkered pattern, the sound of loud—rather pitchy—country music blares overhead, and the dance floor in the middle of the room is pulsating.

There's a small stage up front with a TV screen in front of it. A woman standing front and center up there belts away a tune about a truck and a dog, and the room is thumping with the rhythm.

Tables are set out on the periphery, and to my surprise, and slight horror, I see an entire horde of people I recognize. I don't hesitate to trot their way.

Seated at the table is Carlotta at the helm, Charlie, Cormack, Naomi, Greer Giles, and that cool cat, Leo, purring away in Naomi's arms. It's disconcerting to say the least.

Greer waves our way. "Hey, Lottie! I can't wait to see you up on that stage. You wouldn't be up for one minor possession, would you? I miss karaoke something awful."

I shake my head at her. With my luck, this minor possession might just morph into a full-time gig.

Carlotta stands and pulls Everett in. "Here's the man of the hour."

Charlie sheds a greedy grin our way. "Don't worry, Mr. Sexy. I've already signed you and Lemon up for a duet. You're on in twenty minutes."

A groan expels from me. "First song of the night—the blues." And I'm not singing 'em.

Naomi lifts a dark brow. "I'd lube up the vocal cords with a couple of shots of vodka if I were you."

Carlotta shakes her head. "Lot Lot's still playing the part of milk maid to Little Yippy. She's got to take it like a big girl without any lube."

"I bet it's not the first time." Cormack snickers and the entire lot of them breaks out into wild cackles.

"So not funny," I say, looking around and spot a table full of people I recognize from the courthouse. I see Fiona, Betsy, and even Millicent Meyers, Everett's private secretary, a matronly older woman who looks to be whooping it up with a drink in her hand.

"Just our luck," I say to Everett and Noah. "There's an empty table right next to them." I point their way.

Noah groans, "Yup. Just our luck it butts right up to this table." He glances at the table before us.

"Oh, come on, Lottie." Greer pats the seat beside her, which technically belongs to the empty table in question. "We're gonna have the time of our lives."

"Come on, boys," I say, leading the way. "Greer says we're going to have the time of our lives."

"She's dead, Lemon," Everett says as he warms my waist with his arm. "She no longer has a life to have a time with."

Noah looks to Everett. "I'm sensing the judge has a bad case of nerves."

"I have nerves of steel," Everett says as he pulls a seat out for me and his face goes white.

"Everett, what's the matter?" I try to follow his gaze and spot a couple of men in dark suits glaring right at him.

Either Luke's men or Jimmy's—at this point Everett has both mob families equally as ticked at him—and we can't forget Manny Moretti.

Everett may not have many enemies, but he seems to have all the right ones—or wrong ones as they were.

Noah ticks his head at Everett. "I bet he caught a glimpse of his future—him running away as soon as it was his time to hit the stage."

This is typically where Everett scorches Noah with a zinger, but he simply holds out my seat and we sit down together.

"Okay, there she is." I nod in Betsy's direction. "We're almost up, Everett. So I think I'd like to grill her first in the event *I* feel the sudden urge to run."

"You're not serious," Everett says as his brows pinch in the middle. "Just because Charlie put our names down doesn't qualify as consent. If this were a case in my courtroom, I'd toss it out."

Noah's cheek flinches. "Knew it. Nobody is going to see Judge Baxter strut his stuff on that stage tonight. It's probably best that way. The room would clear out if they heard him sing."

I frown over at Noah. "Don't listen to him, Everett. He's just trying to get under your skin." I do my best to pull Everett my way. "You'll have a blast up there. You have to do it. You only live once." I gasp as the callous words come from my mouth and my fingers fly to my lips. "I mean, I want to live every minute of this beautiful life with you. I don't want you to miss anything." I sniff as the sentiment streams from me, and both Everett and Noah exchange a look. I clear my throat as I pull myself together. It's not like Nell's vision is going to come true tonight. "And you don't have to sing," I tell him. "You can talk your way through the song like Johnny Cash."

"Johnny Cash is one of my favorites," Noah is quick to interject.

Everett glances his way. "Then you'll love me."

"Judge Baxter!" The women at the other table belt out a few catcalls.

I nudge Everett. "We should go over and say hello."

The crooner up on stage brings her song home and the room lights up with a raucous applause. I don't know why, but it feels as if the crowd is getting rowdier by the minute.

A man takes the stage and waves to get everyone's attention. He has dark hair and kind eyes and a boy next-door appeal to him in general. He's wearing a navy polo shirt, and there's something oddly familiar about him. I feel like I've seen him somewhere before, but I can't quite figure out where.

"Thank you to Ms. Tallulah Belle. And good luck getting that ticket to Hollywood next month!" More applause. "Up next is the crimson vixen—the killer catcher herself. Give it up for Detective Ivy Fairbanks!"

My mouth falls open as I stick an elbow in Noah's rib. "I bet this is where Ivy wanted to take you! How about that? You showed up for your hot date anyway."

Everett's lips curve. "It must be like destiny."

Ivy takes the stage in a slinky red dress that clashes with her long and surprisingly loose tresses, but hey, who am I to judge?

"I don't think I've seen Ivy with her hair down," I say. "She's drop-dead gorgeous."

"Lucky you, Noah." Everett winks over at him.

Noah frowns at the stage. "I'm not feeling so lucky."

Ivy pulls the microphone to her lips. "I'd like to dedicate this song to someone special. Someone who I've had my eyes on for a very long time and I'm hoping he'll come around."

The room ignites with whoops and hollers—sans our table, of course.

I'm suddenly fuming. Noah looks disgruntled. And Everett's chest is silently rumbling with laughter.

"Hear that, Noah?" Everett doesn't even bother hiding his mocking tone. "I think we all know she's talking about you. Why don't you make Ivy's night? Run on up there and belt out a few bars with her. Maybe close with a big smooch. A crowd like this is practically begging for a feel-good ending."

Noah growls, "My fist is going to give your eye a feel-good ending—as in it'll feel good for me when I break your nose as a bonus. Let's see how sexy the women find that."

"All right, down, boy," I tease as I watch the man in the navy polo exit the stage and then it hits me. "Hey, I just realized where I recognize that guy from." I do my best to point over to him discreetly. "He was at the lake on the Fourth. I saw him twice—once arguing with Clark, and then after the murder, he was comforting Sammy. Do either of you know who he is?"

The two of them shake their heads as they examine him.

Noah takes a breath. "But I'll make sure to speak with him before we leave."

"Lemon will beat you to it," Everett assures him.

"He's right," I say. "But don't feel bad, Noah."

"I won't," he says. "Because I'll be right there with you. I don't plan on leaving your side tonight."

Ivy croons and swoons, and darn it if she's not just that good.

"Hey, if this detective gig doesn't work out, she can always break into the music industry," I say. And I'm silently rooting for her to do just that.

"Judge Baxter," Fiona teases as she curls a finger his way. "We've made room for the three of you right here." She pats the seat next to her, and I note the seat next to Betsy is free so I fly on over.

A jag of lightning appears before me on the table as Leo materializes, grooming himself in a quasi-offensive fashion.

"Charlie says we're going to a real club after this," Leo growls it out in a deep voice. "She knows all the best places to wiggle and giggle."

"I bet she does. I wouldn't trust her if I were you," I snip, and Betsy turns my way.

"*Ah.*" She nods as she looks past me, and I glance that way to see a bunch of young women all but accosting Everett—heck, they *are* accosting him. "I see the problem."

"Hey," I bark out just a notch above Ivy's crooning, and all eyes at the table are feasted on me. "Hands off, ladies. You can look, but you can't touch."

A few of them offer polite nods my way, but for the most part they're right back to swarming him. Everett is a superstar among them, and each one looks hungry enough to take a bite out of the choicest piece of him. I can't blame them. He's dangerously handsome and exudes enough testosterone for sixty men.

Leo chuckles. "I remember when the ladies couldn't keep their hands off me. Clark would take me everywhere. Sammy used to call me a fan favorite. I've been a fan favorite in paradise, too. Like Sammy used to say, 'You can't hold a good cat down.' She didn't want to hold down Clark, though."

My lips fall open as I try to decipher what he might mean.

Noah clears his throat. "Earth to Lottie." He raises his brows at me. "The waitress asked what you wanted, so I ordered you a virgin cocktail."

"Oh, sorry—thank you." I can't help but notice a few of the girls across from us seem to be drooling at Noah as well. Their eyes run up and down his body freely as if he were the exact snack they were craving, and I bet he is.

I shoot them a look that says *sorry, ladies, but the kitchen is closed.*

"Betsy"—I say, forcing a smile as I turn her way—"how did you like the cookies?"

"Confession"—the cute blonde giggles as she says it—"I ate the entire box on the way over. The fudge brownies were my favorite." Her eyes roll into the back of her head as if she were reliving them.

There's something about her that reminds me of Keelie—not just the blonde hair, but the easy, happy-go-lucky attitude she seems to exude. She leans forward a notch. "Hi, Detective Fox." She gives Noah a friendly wave—maybe a little too friendly. "How's the case going?"

Boy, I love it when a suspect dives right into the deep end of the investigation. And I've had both innocent parties and killers segue into the topic this way, so I can't quite use it as an indicator of innocence or guilt.

"It's going," he says. "But I could still use a few good tips."

Her lips twist as she grips the glass in her hand. "I wish I had them to give you."

"You worked with him, right?" I ask and her mood changes on a dime.

"How did you know that?" She takes a sip of her pink drink and doesn't take her eyes off me.

"Bridger mentioned it." I shrug.

Geez, I didn't realize this would be a point of contention.

Leo mewls and I take up Noah's hand so he can listen in, too. "Maybe she's embarrassed by this? She does have a rather professional career going for her at the moment. She might have felt working weekends at the antique shop was beneath her."

Noah nods my way because Leo could be right.

"I did work with him, but it was just a seasonal thing." Betsy swallows hard, and that action alone makes me wonder if embarrassment has nothing to do with the shift in her mood. "Hey, have you talked to Sammy?" she asks Noah, keeping her eyes pinned to his.

Leo's whiskers twitch. "She's changing the subject. Something isn't sitting right with me. Do you think she had an affection for Clark?"

Noah quirks a brow my way as if to ask the very same thing. He looks back at Betsy.

"I did speak with Sammy. Briefly," he says. "Nothing too in-depth. Have you?"

"We're not close." She shakes her head emphatically. "My connection to the Willoughbys was purely through my employment there."

"How long did you work for them? "I ask just as a red fruity concoction lands in front of me and I quickly thank the waitress.

"Almost a year." Betsy shudders. "And to be truthful, that whole violent break-in they had just hovered in the back of my mind the entire time. I saw the pictures on the internet of the two of them bloodied and being carried out of their home on stretchers. And they continued to live there after the fact. That was the strange part."

"It was after my time," Leo says. "I would have rather been there. I would have clawed at the beasts who dared to hurt the Willoughbys."

I nod his way because I have no doubt it's true.

Betsy leans in, her eyes pinned back to Noah once again. "I've heard rumors for years that Sammy was being abused by Clark. So when I got the job I was terrified of him. But you know what? He was the kindest man on the planet. I guess you really don't know what someone is capable of behind closed doors." She nods to Noah. "It's not talked about a lot, but there was a theory circulating at the time of the break-in that Clark orchestrated the event."

"I heard that, too," he says. "But the reason that rumor got started is because Clark was seen turning off the security cameras. He was questioned about it, though, and as it turned out, he said they were making a loud buzzing noise that night. He said neither he nor Sammy could get to sleep, so he shut them off at about two-thirty in the morning. The armed men broke in at three-fifteen, and Clark chalked it up to bad timing on his part concerning those cameras."

Leo sits straight up and looks regal while doing so. "I don't believe in bad timing. Something smells fishy to me."

I don't either. I'll have to deep dive into that break-in when I get a chance.

"What did you do at the stores?" I ask.

She swallows hard once again. "I ran the cash register. Clark was in charge of procuring the merchandise, accounting, that sort of stuff."

"What about Bridger?" Leo asks and I repeat the question to her.

Betsy shakes her head. "He was my manager, but for the most part, we did the very same things. He ran the register, helped the customers. I guess he does the staff scheduling, too. Clark did all the heavy lifting, but Bridger was his right-hand man. Bridger was interesting, though. He's basically a software genius. We had a few hiccups with the computers and he fixed it in a flash. He said he was fluent in three different coding languages."

"Really?" I say as if I knew what it meant.

"That's right." She bites down on her bottom lip until it turns bone white. "You should really look into Sammy," she tells Noah before leaning in. "I'm just going to say it. I don't know if the rumors are true about her being abused by him, but I did see scratches on Clark's arms multiple times. He always said it was his cat, but when I asked Sammy about their cat, she said their cat died ages ago. And then one day he came in with a banger of a bruise on the side of his head. He said he walked into a hanging plant on his trellis, but something didn't feel right about it. He had bruises on his arms a couple of times, too. And then out of the blue, I heard that he and Sammy were separating. They still lived together, though. I thought that was weird. Anyway, I can't imagine what it would be like to live with someone you no longer want to be married to. It sounds like a miserable existence. It sounds like a pressure cooker." Her eyes hook to Noah's, and it looks as if she's just named her number one suspect.

The music dies down, and that man in the navy polo takes the stage once again, thanking the crimson vixen for belting out a few tunes for us.

Betsy gives a wild applause as she looks his way.

Leo taps my hand with his paw. "Ask her who he is. I saw him the day Clark was killed. He looks familiar, but I can't quite place him."

That's what I said.

"Betsy, who is that man?" I tick my head toward the stage. "I feel like I've seen him somewhere before. Does he work at the courthouse, too?" I just threw that last bit out, hoping she'll correct me.

"Oh no, that's Quincy Calvin. He owns this place." A tiny giggle titters from her. "He's Sammy's longtime boyfriend. They've been together for a while. He'd come around the shop with Sammy. Clark really hated him. It didn't seem natural, you know? Here he was dating Clark's wife essentially. Bridger once told me that Quincy had a habit of staying over at the house with Sammy—overnight. I know Clark and Sammy slept in different rooms, and that Sammy got to keep the master bedroom. Can you imagine having that go on under your nose? It's sickening is what it is. Clark was still in love with her and he had to face the fact that she was sleeping with someone else just inches away. I'm not sure what was really going on in that marriage. But whatever it was—it wasn't good."

"And now"—Quincy waves a small white card in his hand—"I'd like to introduce you to Mr. Sexy and his luscious Lemon!"

I suck in a quick breath. "That's me! I can't do this." A ripe panic enlivens in me just as Charlie, Cormack, and Naomi pluck me from my chair and navigate me to the stage. "I'm a *baker*," I shout in protest but to no avail.

Noah has Everett's hands behind his back as if he's about to arrest him and lands him up on stage next to me.

I glance out at the crowd and I get a bad case of tunnel vision, my stomach begins to churn, and my knees are begging to give out. "I can't do this. Everett, help," I hiss over at him. "Oh dear Lord up in heaven, I can't sing!"

The music starts up. Both Cormack and Noah are handed a

microphone, and just as they're about to hand it to us, Everett tucks his mouth to my ear.

"Follow my lead."

Charlie and Naomi dart off the stage, and as Noah lets go of Everett's wrist, Everett shoves him to the front of the stage. I do the same with Cormack, and before I know it, Everett has us back into the fold of the crowd.

I glance up at the stage as Cormack belts out a few bars of some sappy love song.

Noah spots us and shakes his head in dismay. And as he's about to hop off the stage, Cormack links her arm through his and the crowd goes wild.

Women begin to catcall like mad, and I even hear a few of them chanting *Hot Cop,* an ode to the internet fame Noah procured a few months back thanks to Evie.

Cormack's lyrics come to an end and the music thumps on. Noah looks to the giant screen in front of him as the lyrics roll on without him.

Then in an unprecedented turn of events, Noah talks his way through the next few verses and you would think he took off his shirt the way the women in here are screaming like mad.

Everett nods. "Our work here is done."

I give him a high-five, and as I do it, I spot Quincy Calvin by the bar.

"Actually," I say, taking Everett by the hand. "We're not done by a long shot." I fill him in on what Betsy told me about the man: the fact he was sleeping with Sammy under the same roof Clark was living, and in the same bedroom that she once shared with Clark.

The ghost of Greer Giles zooms our way with her dark brown tresses floating all around her as if she were underwater. Dead or alive, Greer is a knockout.

"I can't believe you two," she says as if she were incensed. "Everett,

I was really looking forward to hearing you sing. And Lottie, I've heard you humming to yourself at the B&B. You have a range. Okay, so it's not great, but still, that's not the point of karaoke."

"Thanks for the vote of confidence," I tell her. "But do you mind? We're about to quiz another suspect. I just love it when I get a two-fer like this."

"Tell me it's not Quincy." She rolls her eyes just as Leo floats over, and she scoops him up before landing a kiss to the top of the celestial kitty's head.

"It is Quincy," I say to her as Everett and I continue to traverse our way through the dance floor. Noah and Cormack are really putting in the work up there. "Did you know him?"

Greer makes a face. "I dated him a couple of times. The thing is, he was a nice guy. And well, nice guys weren't my speed back then. Plus, he didn't have two nickels to rub together."

Leo jerks his face up to get a better look at Greer. "Is this Quincy you're discussing? When you left, Lottie, I heard Betsy say under her breath that she would have taken him for herself but wanted nothing more to do with the Willoughbys."

I shrug over at Everett. "I can't say I blame her."

We hit the bar and Everett and I each order a drink.

Quincy glances our way and his smile expands. "I see you've expertly evaded the stage." He laughs as he closes the distance between us. "The drinks are on me." He points to the bartender, and just like that, Everett and I have our libations covered for the night.

Greer floats in close. "Didn't I tell you he's a nice guy?" She makes a face. "If I had made things work with him, I might still be alive today. Although, I just love Winslow, Lea, and Thirteen so much I couldn't imagine my afterlife without them." She drops another kiss to Leo's spotted little head. "And I just love you, too. Yes, I do."

"Thanks for the drinks," Everett says. "Everett Baxter." He holds out a hand and Quincy shakes both his and mine.

"Lottie Lemon," I tell him. "So a friend of mine just told me you own this place."

"I sure do," he says. "Going on three years. It's not entirely mine. I'm in deep with three buddies of mine. But I like to work the floor." He tips his head to the side. "Wait a minute"—his demeanor darkens—"I think I saw the two of you at the lake that fateful day." He blows out a breath. "That was some tough stuff."

"It sure was," Everett tells him. "I think I remember you as well."

"That's right," I say, playing along with Everett. "I think I saw you with Sammy Willoughby—the widow."

His cheek cinches on one side. "That was me. I was doing my best to comfort her. Actually, we dated for a while."

"Oh? You're not seeing her anymore."

He shakes his head. "We were just having fun in the beginning. She was separated from her husband at the time. And as we grew more serious, I thought she might want to move in with me, but she declined the offer." He gives the back of his neck a scratch. "She was still living with him in that house. At first, she made it sound like a transitional thing that was going to take a minute or two to work itself out, but it dragged on for months, and well, I grew impatient."

"Bingo," Leo says. "We have a motive. Quincy could have dealt those fatal blows to Clark to get him out of the picture."

Greer nods. "He might have thought in was a surefire way to get Sammy to commit to him."

"I bet she put him up to it," Leo yowls. "Clark was a kind man, and he loved Sammy despite all of her flaws. I knew she was trouble. A woman who doesn't care for cats should be watched carefully. I tried to tell him not to trust her. And now look where he's landed?"

Everett and I exchange a glance. It's clear Leo is convinced Sammy is responsible for pumping Clark's chest full of bullets—at least indirectly.

Greer inches my way. "Oh, he's such a nice guy, Lottie. Ask him anything. He'll spill his guts and clean up the mess afterwards. I bet you can ask him outright if he did it, and if he did, I'd bet good money he'd confess."

Everett nods my way. I can tell he's come to the same conclusion.

"Quincy"—I lean his way—"you didn't do that to Clark, did you?"

"No." His expression sobers up quickly. "Nor would I have ever thought about it. Sammy joked about it all the time. 'I should kill him,' she'd say. If I had a dime for every time she said if Clark was dead she wouldn't have anything to worry about."

Everett turns his ear this way. "What did she have to worry about?"

Quincy shrugs. "I assumed she meant the house. I encouraged her to see an attorney. I think she was afraid if she moved out he'd sell it from under her. His name was on the title. And those businesses he had were all something he came into the marriage with. But Sammy could have sued for half. They were together for ten years—technically, at least. It was almost as if she was afraid of him." He winces. "Maybe not quite that. I could never put my finger on it. But it always felt as if he had something over her."

"Do you think Sammy could have done something like this?" I ask without hesitating.

He tips his head back and his eyes remain closed a moment too long.

"That's our answer," Leo says. "Didn't I tell you the woman was evil?"

"I don't know." Quincy shakes his head. "Yes, things were tense between them, but they hardly ever spoke. She went out of her way not to cross paths with him. I mean, I had more of a relationship with the guy than she did. Clark and I spoke about the weather, sports, fishing. Once we even went on a hike together.

The guy was pretty great. But Sammy, well, she can get too wrapped up in herself sometimes. And I don't like to speak ill of the dead, but she mentioned several times that she found Clark boring. To be truthful, I think she found me the same way toward the end."

"Sorry to hear it," I say.

Greer motions for me to hurry. "Don't just stand there. See what he thinks of your other suspects. If anything, Quincy is a straight shooter."

I nod his way. "Can I ask what you know about Bridger Douglas? I guess he's the manager of Clark's stores."

Everett's hand tenses a moment, and I can tell he's not comfortable digging around his old friend. But I needed a transition to Betsy, and the store manager is the best way to get to her.

"Aw yes, Bridger." His brows flex. "He's nice guy. Keeps to himself. Sammy said she didn't trust him as far as she could throw him. She said he and Clark were as close as brothers."

"They seem like good friends," Everett says and I can tell he's ready to segue away from his old friend.

"Yeah," Quincy's gaze drifts into the crowd and stops cold once he gets to Betsy. "I guess it was Bridger who discovered one of Clark's employees was washing dirty money through his store."

"What?" I practically shout the word over Noah's lyrical proclamation of love to Cormack. "Are you talking about Betsy?"

"That's the one." He raises his hands. "But if word gets out, I'll deny it. Bridger told me that she was in bed with a dirty judge. The guy paid her a nice sum to wash some serious cash for him."

I look back at Everett and his eyes expand my way.

That conversation Everett and I had with Betsy that day at the lake comes back to me. He asked how Judge Gorman was doing, and she said she hadn't spoken to him since he moved to Europe.

I bet he was mixed up in some dirty dealings with the mob—just like Everett! And it sounds as if he found someone to wash the money for him. I hope he's sipping something frozen on the French Riviera and not tied to a millstone at the bottom of the Atlantic.

Everett blows out a hard breath. "I take it Betsy didn't quit on her own then."

"Nope." Quincy shakes his head. "I guess Clark caught her changing out the cash, then let her go. Clark was a good guy. But on occasion, he couldn't keep his mouth shut. A part of me wonders if that's why he's dead today. Can't imagine why anyone would want to kill him. But making him keep his mouth shut about illegal activity is about as good a reason as any."

The song comes to a conclusion, and the room breaks out into wild cheers. I look to the stage in time to see Cormack hopping on Noah's back as she nearly topples him to the ground. He manages to land her safely to the floor, and the two of them exit the stage.

"That's my cue," Quincy says with a wave. "Nice meeting you two."

He takes off and Leo zips before me. "Betsy is a crook."

Greer shrugs. "It sounds like Clark was as nice as Quincy. Sammy has good taste in men. I'd better catch up with the girls. You wouldn't believe the juicy gossip they're capable of. They've really got their finger on the pulse of Honey Hollow." She zips off and takes Leo with her.

Everett and I head back to the table just as Noah steps up.

Noah's hair is mussed, his expression is dark, and he looks as if he's up for a bar brawl—with Everett in particular.

"You did great!" I say, jumping over him with a giant hug. I go to land a kiss to his cheek. As I lean in, he turns his face just enough, and I smack him right over the lips instead. "Hey!" I laugh as I pull back. "Okay, fine. You deserved it. Thank you for taking one for the team."

"Anything for you, Lottie." He shoots Everett a dirty look. "I'll get even with you later."

Carlotta snatches me by the hand. "Excuse us, boys, but Cha Cha and I are up next and I want my Lot Lot to join us. Come on, Lottie. Don't let me down. We're singing my anthem song."

"No way," I say as she pushes me in Charlie's direction, and the two of them hook their arms though mine and land me right back on stage. And judging by the stranglehold each of them has on me, there's no hope of ever busting loose. The music cues up, and soon the three of us are three lines deep, belting out the lyrics to "Mamma Mia" with all our might.

In less than ten seconds, the entire house is on their feet and dancing, and soon Cormack, Naomi, and Greer join us on stage, and surprise of all surprises, Suze has appeared and is singing right along with us.

We laugh our way through it, both singing and shouting as we try to stay above the noise of the crowd, and I feel alive in a whole new way, standing up here with the music coursing through my veins. It's a good feeling. Not one I'm looking to replicate anytime soon, but I can see why people love this, and how they can become addicted to it.

The song comes to an end and Carlotta scoops me off my feet.

"Foxy! Sexy! Catch a Lemon if you can!" She tosses me right off the stage, and I bounce softly in a safety net comprised of Noah's and Everett's strong arms.

"Nice work, Lemon." Everett lands a kiss to my lips as they help me to the floor.

Charlie and Carlotta crop up beside me, and Charlie slings an arm over my shoulders.

"You know, Mama and I have sung that same song at karaoke more times than I can count, but not until tonight have I had that much fun."

"Aw, thank you," I say. "I had fun singing it, too."

"I was talking about watching you get thrown off stage," Charlie is quick to inform me.

"Figures."

Ivy speeds this way, breathless, as she steps in close to Noah.

"Rooster is awake, and he's left Honey Hollow General Hospital against medical advice."

Both Charlie and Carlotta let out an ear-piercing scream.

And a part of me wants to scream along with them.

We quickly gather our things and start to make our way out of the club, when out of the shadows those two men in dark suits that were glaring at Everett earlier step in front of us and block our path.

"Judge Baxter?" The taller of the two hands a small paper bag to Everett and they take off into the crowd.

Everett waits until we step outside to open the bag, and we look down to see a dead rat staring back at us.

I jump back and scream at the top of my lungs, and Noah does his best to calm me down. But Everett remains cool as he tosses the bag into the trash can near the door.

"They're not going to hurt him, Lot," Noah breathes the words into my ear.

I nod in agreement.

They're not. I'll make sure of that myself.

LOTTIE

*L*ast night, I drove Everett's SUV back home while he and Noah went hunting for Rooster.

Ivy went out looking for him, too, but to no avail. At breakfast, Noah suggested that Rooster might have skipped town. But Carlotta assured him he was too greedy, evil, and ruthless to do such a nice thing. And I have a feeling she might be right.

It's almost two in the afternoon, and I'm sweltering in my booth down at Honey Lake. Both Lily and Suze threatened to quit if I made them melt in the elements, so I had no choice but to come out myself.

My mother is here pushing Lyla Nell around the lake in a stroller, and neither my mother nor Lyla Nell is deterred by the weather. In fact, the warmer the weather gets, the happier Lyla Nell seems to be. I hope that's not a sign she's going to hate winter. I hate to break it to her, but for most of the year, it's colder in Vermont than it ever is warm.

The lake is teeming with bodies today. Evie and her BFF are not all that far away, soaking in the rays. It seems every soul in town has tossed on a bathing suit, evacuated the premises, and landed toes to the sky as they take a leisurely nap on the beach. I wish I were doing the same.

The Hot Dog House is grilling up a storm, and despite the fact I never thought I'd look at another sausage again, my mouth is watering to get my hands on one.

Across the way, that giant community garage sale is still attracting both townies and tourists like bees to honey.

It's a busy day over here at the lake—everywhere but at my booth.

"I take it no one wants melted cookies and mushy cake," I say to Carlotta as she sticks her head into the refrigerated bakery display Mayor Nash has provided the booth with.

Last month, he had every business on Main Street down here, and this equipment is left over from that. Although it wasn't nearly as lethally hot back then.

Leo, the cool celestial cat, is here, too, and I've been feeding him a steady diet of wilted lemon meringue pie, and he's not only lapping it up at lightning speeds, he's purring like a jet engine while doing so.

"Nope, Lot. No one wants any of your melted goo," Carlotta says with her face as red as a beet and sweat trickling down the sides of her temples. Once Lily and Suze abandoned ship, Carlotta said she'd come down to the lake to keep me company—and eat her fill of the aforementioned goo. "People like their hot chocolate around here, Lot. Just not in July in the form of a melted cupcake. I say we toss in the towel."

"I'm with her." Leo lifts his head away from the pie just long enough to say it.

"I can't do it," I say. "I still have a decent amount of inventory left, and mostly they're all good. But don't think for a minute I'm coming back tomorrow."

"I'm coming back tomorrow," she says as she opens the cash drawer. "And I'm going sit in an inner tube floating around in that lake with a fishing line tied to my big toe."

"Let's hope you don't catch Rooster."

Carlotta speeds over and smacks me on the arm. "Why'd you have to go and say his name? Now he's destined to show up. Have you got Ethel with you?"

"No, I never bring Ethel to work."

"Who's Ethel?" Leo asks, rearing his head again.

"My gun," I whisper.

"I like you a little better already." He winks before getting back to the lemony task at hand.

Carlotta growls, "You'll change your tune about Ethel once Rooster starts shaking you down for all the green you stole from him."

"You mean the green *he* stole from Everett. And Wiley stole from him." It's a rather convoluted trail of thievery that my mind has no desire to wrap itself around at the moment.

A group of teenagers steps up to the booth and on their heels is Bridger Douglas.

"You take the teen scene," I whisper to Carlotta. "Everett's friend knew the deceased. I'll see if I can get anything new out of him."

I step to the right and flag Bridger over, and as I do, a spray of silver stars appears as Leo lands softly over the counter.

"I'm sorry, Lottie," the tiny specter mewls. "But I can no longer partake in the melted madness you have going on here.

Let's get to the bottom of things quickly with this man. I'm heading back to the bakery. There's a raspberry cheesecake that's calling me."

I knew it was bad, but it's even worse than I thought when the dead among us are willing to eschew the delectable delights I have on hand.

"Bridger," I say his name brightly. "What can I do for you on this fine—rather hellishly hot day."

He rocks back on his feet as a warm laugh bounces from him. His salt and pepper curls have a bit more life to them thanks to the humidity, but other than that, he looks comfortable in his T-shirt and jeans.

"Everett Baxter is one lucky guy, Lottie. I never pegged him for the marrying kind, but he's struck gold with you. Not only are you easy-going, but you can bake a mean blueberry muffin. I'd like to treat some of the volunteers helping out with the garage sale. Would you mind if I bought out your inventory?"

"Are you kidding? I'd throw you a tickertape parade for doing it," I say, getting right to work boxing up everything in front of me. Bridger is my ticket to air-conditioning.

"So how's the case going?" He offers a warm smile. "I hope you don't mind me asking, but does Detective Fox have any leads?"

I shake my head. "No real leads. I mean, Sammy is certainly someone of interest." I glance over his shoulder a moment as I lean his way. "I guess Noah learned that one of your employees was fired for laundering money through the stores."

He inches back. "Who told him that?"

"It was Quincy." I twist my lips because I'm not sure I should have gone there. But what the heck. "He said you mentioned that Betsy was laundering money for a crooked judge."

Any trace of a smile is replaced with disappointment.

"I'm so sorry," I say. "I shouldn't have relayed any of that."

"No, it's okay. It was right of Quincy to tell Noah everything he knows. That thing with Betsy is something I probably should have brought up myself."

"Well, I'm sure Noah will get around to talking to you again. He's been working on this big ATM robbery case that's kept him busy."

"ATM robberies?"

"Yes, they've been rampant. But the banks have been cooperating with the sheriff's department, and Noah is actually starting to make headway with it."

"That's great," he says. "How does that work?"

"The banks cooperating? I guess the bills are marked, stuff like that."

I land a large pink box before him and give him the total.

He pulls out his wallet and winces. "I'm running on empty. How about a credit card?"

"That works."

He hands me a card and I go to run it through the machine, but the machine acts as if I didn't slip anything into it.

"Oh no," I say, tapping the side of it. "Don't malfunction on me now." I pull out the card and glance front and back, and it's empty on both sides sans a black strip toward the bottom.

"Ah, my fault." He takes the card from me and gives me another. "That's the keycard I forgot to give back during my last cruise."

"Not a problem. I hope you had fun."

"As always, I had a blast."

The card goes through, and I give it back and slide the box his way.

"Tell Everett I said hello." He gives a cheery wink as he takes off.

Leo mewls my way, "And I'll tell the bakery you said hello. I'm off to eat my way out of a cheesecake." He blinks out of sight, and I wish I could do the same.

Eating my way out of a cheesecake sounds like bliss right

about now.

Carlotta runs down from the south side of the lake with a hot dog in each hand, and I hadn't even noticed she left.

"Oh thank goodness." I flick my fingers her way. "I'm starved."

"Who said I got one for you?"

"You'll hand it over if you know what's good for you."

"Fine, but you owe me four ninety-nine."

"Geez, four ninety-nine for one plain hot dog? I'm in the wrong business."

"That includes my markup. But I don't have time to haggle with you. Great news, Lot! Since the hot dog king bit the big one, the owners of the Hot Dog House have decided they're going to host another competition this Saturday evening right before the big fireworks show."

A hard groan comes from me. "As much as I love their hot dogs, I can't do that to my body again."

"Well, I'm in, and I'm in it to win it. You're looking at the new Hot Dog Queen of Honey Hollow."

A dark chuckle emits from my right. "If you're the queen, can I be your king?"

Carlotta's body goes rigid and both hot dogs slip from her hands as Rooster steps up between us.

He looks a little ruddy in the cheeks, his dirty blond hair looks greasy as can be, his mustache has grown out and is crawling down his face like an upside-down U, and his brown suit is dusty as if he just rolled around on the ground to achieve that look, but otherwise, Rooster is the picture of health.

"You're an immortal," Carlotta bleats with a twinge of fear in her voice.

"Darn tootin'," he growls at her as his eyes bulge with rage. "And don't you forget it. Now you'd better return the money you stole from my room or I'll end you and I'll end Charlie girl, too. I might even go after Mrs. Priss here." He tosses a finger my way without taking his eyes off of her.

"I don't have your money," Carlotta seethes. "Wiley took it. I don't want anything to do with you. If I had any money of my own, I'd pay you to leave town forever."

"You ain't ever getting me out of your life, darlin'. That's what you get for lying on the stand and sending me up the river."

"I had to lie because you lied to *me*," Carlotta riots back at him.

"That's because you were afraid the truth would make you look like you didn't have two brain cells to rub together!"

"You told me you owned that run-down liquor store, right before you had both Charlie and me rob the place blind. I wanted you to fry. I wanted them to lock you up and throw away the key. But here you are, back from prison, and back from the dead."

A hearty belly laugh trembles from him. "That's right, Sugar, and don't you forget it. I'm indestructible. But I tell you what. You come up with a cool one hundred grand, and I'll turn my car around and head back to Higgins Bottom. You won't see me ever again." He leans in so close I think he's going to kiss her. "But you'll miss me." He winks.

"And if I don't?" Carlotta gruffs the words out like a threat.

"I'll turn your little world into hell on earth, woman. You've stole what was mine once before, and I'll be damned if I'm going to let it happen again."

"Wait a minute," I squawk. "That money was never yours to begin with. You stole those briefcases from the boat." I don't dare lay claim to the boat or the briefcases.

"Finders keepers," he roars my way before turning to Carlotta. "Now get me my money or else! Every last one of you will live to regret this."

Carlotta and I watch as he staggers off into the heat of the afternoon, and a flood of relief hits me once he's gone.

"He's right." Carlotta's shoulders sag as she leans against the counter.

"Right about the fact you were afraid to tell the truth in court because it would make it seem as if you didn't have two brain cells to rub together?"

"No, Lot. Finders keepers," she growls. "Don't you pay attention? I owe Rooster one hundred clean ones. And there's only one person who I know willing to give me that kind of money." She quickly taps into her phone.

"Who are you texting?"

"Mr. Sexy. Who also happens to be Mr. Billions."

Her phone beeps and I lean in to see a big fat *no* in response to her bold request for billions.

"There's that." She tosses her hands in the air. "I guess I'm down to my last resort."

"A bank heist?"

"A trip to Red Satin."

"*Ohh*, wait for me. I was thinking of paying a visit to that son of darkness myself."

I take the cash drawer, grab Lyla Nell, and the three of us are off to Red Satin.

"What are you bringing Little Yippy for?" Carlotta grunts as I drive us out of Honey Hollow.

"I dare Jimmy Canelli to look into my little girl's face and threaten to kill her daddy."

"That's ammo from the bottom of the barrel, Lot Lot."

"At this point, that's the only ammo I've got."

NOAH

For as much as I seem to frequent Red Satin Gentlemen's Club, and oddly that's not the kind of gentleman I consider myself to be, I'm constantly amazed by the level of depravity that goes on here.

The joint is dark, muggy, and smells of despair and cheap cologne. It's early evening, and the place is already filling up with men looking to lose a couple hundred bucks to booze they probably shouldn't have and half-naked women they *can't* have. I stepped in a few minutes ago, and Lottie's sister Meg spotted me and offered to get me a beer, so bottoms up it is as I belly up to the bar for a moment.

The lights dim dramatically before they come up again and a series of hot pink spotlights twirl across the ceiling.

"Gentlemen, start your engines"—a disembodied deep voice calls out from the speakers—"and put your hands together for Char—*lay*."

A raucous round of applause breaks out, and to my dismay I see Lottie's look-alike strutting out on stage dressed like a NASCAR driver as the revving of an engine roars through this place. I know she won't have those clothes on for long. I can't believe of all the places in Vermont to find decent employment, she chooses to work here.

No sooner do I bring the beer bottle to my lips than Lottie, Lyla Nell, and Carlotta step into my line of vision, all three with a look that can kill pinned right on me.

"Noah Corbin Fox," Lottie snips with her free hand balled against her hip.

I practically spew the beer out of my mouth at the sight of her.

"What the heck are you doing here?" I put down the beer in haste and pick up the baby. "And with my daughter no less."

"Dada!" Lyla Nell kicks and squeals as she slaps my face silly. Her feather soft hair is scooped up on the top of her head and held together in a giant pink bow.

"We can ask you the same thing," Lottie says, unrelenting with her fury.

I'll admit, it's adorable as anything when she's angry with me like this. It would happen once in a while back when we were together, and I'd take her back to my place and defuse her one steamy kiss at a time, to select parts of her body, of course. My mouth waters just thinking about it.

I say it's time we give Lyla Nell a sibling. I wonder how many beers I'd have to get into Lottie to get her to agree to it? Not that I'd resort to it, but my guess is three.

"Come on, Lot." Carlotta bumps her elbow to Lottie. "I know

you're no genius, but Foxy here is a member of the Fifth Limb Club. And where else is he supposed to go to see the woman he loves take her clothes off? Now that you and Sexy put up curtains in the master bedroom, not only are half the women in Honey Hollow good and ticked, but Foxy has to look elsewhere to get his Lusty Lemon kicks. Good thing Cha Cha showed up on the scene." She leans my way. "Tip her good, Foxy. She's family, you know." She looks to Lottie. "Don't worry. I'll make sure she splits the take. You keep breaking men's hearts and sending 'em her way, and we'll have a nice little side gig going for us."

"Carlotta." She shakes her head before casting those glowing hazel eyes my way. "What gives, Noah?"

Carlotta clucks her tongue. "Boy, a guy can't have a beer after work and unwind with a few buxom beauties without you breathing down his neck. I bet Sexy is going to get tired of the watchdog campaign you've initiated over his life."

Lottie glowers at her. "I'm not a watch dog over my husband. Everett is free to come and go wherever he wants. Besides, I don't need to ask for a schedule of where he's going to be. He's predictable. He's just finishing up at the courthouse, and I bet he's on his way to pick up dinner for us—from the Wicked Wok, his favorite."

"And I was about to pick up Mangias, our favorite." I wink at Lot as I say it.

Carlotta grunts, "What about *my* favorite? Who's gonna pick up a bucket or three of Hennifer's Fried Chicken and plop it down on the dining room table?"

"Carlotta, your favorite dinner is a box of crullers," Lottie tells her. "But now that you mention it, Hennifer's sounds amazing."

Meg steps up and nods to Lottie and Carlotta before turning to my left. "What can I get for you, Judge Baxter?"

Sure enough, there he stands, a six foot three wall of trouble in a suit.

Lottie lets out a wild yelp at the sight of him and Carlotta belts out a laugh.

"It looks like Cha Cha is in for a banner night." Carlotta sings. "Whassa matter, Lot? You forget how to work your twerk in the bedroom?"

"Everett?" Lottie gives a couple of quick blinks in his direction, alerting every one of us that he's in deep.

"Not to cause any waves"—I start—"but Lottie did just mention you were predictable."

Everett growls my way and Lottie holds up a hand.

"This is anything but predictable, Noah," she snips, never taking her eyes off his.

A tiny chuckle works in my chest just as a couple of women wearing nothing but thongs and glittering pink pasties walk between us.

"Um, um!" Lyla Nell jumps in my arms as she does her best to reach out and grab the women by their more delicate, amply endowed, parts. Her little head turns toward the stage just as Charlie takes off that jumpsuit in one quick move, showing off a set of pink pasties of her own and not much else.

"*Mama!*" Lyla Nell kicks me just shy of the cookies as she does her best to stretch in that direction.

Lottie gasps. "No, no, no," she scolds with a whimper. "That's your Aunt Charlie. I'm Mama. *Me.*" She points desperately to herself. Lyla Nell has managed to call both Everett and me Dada, but hasn't given Lottie the same privilege with Mama or anything that sounds remotely like it. However, she's called Charlie Mama a few times already. Not quite sure what's going on there.

"Never mind that." Lottie digs her fists in her hips as she gives Everett a scathing look. "I suppose you're here to knock a beer back yourself."

He shoots me a look. "Nope. I'm here to speak to a dirty rat. And now that I've said hello to Noah, I'd like to speak with Jimmy as well."

"You're hilarious."

"You're hilarious." Everett shoots back with ten times the venom. "What's with Lyla Nell? This isn't bring-your-daughter-to-the-strip-club-night, Noah. You're going to do some serious damage if you keep this up. Damage that I'll have to undo because apparently I'm the one-man Noah Fox cleanup committee."

"You're lucky I'm holding Lyla Nell or I'd wipe the floor with you. I never asked you to clean up my messes."

"You're right," he says. "You just leave me holding the bag and walk out the door like nothing happened. It's been your MO for years. Florenza Canelli was just another body for me to bury."

"Would you shut the hell up?" I grit it through my teeth. "Do you know where we are?"

Lyla Nell tips her body toward the stage about as far as she can go.

"Noah," Lottie says, taking the baby back. "We can't use salty language around the baby. She's soaking everything up like a sponge."

"I'll say," Carlotta clucks. "Check out Little Yippy. It's as if she's entranced with what's going on up there."

"Oh, honey, that's not for your little eyes." Lottie tries to spin Lyla Nell away from the fleshy carnage, but Lyla Nell shouts her head off as if she were angry as heck, and Lottie spins her back that way. Instantly, Lyla Nell is entranced once again, cooing softly to herself as she soaks up the scene.

"Well, lookie here," Carlotta says, inspecting her. "Looks to me as if life choices are being made. I think she's already found a career she's interested in."

Everett growls, "I think Carlotta is right. This is all your fault, Noah."

"I brought her here." Lottie winces. "And believe me, I didn't want to. I was forced."

"Not by me," Carlotta says. "I never want to take Little Yippy anywhere."

"Never mind," Lottie says. "I take it we're all here to see Jimmy."

Meg nods. "Nice cover, boys." She winks to Everett and me. "Your secret is safe with me." She looks to her sister. "Sure, Lot, the first thing Noah asks for when he walks into the place is where he can find the men."

Everett rumbles with a laugh. "You escaped a fire with that one, Lemon." He takes Lyla Nell and pulls her close to his chest protectively and Lyla Nell pulls his head down and begins to gnaw on his cheek.

"See that, Lot?" Carlotta grins. "Who says she doesn't pay attention to what goes on in that bedroom?"

A growl comes from me. "She sleeps in the nursery from here on out."

"That's right, Judge Baxter." Meg sighs. "I'm sure when Lyla Nell is eighteen she'll think back fondly of all the times her daddy held her right here in this very spot."

"That's twisted." Lottie shakes her head at her sister.

"Of course, it is, Lot," Carlotta says. "But it'll just be one in a dozen daddy issues she'll have drummed up by then. And we all know the road to Red Satin is paved with daddy issues."

Everett quickly lands Lyla Nell back in Lottie's arms.

"Let's find Jimmy," Lottie says and we don't take ten steps before Lottie stops abruptly, and to our surprise we find Keelie and Bear seated at a table with a giant platter of nachos between them.

"Keelie!" Lottie shouts her best friend's name. "What are you and Bear doing here?"

Keelie offers a lazy smile our way. "It's Bear's birthday and they give a free platter of nachos if you're celebrating. Plus, I told him we could go wherever he wanted."

"At least he's keeping it real," Carlotta says.

Bear nods to Keelie. "I told you little Bear wasn't too young to go clubbing with us."

Keelie lifts a brow at Lottie. "I'll admit, between the two of us, I thought I'd be the parent with the loose moral compass."

"Have you met Lot Lot?" Carlotta says it deadpan.

Lottie makes a face. "Believe you me, this is Lyla Nell's last night in this pigpen. We'll talk soon. Happy birthday, Bear."

We all wish him the very same sentiment as we make our way down through the bowels of this place and land in the casino with all its whirling, twirling lights, the one-armed bandits going off like a fire drill, and the card tables in the back filling in quickly. There are just as many men down here as there are upstairs this evening.

"Gimme that kid," Carlotta says as she takes Lyla Nell from Lottie's arms. And to be honest, this might be the very first time she's held her.

"Why do you want her?" Lottie looks suspicious, as she should.

"Everyone knows a Little Yippy is good luck gold in a casino."

"Says who?" Everett doesn't look impressed with Carlotta's line of thinking.

"Says everyone, Mister I've-Got-Every-Degree-in-the-World-Hanging-in-My-Office. Didn't they teach you anything in that fancy law school of yours? A diaper dweller in a casino is akin to a leprechaun holding a pot of funny money on St. Paddy's Day."

"Carlotta," Lottie snips. "Babies are not even allowed in casinos. There is no truth to this rumor. It was probably thought up by some woman who couldn't find a babysitter."

"Not true, Lot," Carlotta bites back. "I've spent my fair share of time casino hopping in Vegas, and you'd be shocked to learn how many fine folks snuck in a kid just to have the luck of the draw. I always thought it was an unfair advantage—but lookie here, I've finally found a use for the fruit of Foxy's loins."

Lyla Nell bucks wildly, her foot hitting a slot machine and a handful of nickels crashes to the metal tray below.

"Look at that!" Carlotta shouts with glee as she quickly scoops up the loot. "She's got the magic touch, Lot. I bet Suze's white witch powers are coming through strong with this one. Great news, Lottie Dottie. You've just landed yourself a brand new babysitter. The best part? Little Yippy herself will pay *me*." She looks back at Everett. "She's not cheap like her daddy." She shrugs my way. "I'm in need of one hundred big ones. I would have asked you for the loan, Foxy, but when it comes to money, I'm rooted in reality."

"Good to know." I frown over at Lottie. "Is that what you're here for? Carlotta, are you asking Jimmy for a loan?"

Carlotta makes a face. "After the things I've done for that man, he should be throwing the big bucks my way. I put out a long time ago, and it's about time he pays up—with interest. No use in Rooster having all the fun."

Everett tips his head. "What does Rooster have to do with this?"

Lottie takes a breath as Carlotta snatches Lyla Nell and starts tapping her little feet to every machine in the vicinity.

"Rooster came by my booth at the lake, and he said if he didn't get his one hundred grand back, he was going to rain down hell over our lives." Lottie glances over her shoulder briefly. "Carlotta made a deal with him, or at least she thinks so. He said if she gave him one hundred grand, he'd leave town."

Everett shakes his head. "I don't believe it. Rooster is a liar. He'll rain hell down over us all, regardless."

I shake my head. "I'm not afraid of Rooster. And ironically, I'm not particularly here to see Jimmy. I'm looking for my dad. This was my first stop of the night. But since I'm in Canelli terri-tory"—I look over at Everett—"I was going to have a word with him about you."

"I don't need you to fight my battles," Everett gravels just as a bell goes off nearby and Carlotta whoops it up.

We look over to find a waterfall of quarters gushing out of a slot machine and Carlotta hands Lyla Nell a cardboard bucket to hold while she does her best to scoop up the change.

"Give her to me," I say, taking the baby from Carlotta before Lyla Nell can stick that dirty bucket into her mouth. I'm about to say something when I spot my father seated just two tables away and by his side is Miranda Lemon, both with a set of cards in their hands.

Lottie scoffs. "*Mother*," she hisses as she heads over and we follow along.

"Wait a minute!" Carlotta tries to snatch Lyla Nell out of my arms. "Why don't you leave Little Yippy with me, and the three of you go have a good time? I don't think you've hit that kinky little playroom downstairs in eons. Come on, Foxy. I bet you're just itching to get Lot tied up in five-way restraints again."

She's not far off by any means. There is certainly a dirty club called the Jungle Room on the premises, and oddly, Everett, Lottie, and I have hit it a time or two but purely for investigative purposes. Besides, the next time I head that way with Lottie, Everett's not invited.

Miranda and my father turn around and take us in. Miranda has a tight red dress on, and my dad is wearing a ridiculous red suit, looking like the man downstairs himself. And for all I know, he might be that diabolical persona.

"Great news, Miranda!" Carlotta beats us to the punch. "The prize derived from Foxy's cookies is a powerful good luck charm! Look at the spare change she just drummed up for me." She rattles the bucket of quarters and nickels and it makes an impressive noise.

Miranda's mouth falls open. "Oh, sweet baby Lyla Nell!"

Lottie lifts a brow at Carlotta. "Hear that? A grandparent who is rightfully incensed. There's a reason I let one of you babysit and not the other."

Miranda stands and plucks Lyla Nell into her arms. "Finally, I might be able to get a little luck around here." She looks to Carlotta. "I snuck all three of my stinkers into this casino when they were Lyla Nell's age and they didn't help a bit. It's good to know we've got a wee one that can pay the bills."

Carlotta holds up a hand and Miranda gives her five.

"Lottie, why don't you deal with this madness, while I deal with my father?" I say.

I pluck my older, not wiser, look-alike out of his chair and march him ten feet away while Everett joins us.

"What the hell are you thinking?" Everett shoves a hand to my father's chest.

Dad looks irritated as he glances my way. "Are you going to just stand there and watch as he roughs me up?"

"Yeah, I am," I tell him. "And then I'm going to finish you off. I hope your vision is good because you're going to need a sharp eye to pick your teeth up off the floor. What are you thinking dragging Miranda down here with you?"

"Listen to me"—Everett yanks him in by the shirt—"I'm stopping by the B&B tonight and I'm picking up my money. That's right, it belongs to me. If I find any of it missing, I'm going to shove your head through a wall and not think twice. You won't even know you have teeth when I'm done with you."

"It's not there." His hands fly to the ceiling. "I promise you, Everett. I got rid of every red cent. Rooster is back. He's already tried to henpeck the staff, looking for it. Thank goodness Cormack got to him and subdued him in her bedroom. That was the only thing that gave me a minute to dump the cash."

"What do you mean *dump the cash?*" I squint over at him.

"What I said." He nods. "I had Manny Moretti swing by and I told him to take it. The green wasn't worth the trouble."

"Manny Moretti." Everett drops my father's shirt and sighs. "Great."

I nod to my dad. "So how much did you manage to squirrel away?"

Dad's dimples dig in deep. "Seventy-five grand clean, son. I didn't come to play." He gives his dress shirt a tug and winks up at Everett. "Enjoy your night, boys." He takes off and Everett and I exchange a glance.

"I'm a dead man," Everett says without one ounce of emotion behind it.

And I'm terrified he's right.

We head back and find Jimmy already charming the socks off Miranda and Carlotta. Although judging by the way his hand is snaking up and down Miranda's back, his arrow is pointed firmly in her direction.

He lifts his silver head our way. "Gentlemen, nice to see you. How can I help you this fine evening?"

"We need to talk." Everett hitches his head and the three of us step back about ten paces. "Look, what do I have to do to get this hit of yours off of me? I've already got Luke and Manny crawling up my back. Enough's enough. Tell me what I have to do to be done with this nightmare."

Everett looks both angry and anxious, and I've never seen him quite this way before. I get it. He's got everything else going for him right now. The last thing he needs is the Grim Reaper chasing him down.

"What's with you?" Jimmy nods my way, not so much as giving Everett the time of day.

I feel for the guy. Hell, I should be the one bleeding for him.

I take a deep breath. "I want you to place his hit on my shoulders. I did that to your niece. He was acting on my word. That's the reason I came to see you tonight." I look over at Everett. "And that's the God's honest truth."

Jimmy chuckles. "Such a nice guy." He slaps his hand over my back and shakes his head at me. "I'll have to think about it." He glances to the ceiling. "No can do. You see, I've got you where I need you, Detective. I have no use for a crooked judge. I've already got a few of those in my back pocket." He winks over at Everett. "How's your two-step?"

"You want to slow dance?" Everett doesn't miss a beat.

Jimmy doesn't crack a smile. "Just a heads-up, sometimes my men get frisky and pepper the ground with bullets. It's good to be light on your feet." He shrugs over at him. "Why are you wasting your time with me? Word is Moretti is still hopped up over the fact you wouldn't land him a girl—Carlotta Junior the Third. Luke says Manny wants to blow your house up. And then there's Luke himself. He's not impressed that the money is missing. That's a lot of money, Judge Baxter."

"Fine. I'll cut him a check tonight. Hell, I'll have cash for him in the morning. In the meantime, call your dogs off. I'm as good as under Luke's protection."

Carlotta scrambles this way with Lottie and Lyla Nell right behind her.

"Jimmy!" Carlotta falls over him. "Rooster's back and he's threatening me something awful. You wouldn't happen to be running any specials on hits these days, would ya?"

"Carlotta." Everett shakes his head at her.

Although I might be siding with Carlotta on this one.

Jimmy shakes his head. "Not tonight, Carlotta."

"Well, I need a hundred grand," she snips.

Jimmy shakes his head again. "Why don't you ask the judge here? He seems to have deep pockets. I've already given Ms. Featherby a one hundred K advance. I need to mind my nickels, if you know what I mean."

Carlotta jolts upright. "He's got to you, hasn't he? See that, Lot? Rooster's already running the mob. Didn't I tell you he would be harder to kill than a cockroach?"

"That seems to be the case," I say. "Jimmy, if you're not

budging on anything, we'll get out of your hair. But just know that I'm easier to get along with if someone is nice to my friends."

Jimmy lifts his chin as he inspects me. "You call this man your friend? He's sleeping with the mother of your child—the woman who should rightfully be your wife. You should call him your enemy."

It's probably wrong that I feel a pang of pride at this moment. It's nice to be validated even if it is coming from a killer.

I shake my head at the killer before me. "I call this man my brother."

Carlotta starts in on a slow clap and Lyla Nell squeals and jumps as if she, too, approves.

I nod to Jimmy. "You might have me in your back pocket, but as long as you're firing bullets in his direction, know that I consider you my enemy."

Jimmy's eyes harden like stone. "Duly noted. Now get the hell out of my club before I fire a few bullets myself."

He takes off and Everett shakes his head at me.

"Wrong time to start a bromance, buddy. You're Lyla Nell's father. You need to stay one step ahead of that medieval mastermind." He pokes a finger in my chest. "If I die, the girls are going to need you around to raise them. You do not get to lie in a casket next to me. So help me, I will find a way to mangle your soul in eternity if I see your face show up before another six decades are through."

"Hey." Lottie pulls Everett back. "You don't get to talk that way. Not around me, never around Lyla Nell. Nothing is going to happen to you. Got it, buddy?"

Everett's lips flicker. "Got it."

"Let's get out of here," I say, landing an arm over Lottie's back.

Carlotta waves to Miranda. "Next time you get stuck with Little Yippy, give me a holler, would ya?"

Miranda gives a covert nod as I do my best to navigate us the heck out of here.

I lean toward Lot. "We're going to have to supervise your mother's time with the baby from here on out."

"Yup," Lot says without missing a beat.

We make our way out into the balmy evening, and I nod for Everett to hang back a moment.

"You're not getting outfitted for a casket anytime soon," I tell him without anything real to back it up.

"You're a lousy liar, Noah." His cheek flinches. "But a pretty good brother."

We head back to Honey Hollow, and all the way home I wonder who will take that dirt nap first, Everett or me.

And my heart hurts for Lottie and the girls either way.

Something deadly is coming down the pike. I can feel it in my gut.

One of us is about to hit the ground, but which one and by whose hand?

A part of me doesn't want the answers to those questions.

EVERETT

L ast night's jaunt to Leeds left me with a bad taste in my mouth. I don't know what death tastes like, but I'm betting that was it.

It's Friday, and I've just hauled myself through the wringer in my courtroom, trying to control the defense from talking over the prosecuting attorney's objections. Typically, my courtroom is civilized, but on occasion it breaks out into an all-out circus. And as much as I find the circus draining, a part of me knows it's what a handful of those jurors were wanting to see. The public always seems to want an element of a knock-down, drag-out fight. In fact, I wish Evie were here to see it. I'd bet good money she'd sign up for law school on the spot if she could.

"Judge Baxter," a cheery voice calls out as I make my way down the main hall that leads to the exit. Bodies are streaming that way as the courthouse drains of its employees, and I look up to find Betsy Monroe headed this way with her blonde hair pulsing around her face like feathers.

"Oh, Judge Baxter"—she runs up—"I have to tell you I've been having ridiculous cravings for your wife's cookies. And those blueberry muffins? They were to die for." Her lips twitch from side to side. "Sort of a morbid thing to say, considering Clark Willoughby died with one in his mouth." She gives a little shrug. "At least we know he somewhat enjoyed the last thing he ate." She winces. "That wasn't very nice of me either, was it?"

"Don't worry. Once I've stepped down from my seat for the day, I'm no longer in the business of judging people."

A laugh trills from her. "Thanks."

"Betsy, can I ask you something about Judge Gorman?"

Something hasn't sat right with me ever since Quincy Calvin all but accused Dan Gorman of being a dirty judge. I knew Dan. We talked, we had drinks. Not once did he strike me as a dirty dog who'd wheel and deal with the mob.

"Anything." She blinks up at me and I sense an air of innocence about her anticipation of my question. Not the reaction I'd expect if she were washing cash for the guy.

"Betsy, were the rumors true?" There were no rumors, but there was no easy way to slice and dice this theory either. "Was he knee deep with the wrong people? I just thought you were close enough that you might notice."

Her lips part as her forehead wrinkles. "Judge Gorman? I think we both know he was as upstanding as you could get. What kind of people do you think he was mixed up with? His wife Wanda and I still keep in touch now and again. She sends me pictures of them on what she calls their retirement tour. They look so happy. And believe it or not, Judge Gorman is actually smiling in a few of those pictures." She's back to giggling. "Anyway, it sounds like maybe you got him mixed up with someone else."

"I think maybe you're right." If she wasn't washing money for Judge Gorman, what was she doing that got her canned? "Betsy, can I ask you bluntly why Clark fired you from the antique shop?" Her entire body seizes. Her eyes grow wide and she looks as if she were caught red-handed.

Caught doing what exactly? Was she really washing money?

She sighs hard as she looks to the floor. "I don't know what happened. We were in the middle of the Christmas season. Clark still needed me in the shop. But the way he went about it, you'd think I was taking off with some of those pricey watches he kept under lock and key. I wasn't. I would never steal. I work in a courthouse, for goodness' sake. I love the law. And to be truthful, that night at the lake, I was hoping to get an answer. Instead, well, I think we both know what Clark got." She nods to the entry. "I'm sorry, I have to go. I'm late for a dinner date. Will you be at the lake tomorrow? I hear they're having that hot dog eating competition again. I might actually enter this time. But it's the fireworks that bring me back each weekend. I just love that they're shooting them off each Saturday night this month."

"It's something they do." I nod. "I'll be there. And I'll be at that competition right there with you."

"All right, bring it on." She lets out a howl. "Game on, Judge Baxter." She laughs as she strides out the door.

"Essex," a sharp voice calls from behind, and I see Fiona clip-clopping her way in my direction. She looks just as impeccably put together at the end of the day as she did at the beginning. Something I've come to expect from her, considering Fiona is impeccable at just about everything when it comes to her career. "Please tell me you aren't back to your tomcat ways."

"Tomcat?" I shake my head at her. "I thought you knew I was a tiger."

Her voice hikes as she laughs. "Fair enough."

"And no, I'm not interested in any woman other than my wife."

"You're really smitten with this one. If I knew better, I'd be jealous. You really are a catch. If I were ready for a commitment, I might have fought to keep you." She grins as she says it because we both know she's well content on her own.

Fiona has always been a female version of the aforementioned tomcat I was.

"Judge Baxter?" a man calls out and I lift my head to see Luke Lazzari heading this way. Dark suit, henchmen ensconcing him on either side, and a smirk on his face because he knows he has the upper hand.

Fiona leans in. "What the hell is he doing here?" she whispers.

Luke tips his bald head my way. "May I have a word with you? It will only take a second."

"Sure." I lead us a good twenty feet from Fiona and her prowling ears. "What can I help you with?" My lips cinch because I know darn well what he wants—something I can't give him. And I'm also well aware of the consequences he outlined for me a few weeks back. If Manny Moretti walked, and he did when he made bail, I was to find that mad money he had in that briefcase and wash it for him.

"My money." He sheds a greasy grin. "Did you ever manage to get that patina off of it. You know the one, the greedy slime that makes it look dirty?"

"That's because it is dirty. I don't"—I'm about to tell him I don't have it when a thought occurs to me. "Not all of it made it back to me."

"Moretti's man took his take?"

By *Moretti's man*, I assume he means Rooster.

"Yes." I nod. "But the good news is, I managed to get a good chunk back, and I'm plowing my way through it for you." Luke won't know if the clean money I give him is mine or not. I don't know why I didn't think of this before.

"Oh." His head bobs up and down as if he were amused. "I see. And what fine establishment are you using to pencil this out in?"

I hesitate a moment. I'd lie, but I don't have one handy. "The B&B up in Honey Hollow. A few fake guests added up pretty quickly. The books look good."

"Brilliant." His brows dip and I can tell he's got my number. "Now that I know you were able to eat the appetizer, I'm going to give you the whole meal. The one hundred K was the tip of the iceberg. I'll have a lot more coming your way. It's a lot of cash, so you might want to start thinking of where to store it. Maybe buy a safe."

An expletive slips from me. "No."

"Excuse me?" He gives an amused blink.

"I said no. I'm not turning my home into a holding tank for your dirty money. I get it. You want me in your back pocket."

"That's where you're mistaken. I don't want you in my back pocket; I have you in my back pocket. Now I'm going to tell you what your next step is, so you can keep that ticker going and I can make some use of those government-issued bricks I've got lying around from the sales of some very fine weaponry in the event you're wondering. I don't dabble in illegal substances like some people." His shoulders jerk as he mentions his nemesis in not so many words, Jimmy Canelli. "You'll open a shell company, get creative. Maybe you and the missus can go in on this venture together? We'll make the money dance until it finds its way back into my bank account. Just like you're going to make the money you're cleaning through the B&B trickle back home where it belongs. I have a feeling we're going to make great business partners." He winks. "You'll be in the business of protecting my financial interests, and I'll be in the business of protecting you."

I'm about to say something when he holds up a finger and cuts me off at the pass.

"This might be your house, Judge Baxter, but I get the last word no matter whose roof we're under." He takes off and his henchmen take a moment to glower at me before accompanying him outside.

Fiona trots up, looking more than a little miffed, and slaps me hard across the cheek without warning.

"Oww," I say as my hand comes up to comfort the sting. "What the heck was that for?"

Her eyes breathe a fire of their own. "I'd ask what the heck that was for, but I think I know," she says, pointing in the direction Lazzari left in. "I don't know how or why, but you've mixed yourself up with the mob again. As if the Canellis weren't trouble enough for you a few months back." She takes in a quick breath. "Oh, for Pete's sake. Jimmy wanted his own justice when the courts wouldn't allow for it, and he's put a hit out on you for kidnapping his niece." Her eyes move slowly to the ceiling as she takes an exasperated breath. "And then *you*, being motivated by your malfunctioning noggin, thought you'd hire Lazzari to counteract the hit. And what exactly is his payment for protection, Essex?"

My jaw clamps shut.

I always knew Fiona was good, but now I see she's excellent at winnowing out the truth.

"You don't have to tell me," she growls. "We can go the long way. We have time—or at least I do. You might be dead in a day for all I know. You're playing with dynamite, and the fuse is a heck of a lot shorter than you think. This is all going to blow up in your face sooner than later." She shakes her head. "And I'll charge you twice the retainer when you're ready." She stalks off and a dull laugh thumps through my chest.

I'd gladly pay it if it meant I was getting out of this pickle.

Then again, she's right. I could be dead in a day.

But by whose hand? Canelli, Lazzari, Moretti, so many bullets, so little time.

I'm a walking, talking fish in a barrel. Heck, I was safer to be around when I just had Jimmy after me.

And the kicker?

No matter how much I preach it, I have no idea how I'm going to fix this mess.

There is not one outcome I can imagine that would be a good one.

Whatever is about to happen—it's going to be bad, bad, bad.

And it's going to happen to me.

"*E*verett, you came right out and asked why she was fired?"

Noah ticks his head to the side. "There's a reason he's not an investigator. He's not one of us, Lottie. He's an imposter. You should cut and run while Lyla Nell is still young."

I frown his way for even suggesting it. It's Saturday evening and the hot dog competition is set to begin. Carlotta is dancing side to side, jogging in place, and throwing jabs at Mayor Nash as he dabs her down with a towel as if she were a heavyweight fighter looking to score a title belt—and in a way she is.

The sun is getting ready to set and the sky is streaked in

tangerine and pink hues that reflect off the water of Honey Lake. The crowds have shown up tonight en mass, but I'm assuming they're here to witness the fireworks display that will be going off in an hour or so, not so much a handful of people looking to shove a pile of hot dogs down their throats.

Lyla Nell coos in Noah's arms as she points up at the twinkle lights hovering over the stage set out for the sausage spectacle about to take place. To the right, there's a refreshment table laden with platters of my sweet treats for sale with Suze at the helm. She said she didn't mind working in the evenings, seeing that she prefers dark to light. I'm not all that shocked to find out Suze is a creature of the night. To be honest, it explains a lot.

Everett just finished telling Noah and me about his conversation with Betsy yesterday. Last night when he came home, I arranged for us to have a little date night and I forbade either one of us from talking shop. Then we spent all day apart, with him trying to figure out a way to proceed with the building of our dream home and me down at the bakery with the baby.

Lyla Nell is so good while she's at the Cutie Pie, Lily actually accused her of gunning for employee of the month.

Everett's chest broadens as he takes his next breath. "I had to cut to the chase. It was quitting time. I could tell she was ready to sail out the door."

Noah doesn't look impressed. "So what did Betsy Monroe say? Why was she fired?"

"She didn't know. She seemed genuinely baffled and a bit embarrassed by it."

"That doesn't jive with what Bridger told us," I say. "Hey, maybe she didn't realize what she was doing for the dirty judge?"

Everett nods. "I'm thinking the same thing."

Noah rocks back on his heels. "Speaking of the Willoughbys' antique shop, that ATM ring we're tracking has used all four locations of the Willoughbys' shops to siphon a majority of the funds. The bank drops from the shops are loaded with dirty money."

"How are the thieves stealing that money?" Everett asks as if he were suddenly interested in a career change.

"Skimmer card, we think. A blank credit card programmed to circumvent the system."

A chill runs through me just hearing it. "I'm not sure why, but Sammy comes to mind. Noah, did either of the Willoughbys ever have a history of domestic violence? That conversation we had with Betsy at Limelight still doesn't sit well with me."

Lyla Nell slaps Noah on the face and shouts something at him.

He shakes his head and his dimples invert. "I dropped the ball. I'll look into it tonight. I can make a few calls and tap into the database with my phone."

"Hear that, Lemon?" Everett's lips curve for a moment. "Maybe he's not an investigator. *He's* the imposter around here."

I can't help but chuckle, but any joy I might be feeling is cut short as I spot a couple of men in dark suits coming down from the woods across the way with marked determination. One of the two points our way and they pick up their pace, getting lost in the crowd the closer they get.

"I think I see trouble," the words come out lower than a whisper.

"I see them, too," Everett says. "I've been seeing them everywhere. Don't worry, Lemon. I'm confident this will all go away soon. It has to."

Noah cranes his neck in the direction of the woods himself. "Maybe the solution here is getting Luke to give you a briefcase full of illegal drugs. It seems to be far less complicated than money."

"Everything is less complicated than money," I say. "And I'm not laughing, Noah. You're in grave peril, too. I think you should both go to the sheriff's department and file a complaint to have every mob boss in the state arrested. I hate feeling as if our hands are tied. And I can't stand the thought of living in fear every day because I'm afraid I'm going to lose you."

I look right at Everett when I say it, because let's face it, Everett was the one that took a few bullets to the chest in that vision Grandma Nell gave me. And that's exactly why I brought Ethel along tonight. I've got her tucked safely away in a holster that straps to my right thigh, expertly hidden under my sundress. Usually I stay away from Ethel when I know the baby will be with me, but time is running out for Everett, and I'll pump a bullet in Jimmy and Luke myself to save my husband. And I have a feeling that's exactly what I'll have to do.

Noah presses those lawn green eyes to mine. "Lottie, I am the sheriff's department. I'd make this go away if I could without breaking my own neck in the process. If the department knew about half the things I've done, I'd be flipping burgers for a living."

"You can work at the Honey Pot Diner," I tell him. "It would be a much more peaceful life than dealing with Jimmy. Same with you, Judge Baxter."

Everett's cheek flickers. "I'm not opposed to honest hard work. But Jimmy and Luke aren't going away no matter what career change either of us makes. I need a new plan to get us out of this."

Noah grunts, "What's with the savior complex? I'm perfectly capable of coming up with a plan myself."

"Prove it," Everett shoots back.

Before Noah can answer, Evie runs up holding hands with a tall, dark, and handsome college man that sends both Noah and Everett in an instant rage.

"Hold up!" Carlotta calls out. "I'm not missing the show." She dances over with a look of abject glee on her face. "Go on, Evie Stevie, what ya itching to get off your mind?"

"Dad, Mom—" Evie hops a little in her cut-off shorts and bikini top. I can tell Everett isn't thrilled with her accouterments, but it's a stifling summer night in July. It's not exactly fur coat weather. "There's a strawberry festival up near Maple Meadows Lodge next weekend and Bradford, Dash, and a couple other of our friends are heading out there. We may spend the night, but only because there's a concert at ten at night and I know you don't want me driving home at two in the morning down mountain terrain. Can you get us rooms at the lodge?"

The Maple Meadows Lodge is a resort in a ski town not too far from here that Noah, Everett, and I own together. Noah wanted to invest in a solid piece of real estate to pass down to his children one day, and now all these years later we have Lyla Nell to give it to one day.

"No." Everett doesn't miss a beat as he gives a dark look to Bradford. "Aren't you a little too old to be running around with sixteen-year-old girls? Why don't you go pick on someone your own age? My kid is off-limits."

"Your kid?" Evie blinks so hard her long, dark curls spring into action. "You had better be talking about Lyla Nell, Judge Baxter."

Bradford leans in. "Dude, your dad is a judge?"

Bradford is handsome, reminds me of a younger version of Everett, and in all the wrong ways.

"Not now." Evie waves him off without taking her eyes off Everett. "Weren't you the one who told me to break up with my boyfriend last month? Well, I listened to you, Daddy Dearest," she smears those last few words out with an extra helping of sarcasm and Carlotta rubs her hands together with glee. "And now that I'm moving on with my life in a direction you apparently don't approve of, you think you can just manipulate a few pieces on the chess board once again until my life is going in the exact direction you want. I'm surprised you haven't shoved me into the nearest monastery."

Carlotta nods. "I bet he's looked into it, kid."

"Carlotta," I hiss.

"She's right," Evie snips. "I bet he's looking into a lot of ways to mold me into his mini-me."

"Would that be so bad?" Everett's voice hikes a notch as if he were offended by the thought.

Evie scoffs. "You're not even denying it! Fine, I won't go to that concert of a lifetime. I'll stay home and read law books all night. Oh wait, you don't spend your evenings doing that. You chase Mom all around the house trying to get lucky. Maybe I will follow your lead. Come on, Bradford. I think I'll chase you around the lake tonight as I hone my Baxter chops." She takes him by the hand and abruptly leads him off into the crowd.

"Geez," Everett growls in their wake. "Noah, I want your men patrolling the vicinity. If that boy so much as looks at her the wrong way, I want him arrested and in my courtroom come Monday morning. Lemon, I'd find out his favorite dessert because I know who will star in the next The Last Thing They Ate Tour of yours. I'm about to kill him."

"*Everett.*" A tiny laugh gets caught in my throat.

Noah chuckles. "Let him go, Lot. It's about time you see him in his prime."

Carlotta slaps her knee. "Evie isn't even official with her new man and Sexy's got an APB out on him."

"Sorry to break it to you"—Noah pats Everett on the back—"but there's no overbearing dad division down at the sheriff's department."

Everett slices a lethal look to Noah. "We'll see who's the over-bearing father once Lyla Nell wants to date a college man while she's in preschool." He does a double take as he looks past Noah. "Conner," he barks, and Conner Saint, linebacker extraordinaire and Evie's ex-boyfriend, shows up on the scene.

He's tall, built like a brick wall, has dirty blond hair, and an overall boy next-door air to him compared to the barhopper in training Evie has suddenly taken up interest in. Okay, so that might have been a little harsh, but Evie is my daughter, too. Evie actually used to date both Conner and his best friend Kyle about a year ago. It was twisted, and sadly I think I modeled that behavior for her. I suppose it could be worse. She could be dating *two* college men.

"*Conner.*" The muscles in Everett's jaw pop as he says it and about six different women crane their neck in this direction. Everett is maddeningly handsome when he hits this level of distress. "You need to go and find Evie."

"Why? Is something wrong?" He gives a quick glance toward the lake, but there's no real urgency behind it.

"Yes, something's wrong," Everett says. "She's interested in someone else. You need to go and fight for her. Get her back."

Carlotta starts in on one of those choo-choo train laughs that you know is not only going to be raucous, but it's going to last a lifetime.

I'll admit, it's a bit laughable to ask Conner to get Evie back when Everett was the one that convinced her to give freedom a chance just a few weeks back.

Conner shakes his head as he backs away slowly. "I'm not going there. Evie threw us away like yesterday's news."

"You have to go there," Everett barks again. "You need to find her and beg her to take you back. You need to woo her." He whips out his wallet and hands the boy a twenty. "Take the cash and buy her some flowers or whatever you give to girls these days to make them like you."

Noah nudges me with his elbow. "Hear that? He gives you flowers to make you like him."

"Everett doesn't need flowers to do that, and neither does Conner." I give a sharp look to Everett. "Evie likes you just enough on your own."

"No, she doesn't." Conner looks at me from head to foot and back again as if I were nuts. "She dumped me. She made her choice. And I have, too. I've moved on. I'm dating the head cheer-leader now."

"What?" Everett roars as if it were heresy. "What's she got that Evie doesn't?"

"Sane parents," Conner says without missing a beat. "If you don't mind, I've got a hot dog eating competition to get ready for."

Carlotta gasps. "Wait, blondie," she calls after him. "I just saw the head cheerleader taking that lanky kid you used to hang out with into the woods."

"*Again*? Kyle!" Conner shouts as he stalks off. "I'm going to have to kill you this time."

Carlotta swats me. "Quick, find out Kyle's favorite dessert, Lot Lot. Here's hoping it's something with a bit more chocolate in it this time."

We watch as Conner sprints to the other side of the lake and Noah shakes his head.

"Way to go, Carlotta. Eliminating your competition one at a time. Not a bad strategy."

"I'm next," Everett says. "My appetite has up and disappeared. I'm hunting down Evie. I think I'll have a private word with Bradford, too. I'll be back, Lemon." He lands a kiss to my cheek before stalking off into the crowd.

Noah takes a breath. "I'd better go with him before he gets taken in with assault charges."

"Good idea," I say, taking Lyla Nell from him.

Noah takes off just as Charlie comes this way with a pesky Rooster on her heels.

"We got to do something, Carlotta." Charlie's eyes are bulging in the exact way mine are prone to do when I'm angry. Come to think of it, Charlie is basically an angry rendition of me. "You got that gun on you, Lottie?"

"Actually…" I waver on whether or not I should tell the truth just as my mother and Wiley show up.

"Give me that baby." Mom plucks Lyla Nell out of my hand and Lyla Nell cheers as if she's just escaped hard time. "Come to

Glam Glam. Let's walk down to the water and look at the baby fishys." She takes off with her and I'm tempted to join them, but Rooster seems to be having a standoff with everyone left in our midst.

"Wiley Fox." Rooster stabs him in the chest with his finger. "You done did me dirty."

"That's right. He did," Carlotta chirps, and I can see the glee percolating in her eyes twice in one night.

"You did me dirtier," Rooster crows her way before growling over at Charlie as well. "You're all going to pay. I've got connections—men who will do whatever I say."

Charlie steps in close and gets right in his face. "I've got connections myself. In fact, one of my connections happens to own a brood of vipers." She winks over at him and it feels like a threat. "Just try to hurt us. You won't live to regret it because I'll make sure you don't live at all this time."

Carlotta chokes. "That's where you went wrong, Cha Cha. You gotta double the dose. All you managed to do was get him mad."

Rooster backs away slowly, glaring at Carlotta and Charlie.

"I don't get mad, honey. I get even." He takes off and I shake Charlie by the shoulders.

"Are you nuts?" I tell her. "You all but copped to a felony. And by the way, I'm a bit impressed with your intended murder weapon. I've yet to see that, and I've seen more than my fair share of homicidal intentions play out."

"I didn't do it." She shakes herself free of my hold. "Manny did. His snake is pretty impressive and so are his vipers." She flashes a short-lived smile at Carlotta.

Wiley steps in, looking ever so much like a dark-side version of Noah.

"You girls stay out of this before you get me killed," he bellows. "Let the menfolk take care of Rooster. We know what we're doing." He starts to take off and trips over a chair and lands flat on his face.

"Don't listen to him, Mama," Charlie pants. "He can't even keep upright. I'll take care of this myself." She takes off and Carlotta eyes the stage.

"With Rooster walking the dead man's plank, this is panning out to be my lucky day," Carlotta unbuckles her jeans. "Wish me luck, Lot, I'm going in." She takes off for the stage as the competition is set to begin.

A spray of red, white, and blue miniature stars appears next to me and they glow like lanterns as the sun dips behind the evergreens.

Leo appears in all his ghostly Bengal glory and lets out a sharp *rawr* my way. "Come quickly, Lottie. Sammy and Quincy are having a terrible argument." He speeds ahead and I follow that floating cat right over to the shadowed side of the lake where that garage sale spectacular looks as if it's winding down.

"Where did they go?" Leo mewls. "They must have wandered deeper into the forest. Let's go find them."

"No way am I going in there," I say. "It's a maze I've gotten lost in a time or two. Can't you patrol from the sky and figure out their location before I meet up with a bear and become his dinner?"

"Fine," he says, rising into the sky. "They were shouting. This should be easy."

Leo turns into a supernatural speck in the sky in less than three seconds when I spot Betsy and Bridger having a terse conversation. I take a few steps in their direction, pretending to be suddenly interested in the tools laid out on one of the tables marked *half off*, but no sooner do I get within listening range than Bridger stalks off—and he's headed in this direction.

"Hey, Lottie," he pants and I can't help but notice he looks distressed. "Looking for something for one of the men in your life?"

"No, actually, it was for me." I shoot him a wry smile. Women need tools, too. But I know he wasn't trying to come across that way. "I've been needing a good drill," I say, picking up a round flying saucer looking contraption the size of a hardback.

"That's an orbital sander." He chuckles. "If you're looking to refinish your floors, it'll become your best friend."

"I'd do it, but my landlord might become my enemy."

"Is Noah here?" He glances behind me as if he was expecting him.

"Yeah, he's actually somewhere on the grounds. There was a small crisis he had to deal with."

Bridger closes his eyes a moment. "I can relate. I'd better close up shop for the night." He gets busy doing just that and I spot Betsy holding herself as she walks this way.

"Hey, Betsy, nice to see you here," I say, trying to capture her gaze.

She shoots a quick look my way. "I'm sorry, Lottie. I'm in a terrible mood. I think I'll skip out on the fireworks and just go home."

"You can't do that. They're about to go off in less than a half hour. Is everything okay?"

She looks back at Bridger. "You know, all I wanted was some answer as to why I was treated so horribly. And do you know what he told me? That it's not all about me. He even threw in the word *sweetheart*." She shakes her head. "I can't stand it when men placate me that way."

"Don't let him win. You go buy yourself a hot dog, have as many of my desserts you want, on the house, and watch the fireworks show. Bridger might be right. Sometimes it's not all about us—it's about not letting the hotheads firing us without explanation get to us."

A tiny laugh emits from her. "Thanks, Lottie. You made me feel better."

She disappears into the murky darkness as Leo floats down

my way with all the elegance of a feather in the wind.

"Follow me, Lottie. They're still going at it." Leo leads the charge, and soon we're about ten feet into the woods and I can hear angry voices.

"All you care about is controlling other people," Quincy growls. "That's why you got rid of me, and that's exactly why you got rid of Clark." He stomps off and right into me before I can move out of his way.

"Lottie?" He looks thoroughly confused all of a sudden. His fingers tap over his face, and I can see three crimson lines, a fresh scratch. I have a feeling I know who delivered it, too.

"I was taking my cat out for a stroll," I say, pulling Leo in toward me. "Gah!" I cry out as I toss the celestial kitty because for one—he can't see him!

"What's that?" He leans in. "Sorry, the night is getting to me. I need to get a drink. I'd step out of the woods before you get lost." He brushes by me and I see Sammy standing at the edge of the woods, looking out at the lake as the anticipation of the fireworks show only grows among the unruly crowd.

Leo lands on my shoulders and whips his glowing tail over my face. "Did you hear what he said to her? She got rid of my Clark. She pulled the trigger that night, Lottie. I don't know why it's taking so long for someone to arrest her."

"I don't know either," I whisper as my feet take me in that direction.

"Sammy?" I call out and she turns my way with the moonlight shining over her dark tresses, giving them an electric blue tint.

"Lottie?" She looks past me. "Is everything all right?"

Leo snorts. "I bet she's looking for your pistol-packing boyfriend. She knows her days are numbered."

I nod as I agree with him in silence.

"Sammy, I heard you and Quincy arguing."

"Oh that." She lets out an exasperated sigh. "Let me give you a bit of free advice, honey. Don't trust a man any more than you can throw him. A round or two in the bedroom is all you need to satisfy that itch. After that nightmare with Clark, I should have known better than getting involved with someone else. You'd think I'd learn my lesson." She huffs out at the lake as if she were genuinely angry with herself.

Clark and his dead body lying on the sand not too far from here flits through my mind, and a river of words begs to percolate from me.

Leo twitches. "She's done this, Lottie," he purrs in my ear with anger. "Do something or I'll be forced to do something myself."

I don't need his threats to spur me on. I'm long past the point of wanting to put the Willoughby case to rest.

"Sammy"—my voice shakes as I try to control my budding anger—"the night you came upon Clark's body, you asked Everett and me if we had done that to him. You asked us specifically if Clark had owed us money."

She blinks my way. "My goodness, did he?" She looks delighted in the fact.

"No, he didn't owe us anything. But it got me thinking." That story Betsy told me about Clark's bruises is still circling through my mind—that coupled with that scratch I just saw Quincy wearing on his cheek. "You were physically abusive to Clark, weren't you?"

Her features harden as she glares my way. The tension is so thick you can build a ladder to the moon with it.

"As he was to me." She doesn't bother to deny it.

Leo growls her way, "I knew it. She's been harmful to him for years. And the end result was death."

My breathing grows erratic. "The night of the break-in, Clark said he turned off the security cameras to your home." I nod her way because I know I'm right. "There was no break-in, was there? You were going to kill him that night."

"I was going to *divorce* him. I deserved half of everything that man had. He was just too greedy to give it to me."

Leo lets out a yowl, "I think I have to agree with her on this one."

My mouth opens as I look to the long-deceased kitty among us.

"Divorce?" I shift my gaze back to Sammy. "You set up a home invasion instead of retaining a lawyer?"

"Oh, I knew the only way to get rid of him was through a casket. Clark Willoughby was stubborn and cold-hearted. He said since I was his second wife, I didn't deserve any of his assets. Those were my assets, too. Any divorce lawyer would have sided with me. I lost my temper." She closes her eyes. "But I didn't set up the home invasion, Lottie. *He* did."

Both Leo and I gasp at once.

"That's right," she says. "After I asked for the divorce, he turned off the cameras because we were about to make cage fighting look like a playground for toddlers. He came at me with a knife, and I armed myself as well. I carved him up pretty good that night and him me." She shudders as she glances out at the lake. "Clark said he'd pin it all on me, that he had been storing up evidence to prove he was an abused husband for years. He said the only way to avoid jail time was for me to stay at the house and for the two of us to stay married. And we did. But we led separate lives."

"And you couldn't take it anymore so you shot him."

She inches back, looking stunned. "I didn't shoot Clark that night. *That*, my friend, was my lucky break."

Leo yowls once again, "She's lying, isn't she?"

"Then who killed him?" I ask without taking my eyes off hers.

She scoffs as she looks to the sky. "Whoever he was skimming money off of. Let's just say the antique shops have all had a spike in sales these last few months. Each one of those stores has what Clark used to call a 'sucker born every minute piece.' Usually a raunchy painting he marked up to some ridiculous price. Well, they all sold out, and then some. The night he died, I had asked him about those booby prizes he'd been pushing. I still have access to the accounting software at the stores. Bridger never changed the passwords when I stepped away from them."

Leo taps his paw over my shoulders. "It's a wonder he didn't. Everyone knows Sammy can't be trusted."

I nod.

It is a wonder.

"Clark was inflating merchandise and they were selling like hotcakes?" I quirk a brow at Leo. Sounds like he was cleaning dirty money to me.

"That's right." Sammy nods. "And do you know what that sounds like to me? Like he was cleaning dirty money. That's what we argued over just before someone tracked him down and put a bullet in his chest. If you're looking for the killer, I'd look in the direction of whoever bought those pricey objects."

"Do you have access to the records of who could have bought them?"

"No, but Bridger does." A hot breeze whistles by and she wipes the sweat off her forehead with the back of her hand. "Excuse me, Lottie. I need to see about getting something cold and fruity to drink."

She takes off and I look out at the lake just as Bridger steps into my line of vision as he closes up shop for the night.

"Leo," I pant as I take a blind step forward. "I think we've been looking in all the wrong places. I have a feeling the answer has been right in front of us all this time."

Leo lets out a sharp meow, and it echoes off the evergreens and comes back as the roar of a ferocious lion.

I'm feeling a bit ferocious myself at the moment.

"Let's go talk to him," my voice shakes with anger as I whisper.

If I'm right, I'll not only blow Clark's homicide investigation right out of the water, but I just might put a stop to those ATM thefts as well.

LOTTIE

$\mathcal{T}$he lake shimmers and sparkles as if the stars had fallen onto the water.

The crowd is jovial, and a few catcalls go off across the way, along with the sharp drill of a buzzer.

"And now"—a booming voice calls over the crowd—"let me introduce you to the newly official hot dog queen herself, Carlotta Sawyer!" He draws out her name as a smattering of cheers breaks out, but I can't break my gaze from the man in front of me.

Leo purrs as he strikes me over the head with his tail. "Did you hear that? Carlotta won the contest. I believe the rules state she gets a free hot dog every day of the year. I'd be nice to her now that she's struck it rich. She might even share one of those wieners with you."

"I don't want any of Carlotta's wieners," I grunt as I step out of the woods.

"It's probably for the best." Leo sighs. "She almost clawed my eyes out when I tried to take a bite out of one of her spicy pickles."

"Spicy pickles?" My ears hike a notch with sudden interest in Carlotta's dietary habits. For most of my pregnancy with Lyla Nell, I enjoyed more than my fair share of *fried* pickles. I'll admit, a spicy fried pickle sounds good right about now.

"Lottie?" Bridger calls out from the murky darkness before me. "Is that you? Did you say something?"

"Let's go," Leo says, floating on ahead like a luminary in the night and he doesn't have to tell me twice.

A sea of tables lies barren as Bridger works to pack up the leftover inventory into storage bins.

"Yes, it's me," I say as I come within ten feet of him and pause. "Everett took off looking for Evie, our older daughter, and I thought maybe they were out this way, but it looks as if I was wrong."

Bridger's dark curly hair has a halo of moonlight over it as he offers a quick smile my way.

"Well, I wouldn't go too deep into those woods without a flashlight. I'd hate to see you twist an ankle."

"I won't go back." I make my way carefully through the maze of tables until he's just a few feet in front of me. "It looks as if you've buttoned everything up."

"The big Garage Sale at the Lake event is officially no more." He sheds a quick grin and his teeth illuminate as if he had a mouthful of fireflies. "It's our last night and we managed to do better than I thought. But you know, a lot of people came by after Clark's death. Not only was this his baby, but he died just a few feet from here. People came out and brought flowers. It was sort of a memorial. It's been a tough month."

"Not that tough," Leo grunts as he holds up his claws to the moonlight. "But I suspect it'll get tough for good old Bridger here in just a few moments. I plan on taking him back to paradise with me."

I shake my head over at Leo because that's not how this works —although sometimes I wish it would. It might unclog our legal system a bit, and come to think of it, cost my husband his job.

"It's been a tough month, indeed," I say. "Bridger, what kind of a relationship did you have with Clark?"

"We were good friends. The best. Sammy and he had been on the outs for so long, some days I was the only person he talked to. He has grown children, but they're not even on the same coast. I guess you might even say we were best friends."

Leo growls, "I detest liars as much as I do killers, Lottie. Let me at him."

I hold up a finger.

Soon enough, Leo. Soon enough.

"Bridger, that day at the lake when we met, the Fourth—you called Clark your partner in crime and then you winked at him. You were trying to get under his skin, weren't you?"

He hoists a plastic bin onto the table next to him and his brows pinch together as if he were trying to recall.

"I suppose I could have." He shrugs. "We jested like that. It wasn't anything big. In fact, I bet had Clark survived the night, we would have gone out for drinks afterwards." His lips curve into an eerie grin at the thought.

Leo distends his claws and poises them in Bridger's direction. "He'll drink blood before midnight—his own."

I take a breath. "Last week, when we had dinner at Mangias, you looked stymied when Noah suggested that there were two homicides at the lake the night Clark died. You said you found that hard to believe. You thought Rooster died of natural causes.

That's because you knew exactly what happened to Clark, isn't it?"

"Excuse me?" He pauses from picking up another bin.

"I had mentioned that maybe it was the work of a serial killer and you jumped all over that theory because you knew it could not only help cover your tracks—it could bury them. But you doubled down on covering your tracks that night. You told Noah he should investigate Betsy Monroe—you whet his appetite just enough, letting him know that Clark fired her after she begged him not to call the sheriff's department."

"That was true. Did he ever speak to Betsy?" His eyes narrow over mine and he takes a moment to ride his gaze down my body.

"He's gauging you," Leo mewls. "He thinks you'll be easy to knock over, or knock over the head. Perhaps I should handle the rest of *thissss*," he hisses out that last word like the threat it is.

"Yeah, Noah and I both spoke to Betsy, and she had nothing but nice things to say about you. She called you a software genius. She said you were fluent in three different coding languages. You utilized your know-how, didn't you? That's how you made that blank ATM card—the skimmer?" I don't know why I didn't put this together earlier when Noah mentioned the blank card.

The whites of Bridger's eyes expand. He knows his time as a thief has come to a close, and I'm about to ensure his time as a killer on the run has come to a close as well.

"That was the card you inadvertently gave me the other day when you were buying my blueberry muffins. You knew how to code it to get those ATM machines to spit out however much money you needed. You are proficient, after all, in three different coding languages—at least according to what you told Betsy. And then you took the money you stole and washed it all around town, but primarily through Clark's antique stores. That's where you cooked books to make Clark's accountant believe you were selling some of the merchandise at ridiculous markups. A painting here, a vase there—and then what? How did you land the money back into your own account? My guess is you not only stole from the banks, you stole from Clark, too. It was easy enough. You were the manager." A thought comes to me. "Clark caught on, didn't he? And you lied. You made up a story about a dirty judge, and you got Betsy fired for something you were doing. And when Clark caught you red-handed, well, you knew your jig was up because there was no one left to blame."

An amused look crosses his face. "What about Sammy? I'm pretty certain she's a viable suspect when it comes to stealing from Clark."

"You should know, you set her up expertly. You didn't change the password on the accounting software at the shops because you knew, that way, Sammy would still be able to poke around. And each time she did, it would create a cyber fingerprint as she logged in and out of the software. You timed your thievery of the shops to coordinate with her visits. And with that, there would be just one more person to blame should things go south for you. Is that why you killed Clark?"

Bridger purses his lips, his eyes never leaving mine.

"Yes," he says as his breathing picks up. "You figured it all out. I guess you're not just another pretty face." A dark rumble of a laugh infiltrates his chest. "Everett was lucky to have you. But just like I couldn't let Clark live to tell the tale, I'm afraid I can't let you live to tell it either."

He picks something long and dark out of the bin in front of him and swings it at me with great force and I duck just in time to evade, taking a hit to the temple.

"Fireplace poker," Leo says as he pounces over at him.

Bridger lets out a howl of a cry as Leo does his best to slash at the man's face, and achieves the bloody feat, too.

"You witch!" Bridger howls as he lunges right at me and knocks me to the ground.

"Lemon?" Everett's voice booms from the woods.

"I'm down he—"

Bridger lands his hand over my mouth before I can finish shouting for help.

I bite down hard, causing him to move an inch and let out a shrill scream before he clamps back over me.

"Be quiet!" he growls. "I'm going to have to drown you, Lottie. It'll look like an accident. And while you're dying, I want you to think about the fact you did this. You put this pain on Everett's heart, not me."

Leo appears standing on Bridger's back. "Don't worry, Lottie. Those slashes over his face are just the beginning of the affection I'm going to show him."

My hand glides down my thigh before I inch up my dress. And then slowly, blissfully, my hands curl around my good friend, Ethel.

"Are you ready, Lottie?" he pants as he strengthens his grip over me. "Are you ready to meet your maker?"

I give a quick nod and feel his hand loosening just enough, so I do the only thing I can—I clamp down over it with my teeth once again.

Bridger pulls back his hand just enough for me to kick him in the cookies.

"Good shot," Leo muses.

Bridger lets out an awful groan as he doubles over his crotch and I use the opportunity to shove my foot in his chest. I send him flying back before pulling Ethel out of her holster—and just as I'm about to lift her up, he swipes that fire poker off the ground and raises it over his head.

A hand comes up from behind him, snatches the poker away, and the two of them break into a fistfight.

I recognize that dark head of hair, those flaming blue eyes.

"*Everett!*" I shout as they crash over a table. "Get away from him. I have Ethel!" The gun shakes in my hands as I say it, but the two of them just keep going at it.

"I'm sorry, Lemon," Everett grits the words out as he throws another punch. "This is personal." He grabs Bridger by the shirt and pulls him in. "Nobody hurts my wife," he thunders.

Leo zips before me and a trail of tiny silver stars glimmers all around him.

"It's happening, isn't it?"

I give a mournful nod his way. "I'm afraid your time has come —again."

His striped and spotted fur begins to dissipate.

"Goodbye, Lottie. Do lick Lyla Nell over the cheek for me. If I'm going out, I'm going out in style." He bullets over to where the bar brawl is still taking place and lets out a sharp roar before giving Bridger's face one final slash. And then just like that, Leo disappears in a plume of silver stars.

"Magnificent," I whisper as those miniature stars trail all the way through the night sky and straight up to paradise where they belong.

Noah runs this way, knocking down tables as he hops over them.

"*Freeze*," he shouts, pulling out his weapon, but Everett continues to get a few good right hooks in.

"Do something, Noah," I say, wagging my gun in their direction.

Noah puts his weapon away. "I'm calling it in." He fires off a text before putting away his phone. "Keep Ethel trained in their direction. Try not to shoot me. Shooting Everett is optional."

"Very funny," I growl. "Get in there."

Noah jumps into the fray, knocks Bridger to the ground, and in five hot seconds, Bridger is cuffed with his hands tight behind his back.

Noah helps Bridger up while Everett staggers my way.

"Lemon." He pulls me in hard, and I can feel his heart hammering hard over my chest. "Did he hurt you?" He pulls back and examines me as he struggles to catch his breath.

"I'm sorry," Bridger calls out with striations of blood across his face.

"Sorry you were caught?" Everett says as he holds me close.

"That too." Bridger closes his eyes a moment.

"He did it." I nod to Noah. "He confessed to killing Clark. And Noah? That ATM thief you're after? You've already got him. Bridger did it. He programmed a skimmer card and stole the money. He washed it all around town and through Clark Willoughby's shops, just like you said."

Everett groans, "You were a good guy, Bridger. What the heck made you steal?"

Bridger winces as if it pained him to say. "I could, so I did." He sighs hard. "I did it once to see if I could pull it off, and after that, it was addictive. The high I got doing a heist was just as powerful as holding all that money. One thing led to the next, and before I knew it, I was firing a gun in Clark's direction. He didn't deserve it. I fell so fast, so far, I had lost all hold on reality."

Red and blue flashing lights speed this way, no siren.

"That's my ride." Bridger shakes his head. "I'm sorry," he says one more time as Noah leads him toward the patrol car.

An explosion of light goes off overhead and Everett holds me tight as we watch the sky ignite in a red, white, and blue spectacle.

"Come on." Everett gives me a kiss to the nose. "Let's find Lyla Nell and enjoy the show with her."

We do just that, and soon Noah joins us, too.

Lyla Nell squeals and screams with delight as the firework display lights up all of Honey Hollow as if it were noon. Noah bought a pair of cute little pink earmuffs, noise reduction headphones, that are safe for Lyla Nell to wear around loud noises. And because of that, we've decided to let her stay and watch the fiery spectacle with the rest of us.

But I don't keep my eyes on the sky. I keep them on my baby

girl. It turns out, the show is that much better if I watch it through my daughter's eyes.

I want to see her smiling like this forever, and I know that Everett wants to see it, too.

That's exactly why I need to be vigilant. Time is running out, and like Nell said, by my own actions I have the power to stop this.

"Well done, Detective," Ivy says as we finish up with a meeting of the ATM task force for the last time right here in my office.

The task force is comprised of five men and three women, myself included, and we've just enjoyed a box of crullers from the Cutie Pie Bakery and Cakery that I picked up on the way over, still piping hot.

"Thank you," I say. "But like I mentioned, it was Lottie who put it together."

"What can we say?" An exasperated sigh comes from Ivy as she shakes her head at the thought. "Lottie sure seems to be generous to you in every capacity."

The door to my office flies open and in jump not one but two Sawyer women, each whipping open their very own tan trench coat, exposing us to far too much flesh, and not a stitch of clothing to go with it.

An expletive flies from my lips as the two of them stand there with a mild look of surprise before closing up shop.

"Like I said," Ivy muses. "She is generous in every capacity."

"Meeting's over," I shout and motion for my coworkers to bolt to the four corners of the earth.

Ivy takes a breath as she passes by Carlotta and Charlie. "Nice work last night, Lottie."

About a thousand words choke their way up my throat, and not one of them makes it out alive.

Carlotta shuts the door and the two of them fall into the seats in front of my desk.

"Good going," I say to Charlie, and it comes out rough. "They thought you were Lottie."

She shrugs. "I'll let *you* think I'm Lottie all you want." She claws at the air and winks my way.

Carlotta tips her head. "I'd take her up on the offer if I were you, Foxy. Just close your eyes, they're one and the same more or less. Who knows when Lot will come to her senses and give you the golden ticket back to her bedroom? And this way you could give Little Yippy a sibling to pick on her once in a while. Lord knows someone's got to set her straight." She turns to Charlie. "Just drop the rugrat off at Lot's place in a basket and play ding dong ditch. She'll raise it as her own. Miranda Lemon injected just the right amount of her gullibility into Lot."

Charlie dips her chin my way. "What do you say, Detective? Is it baby making day?"

"It's a hard no," I tell her and she proceeds to flip me the bird before snagging a donut out of the box.

I slide a pile of napkins their way. "Now what did you come

here for? Are you trying to get me fired? Because you're off to a good start."

"I'll cut to the chase, Foxy." Carlotta leans my way. "We need one hundred big ones to get rid of Rooster. Sexy and Jimmy already shut me down."

"We talked about this the other day at Red Satin," I remind her. "There's no guarantee that Rooster is leaving town even if you give him one hundred G's. If I can give you one word of advice, it's don't negotiate with terrorists. You'll only live to regret it."

My phone rings and I look down at my desk to see the initials JC staring back at me.

"That's Jimmy Canelli, isn't it?" Charlie nods.

Carlotta gasps. "Well, don't just sit there, Foxy. He's probably trying to get in touch with me to give me my money. I knew Jimmy would come through."

Charlie frowns over at her mother. "Now why would he call Noah to get in touch with you?"

"It's his way of letting Foxy know he's watching him like a hawk. Jimmy Canelli is always one step ahead of the game."

I pick up and put it on speaker just in case he decides to say something that should be relayed to Lottie in the event I meet my demise.

"Noah here." I twitch my brows at Charlie and Carlotta as I wait for a response.

"It's Jimmy." He takes an audible breath. "I hope you're doing well this fine day. I saw you made another arrest last night. Well done, Detective. Now that your schedule has freed up a bit, I'd like for you to find a way to make Moretti Jr. disappear. Just a heads-up. His boys are planning something big, and according to my sources, it's coming down the pike next month. I'm hearing rumblings, and I don't like it. His men are making threats.

They're getting personal. If anything happens to me, I've arranged for something to happen to you. How do you like that, Detective? We're sort of tied at the eternal hip. See you around or see you in paradise. I guess it's your choice."

The line goes dead and Carlotta slams her hand over the table.

"Way to go, Foxy." She glowers my way. "You had a line to the big guy and you hogged it all for yourself. All you had to do was say you'll get your way if Spider gets hers."

Spider is a nickname given to Carlotta by one of her good friends who also happens to be a Canelli.

I nod her way. "I'll try to be more considerate the next time I speak to him." I lean back in my chair and try to absorb this new threat Jimmy just leveled me with.

Charlie narrows her eyes over mine. "Manny Moretti is trouble. He's lethal, Noah."

"Not lethal enough," Carlotta grunts. "He couldn't even finish off our troubles."

"Are you talking about Rooster?" I sit up, suddenly interested in the turn of events.

"That's right." Charlie's lips knot up. "I think I'll go pay good ol' Manny a visit and let him know exactly how I feel about the fact he can't do anything right." She cinches her purse to her shoulder and disappears faster than I can open my mouth to stop her.

"Charlie, wait," I call after her, but she's halfway to that hotel Manny is holing up in. "She's going to make things worse."

"She always does." Carlotta shakes her head. "But there's no getting rid of her either. She takes poison about as well as Rooster."

I'm not even touching that one.

I lean my head against my chair and close my eyes.

Jimmy and I are tied at the eternal hip.

I'll admit, I did not see that one coming.

207

Let's hope Manny and his men don't see what I have coming for them either.

Now just what could that be...

EVERETT

*T*wo sessions at the bench wrapped up in record time, so I cut out early for the day, just an hour before quitting time, but even that feels like a vacation at this point. I sent Lemon a text, and she let me know she was still at the bakery, so that's exactly where I've landed myself.

I step inside, and the scent of fresh baked blueberry muffins hits me in the very best way.

Lily gives a friendly wave from the register as she helps out the customers, just as my beautiful wife makes a beeline for me and I land a kiss to her lips before she can close the distance between us.

My heart thumps just being near her.

I've never had a woman affect me in this manner before.

I knew Lemon was special the day we bumped into one another, physically speaking, just outside of the courthouse the day we met. She stirred things up in me immediately, and I couldn't for the life of me put my finger on why. I was flooded with thoughts of her instantly. I couldn't see straight until I tracked her down again, and that's when I found out Noah was already doing his best to lay claim to her. I wanted what was best for Lemon even then. And if that was Noah, then so be it. But I couldn't leave her. I had zero intention of stepping out of her life.

She had me wrapped around her little finger. She caged me in so efficiently, I didn't even realize what had happened.

"Everett." Lemon has a huge grin on her face as she wraps her arms around my body, and if I didn't know better, I'd think I just heard her sigh with relief. "Thank goodness, you're okay."

I pull back, puzzled. "Why wouldn't I be?"

"Oh"—she gets flustered for a moment—"you know, traffic at this time can be a real killer." She shudders in my arms as she says that last word. "I'm just glad to see you. How about I get you something sweet to eat?" She winks my way while quickly landing a plate of fudge brownies and a cup of coffee in front of me.

Lyla Nell screams and cheers my way as Evie holds her by the counter. And sitting right next to them is Carlotta.

"There are my girls." I head over and land a kiss to Evie and Lyla Nell.

"What about me, Sexy?" Carlotta quips. "Am I chopped liver?"

I pull up Carlotta's hand and kiss the back of it.

"*Woo wee!*" Carlotta belts it out as if she were riding a bull at the rodeo. "No wonder Lot Lot spends so much time holed up with you in the bedroom. Even your innocent hen pecks are hotter than a grease fire. I can only imagine the inferno you bring underneath the sheets. It's no wonder you have a history of setting houses aflame."

"Like *eww?*" Evie looks physically ill at the thought. "Unless we change the subject in three seconds flat, those muffins I just inhaled are going to land right back on the counter in a different form."

Lemon cringes a moment. "Fine, but you asked for it. What's going on with the concert?"

I nod to my look-alike in teenage girl skin. "Your mom and I can go up with you. We'll stay at the lodge while you're at the concert, and that way if your friends want to spend the night at the lodge, too, I'll feel better about the whole thing."

Her mouth falls open as if I just threatened to enroll myself at Honey Hollow High.

"Cray Cray"—she growls out the nickname she has for Carlotta—"hold me down before I hurt someone."

Carlotta chuckles. "Don't worry, Evie Stevie. I had fuddy-duddy parents in my young days, too. They may have secured the gate, but I knew how to scale a wall. You'll figure it out. When there's a concert, there's a way."

Evie gives a sly nod to Carlotta.

Lemon shakes her head at me as if I shouldn't have gone there, and Lyla Nell jumps in my arms and slaps her hands over my face while laughing hysterically as if she were trying to teach me a lesson, too.

"*Dada! Dada!*" she cries out as her forest green eyes look right at mine and her dimples dig in deep.

My heart melts and I can't help but curve my lips at her. I love this little girl—both of my girls more than I knew was possible, and with far more ferocity than I knew I was capable of. It's the exact way I feel about their mother.

"You tell him, Lyla Nell," Evie says.

"Okay." I sigh. "We still have a few days to decide."

"It's this Sunday, Dad," Evie says. "All my friends are going. I *have* to go. It's not my fault Bradford and all his friends will be there, too. This is the concert of the century. Everybody is going to be there. You don't want me to hold this over your head forever, do you?"

"Everett," Lemon says my name softly as she bites down on her lip, and I can tell she feels bad for Evie.

Heck, I do, too.

"Don't worry, Evie. It'll all work out," I tell her.

But nothing had better not work out in Bradford's favor or I might be forced to commit another felony. And this time, I won't have Noah to blame.

Speaking of the useless scapegoat, the bell on the door rings and in walks Noah himself.

We offer up a collective greeting and he scoops Lyla Nell right out of my arms.

"How's it going?" Noah says as he lands at the counter next to me, and Lemon lands a plate of chocolate chip cookies and coffee in front of him with lightning agility.

"*Dada, Dada*," Lyla snips as if she were laying the brunt of her day on him and a warm laugh breaks out.

"No fair." Lemon wrinkles her nose. "She calls the two of you Dada, and it's like she doesn't even know who I am. I'm nothing but the scullery maid to her."

Evie laughs. "You're the *milk* maid, Mom."

Carlotta nods. "She's right. Lyla Nell hardly recognizes your face, Lot. And that's because all you ever let her see is your boob. I bet she calls your boobs Mama all the time."

"Stop." Lemon plops another blueberry muffin in front of Carlotta in an effort to silence her. "And it's not true. Lyla Nell recognizes me, all right. She's already called Charlie Mama a handful of times." Her expression sours just thinking about it.

"Well, there ya go." Carlotta toasts to Lemon with her muffin. "Calling Cha Cha Mama is just as good as saying it to you, considering the fact she's walking around wearing your face."

Evie nods. "She's right. Last week, I had a heartfelt chat and spilled all of my deep, dark secrets to Charlie, and the whole time I thought I was talking to you."

"*Evie.*" Lemon presses a hand to her chest. "Oh, I feel terrible. I'll tell you what, when we get home, I'll whip us up a fresh batch of those snickerdoodle cookies you love so much. We'll hang out in the kitchen and have that heartfelt talk, and you can even spill all of your deep, dark secrets to the *real* me."

"Nah. There's no point," Evie says, breaking apart the cinnamon roll on her plate. "I feel a lot lighter now that I've got everything off my chest. I really had a good time with her. Speaking of good times"—she wags her phone at us—"if you'll excuse me, I need to text Bradford about a certain driving session after dark."

"It's not happening," I call out after her, but Evie is already in zombie mode as she taps into her phone at the other end of the bakery.

"Great," Lemon says as she visibly deflates. "Both Evie and Lyla Nell have no problem swapping me out with Charlie. Where is my wily sister, anyway?"

"I can take a stab at it," Noah says with a sigh. He glances to Carlotta before looking to Lemon and me. "Carlotta and Charlie dropped by my office today."

Carlotta tosses up her hands. "Who knew you were such a tattletale, Foxy?"

"I did," I say under my breath.

Carlotta huffs, "I wish you'd given me a clue, Sexy. Foxy is an alligator traitor with a heart of barbed wire."

Lemon shakes her head. "That hardly makes sense."

"Oh yeah?" Carlotta grumbles. "Did it make sense when Cha Cha and I stormed his office and shed every stitch of clothing just to put him in a good mood? The man didn't even bat a lash. Foxy didn't get happy. He got angry."

Noah straightens. "I got angry because I had seven other

people in the room with me to witness the event. Ivy thought Charlie was Lottie. And despite the fact, I only have eyes for one woman." He smiles over at Lemon. "That's you."

Lyla Nell jumps into his arms and shouts something up at him that sounds like a reprimand.

Carlotta shakes her head. "Hear that, Lot? Little Yippy wants all the manly attention for herself. Looks as if you spit out a carbon copy of yourself, haven't you?"

Lemon shakes her head. "We're not changing the subject. Noah? What the heck went down in your office this afternoon?"

Noah tells us all about his adventure with Carlotta and Charlie, about the fact they were fishing for funds because they mistakenly believe money has the power to slingshot Rooster back to Higgins Bottom.

I doubt it would slingshot him across the street. The man is the embodiment of a lie.

"But before they left"—Noah blows out a breath, and Lyla Nell tips her head up at him as if she, too, were waiting for him to continue—"I got a call from Jimmy Canelli."

My blood runs cold at the thought.

That shell company Luke Lazzari wants me to open for him comes to mind.

A part of me is afraid I'm going to do it. That somehow I've sunk deep enough to where I feel my only option is to help a mobster convert the heaps of dirty money he's obtained through the sales of weaponry in order to keep pumping air into my lungs.

I'm terrified to hear what Canelli has to say. Sure, his dealings are with Noah. But for as much as I can't explain it, I feel the need to protect Noah, too.

His chest expands. "He said Moretti and his men were planning something big next month, and that if anything happens to him, he's arranged for it to happen to me." He looks in my direction. "I wouldn't have said that last part in front of Lottie, but Carlotta heard the whole thing."

"Gee, thanks, Noah," Lemon growls over at him.

"I'm sorry, Lot." Noah reaches over and takes up her hand. "But I never want you to have to worry about me."

She closes her eyes a moment. "And now I'm worried sick." She shakes her head. "Does this have something to do with you knowing where Charlie is right now?"

Noah nods. "I don't know about right now, but when I let her and Carlotta know that I couldn't help with the cash to get rid of Rooster, Charlie got in a rage. She said she was going to find Manny Moretti and give him a piece of her mind for not offing Rooster the right way the first time."

Crap.

Manny is lovesick over Charlie. She was the sole reason he chose to lash out at me. The only reason Manny Moretti has landed a target over my back is because I couldn't land him a date with his new obsession.

My phone buzzes and I can feel the air getting sucked out of my lungs when I look at it.

It's the devil himself. Manny.

I'm here in the alley. We need to have a word. Come alone or regret it. I've got a message for you, big guy.

I sink my phone into my pocket but not before Noah laid eyes over it.

"I'll be right back." I give Noah a stern look that serves as a warning not to say a thing to Lemon. "I need to get something out of my car." I rise to my feet. "Lemon, do you mind if cut through the bakery?"

"Not at all," she says as I make my way around the counter. She hikes up on her tiptoes and lands a heated kiss to my lips. "But you're sure taking the long way, considering you parked out front." Her left brow hikes because she knows she's got me.

I tick my head to the side. "I should know better than trying to pull something past the best detective in all of Vermont. I'll only be a minute." I give her another far deeper kiss before making my way through the kitchen and stepping out the back door of the bakery.

The air is heavy and humid as a scorching breeze blows through the alley, causing the leaves in the tree across the way to rustle like a death rattle. I take a few steps into the alleyway and give a quick look around.

"Manny?" I call out just as I'm knocked to the ground from behind, face-first and what feels like a dozen fists pummeling me at once.

I'm flipped and turned, my head bashed into the asphalt, as I take blow after blow to my gut and my face. Before I can properly defend myself, two men take off running, and the sound of a car peeling away screams through the air.

"Everett," Noah bellows as my head hits the ground one last time. His gun is drawn and I see Lemon on his heels.

"*Everett*," she screams as she lands by my side and shakes me by the shirt, but I can feel the world going gray and I can't seem to fight it.

A splash of cold water lands over me, and I open my eyes with a start as I try my best to sit up.

"Works every time," Carlotta snorts.

I give a few groggy blinks as Lemon lands a careful kiss to my lips.

"Oh thank goodness, you're going to live." She sighs with relief.

Noah shakes his head at me because he knows as well as I do my days are numbered.

Manny sent his men to jump me as a warning.

But if I had to place a bet, I'd say Lazzari is going to finish me off.

LOTTIE

*E*verett's ego was more bruised than his body. But as soon as we got home, I made sure to kiss all of his boo-boos, and there were many. Noah and I begged Everett to head to the hospital and get checked out. Heaven forbid there was any internal bleeding, but he flat-out refused. Everett can be as stubborn as he is gorgeous. But he can also be as generous as he is gorgeous. After I kissed all of his boo-boos, he kissed me in all the same places, then added a few dozen other locations, too. He sure didn't let a few bumps and bruises stop us from setting the night ablaze.

A few days have drifted by, and we've landed ourselves at Honey Lake for one last firework spectacular of the season. It's Saturday evening, and it seems all of Honey Hollow has shown up to witness the sky light up in a fiery show of splendor.

I brush my finger gently over the bruise under Everett's left eye, and Lyla Nell reaches up as if she wants to do the same.

"It's looking so much better," I say to him.

"Don't listen to her," Noah says as he goes for another slice of pizza. "You look like crap."

I make a face at him as all of our friends and family load up their plates as they partake in the virtual buffet we've brought along.

Everett shakes his head at his old stepbrother. "All right, I got jumped in an alley. What's your excuse?"

Carlotta hacks out a laugh. "He's got you there, Foxy."

"I think you look as sly as a fox." Charlie winks over at him. "I hear that every fox has his tricks. I've got a few tricks of my own. How about we do a little show and tell tonight? After the fireworks, we can go back to your place and light up the rest of the night."

"Charlie," I hiss and Lyla Nell does her best to mimic the sound.

"What?" Charlie says, scooping a heap of orange chicken onto her plate. "I'm having a conversation with Noah. It's not my fault you decided to eavesdrop." She grazes her lower lip with her teeth as she looks at him. "I'm not afraid to ask for what I want in the bedroom."

"Charlie." Noah shakes his head her way. "But thank you for thinking of me."

She lets out an exasperated sigh. "At least Lyla Nell loves me."

"Mama!" Lyla Nell laughs as she looks to Charlie and an echo of laughter circles around me.

Mom bops over with her creamy vanilla locks bouncing like springs. "Isn't that the cutest thing, Lottie?"

"Adorable," I growl as I look at Charlie. "Hey, can I ask you a question?" I pull my mother aside for a moment as Lainey and her husband, along with Meg and Mayor Nash, move in to help themselves to the buffet. "You and Wiley aren't partaking in any more of those role-playing games, are you? Noah told me about the money laundering scheme."

She waves me off. "We finished those last week." Her lips twist as she looks to Lyla Nell. "Give me that little angel." She quickly scoops her out of my arms. "You wouldn't happen to need a babysitter anytime soon, would you?"

"Actually, I do. Everett and I are driving Evie to the Maples Meadow Lodge tomorrow for a concert. But we'll be home very late." Evie didn't want to spend the night with her friends with her parents in the next room.

"The later the better!" Her eyes widen at the prospect. "Wiley?" She waves to him as he talks to Noah and his brother Alex across the way. "It's a go!" She gives him a thumbs-up. "We've got our little good luck charm tomorrow night! And they won't be back until late." She trots off with the baby in their direction just as Everett pops up next to me.

"Hey." I shake my head at the woman who just scampered off with our daughter. "I think she might be up to no good," I tell him.

"I heard the whole thing," he says. "We'll have to write up a no casino clause for the next time she babysits."

"But that won't change the fact I'll have to worry the entire time we're up at the lodge."

"No, you won't," Evie says as she pops in front of us. Her hair is up in a ponytail, and she has a tank top and cut-off shorts to complete her summertime look. "We're not going to the concert."

"What happened?" Everett says in haste. "Do I have to break his legs?"

"Would you?" Evie hitches a brow as she leans in. "Kidding. Sort of."

Everett wasn't kidding, but I don't dare say it.

"Evie, did Bradford do something to hurt you?" I ask with an air of caution. If she says yes, Everett might be moved to give Bradford a set of matching bruised eyes—and the aforementioned broken legs.

"Yes, he did," Evie says it emphatically, and Everett's chest triples in size. "He went and got a girlfriend."

"A girlfriend?" Everett breathes a sigh of relief. "Not one of your classmates, I'm assuming."

"Nope. They go to the same college. I guess I was never really in the running. It turns out, he really *was* trying to teach me to drive." She glowers out at the crowd peppering the shoreline. "Anyway. Your weekend just freed up. I'm going to find Dash and hang out with her. I'll track you down when the fireworks start. I want to see the look on Lyla Nell's face as she's watching them."

She takes off, and I wrap my arms around Everett.

"And just like that, the book closes on Bradford." I bite down on a smile as I look up at Everett.

His cheek flinches. "The book might have closed on Bradford, but I predict Evie is on the prowl to start a new story with someone else."

"Let's hope that's one prediction that doesn't come true for a long, long time."

I press my lips together as I gaze at my lethally handsome hubby. I'm hoping that prediction of Nell's doesn't come true at all.

Come to think of it, more than enough time has gone by. The month is practically over.

Hey? I bet I've circumvented the atrocity just the way Nell suggested.

No sooner did she show me a vision of Everett taking a bullet for Noah than she told me that I had the power to stop this by my own actions.

"I must have stopped it," I whisper as I glance out at the lake.

"What's that?" Everett dips down and captures my gaze again.

"Oh, nothing." I breathe out a sigh of relief of my own as I hike up on my tiptoes and land a steamy kiss to his lips. "There's more where that came from, Judge Baxter."

"You know what I'm going to say next." His lips twitch with the hint of a wicked smile.

I nod. "That's a binding agreement."

"And I'm going to hold you to it, too."

A laugh bubbles from me. "We should probably take Carlotta's advice and move a fire extinguisher into the bedroom. If things get any hotter, we're liable to set our third house on fire."

He gives a long blink. "It might be our only house for a while. The butterfly seems to be settling in pretty well."

I make a face. "I think I'm going to spend the rest of the summer trying to figure out how to rehome a butterfly."

"You won't have to," Bear says as he and Keelie step up beside us. He tips his head to my blonde bestie.

"That's right, Lottie Lemon. I have a gift for you." Keelie blows a kiss my way, then one to Everett as well. "It's a gift for you, too, Judge Baxter." She gives his cheek a playful pinch. "My mom is in charge of the local horticulture group, and just yesterday she and her plant-loving cohorts went on a nature walk and found an entire army of Honey Hollow Blue Butterflies just over the ridge near Trickle Stream."

"What?" I shout so loud half the town turns my way for a moment.

Everett nods to Keelie. "An entire army? As in the butterfly is no longer endangered?"

"That's right," Bear says. "I'll start up on the house again Monday morning. I should be done with it later this fall."

I let out a hearty whoop. "Thank you both!" I pull them in for a group hug. "Best news ever. This entire month is turning around." I smile up at Everett. It looks as if every last curse, every bad vision has taken a turn for the better.

I can feel Ethel warming against my thigh. I won't need to be lugging her around, wherever I go, for much longer.

I've been sleeping with one eye open—not that I get much sleep to begin with—and glancing over my shoulder ever since the Morettis jumped Everett. I'm sort of rooting for the Lazzaris and the Canellis to give the Morettis the boot out of Vermont, and out of my husband's life for good.

"We'd better load up before it's gone. I'm starved." Keelie pats her belly while looking at the table laden with food from Mangias and Wicked Wok. "Your mom snatched little Bear right out of my arms as soon as we got here. She even offered to babysit for free whenever we wanted."

"Do not trust her with your child," I tell her, but both Keelie and Bear laugh it off and claim they want in on the action as they zip off toward the food.

"Hear that, Lemon?" Everett warms me with his body. "The blue butterfly is no longer an obstacle in our path. I was beginning to feel as if I were jinxed."

"You are anything but. In fact, it feels as if the universe is righting itself. I bet any minute now we'll find out that those hits have been called off for good."

"Now that would be a miracle."

Noah comes over, and that serious look on his face has the power to wipe the smile right off my face, and it does.

"What is it?" I ask as my breathing picks up pace.

Honestly, unless it's more good news, I don't want to hear it.

Noah glances to the lake. "Jimmy Canelli just sent me a message. He wanted to give me a heads-up. He said his men saw a couple of Moretti's boys casing the lake. I'm going to go check it out."

"No," I tell him. "Manny had some nerve jumping Everett just because my sister won't give him the time of day. I don't want a single thing happening to the two of you."

"It won't," Everett says with a look on his face that could eviscerate every one of Manny's boys. "I can identify them. I got a few good looks while they were razzing me over. We'll be right back, Lemon."

They take off before I can protest.

"Lot Lot!" Carlotta waddles this way with Rooster on her heels. "Great news!" She grabs Charlie and pulls her in. "You might want to hear this, too, Cha Cha. Go ahead." She swats Rooster on the stomach.

He's donned a tan felt cowboy hat, his requisite brown suit, and that greasy grin he's known for emboldens him.

"Well, if it isn't my favorite kittens." He winks my way as he says it. "Carlotta is right. I've got me some great news."

A moan works its way up my throat. "Carlotta, please tell me you didn't pony up a hundred G to try to get rid of this goofball."

"You can bet your bottom dollar I did." She nods. "Or better yet, Manny Moretti's bottom dollar."

My body seizes just hearing his name. "What about Manny Moretti?"

"Yeah," Charlie grouses. "What about Manny?"

Rooster gurgles out a dark laugh. "Now, now, honey." He takes a step closer to Charlie. "Don't go getting testy on me. You know how much I love it when you get feisty." He bites the air between them, but Charlie doesn't flinch.

Carlotta grips me by the arm. "I had a brainstorm, Lot. I thought—who could I shake down next to help me get rid of this scumball, and KABOOM!" she shouts so loud half the people around us let out a whoop as they look at the sky, positive that the fireworks show has started early.

"Kaboom?" I narrow my eyes over hers. "What exactly is about to blow up in our faces?"

She waves me off. "I just bumped into Manny Moretti, and I

told him I'd get Cha Cha to go out with him again—for a month straight if he gave me the big ones to make Rooster disappear."

"That's right." Rooster cocks his head to the side. "And I'm taking the money and running. All you gotta do, Charlie, is put on a snazzy little dress and let the gentleman show you a good time."

Carlotta nods. "There may have been something or other in there about a penthouse suite and a whole new lingerie wardrobe, but what girl couldn't use a little more variety in her naughty stitches collection?"

Charlie takes in a huge breath. The look of fury in her eyes is one I've never seen before—not even in mine.

"*Carlotta*," I hiss. "There's no deal. How dare you treat my little sister like some high-priced call girl."

Charlie holds a hand up my way. "Where's Manny, Mama?"

Rooster chuckles. "That's my girl. She's looking to negotiate. I say let's not get greedy. I'll cut both you and your mama in on the deal. You'll each get a cool one thousand dollars for the trouble."

Both Charlie and Carlotta choke on the offer—as they should.

Carlotta should choke on the fact she started this pricey party to begin with.

Charlie lifts her chin. "I get fifty K. Mama gets five hundred."

"Five hundred?" Carlotta snorts. "In your dreams, Miss Hoity Toity. I think you've been hanging around your sister a little too long."

"Never mind you," Charlie tells her. "I've gotta find Manny." She bolts for the lake with both Rooster and Carlotta shouting for her to slow down.

"Manny is here?" I look out at the crowd as the sun dips behind the evergreens and the scenery looks murkier by the moment. "Oh no...Everett." I don't take but a few steps toward the lake before spotting a couple of men in dark suits heading into the woods. "Oh Lord, help Everett," I pant the words out as I speed that way after them. "*Everett*," I call out, but a loud boom goes off just as an explosion of light ignites overhead. Every last person at the lake howls and screams with approval.

Evie runs up with her bestie Dash. "Where's the baby?" she asks, hopping with glee.

"Glam Glam has her," I tell her. "Evie, the diaper bag is under the table. Put the earphones on Lyla Nell. I'll be back."

I bolt into the woods without thinking twice as one loud boom after the next goes off.

A loud pop comes from the forest, and I head that way without hesitation. I pull Ethel out from her sheath and hold her in front of me with both hands, my heart beating wildly inside of me with atomic force. Another round of horrific booms emits in front of me, and I see a spark of light to go with it. The woods swallow any light from the moon above, and it's hard to see the trees in front of me. A couple of men in dark suits move up ahead. Their white dress shirts glowing in the dismal light act as homing beacons.

"There they are," I whisper as I inch in that direction.

Voices murmur—men's voices—as I strain to listen.

"Fire on sight," one of them says. "We've got ten minutes, tops."

Ten minutes?

Another loud boom goes off overhead as a spray of red and blue sparkles fills the night sky.

They're timing the hit to the fireworks show. I have to find Noah and Everett. I reach for my phone and come up empty. I must have left it in the diaper bag.

My hands close around Ethel once again, finger on the trigger.

There's only one thing left for me to do. I have to incapacitate those men before they hurt Noah or Everett. A shot to the knee wouldn't be lethal, but it's dark, and let's face it, I'm not that good. I'm going to have to do my best to stop them both, no matter what the cost may be.

My feet move quickly in their direction, and I see their white dress shirts threading through the woods as they head in this direction.

This is it.

Kill or let Everett be killed.

Ethel shakes in my hand as my finger squeezes the trigger and the intrusive blast of a gun firing fills the air.

The sound of men shouting comes from up ahead. They're still there, so I fire again, and again, and again.

"Freeze," a familiar, deep voice booms, and the next thing I know, I'm staring down the barrel of a gun with Noah at the helm. "*Lottie?*" he barks my name out as he runs my way with a wild look on his face. He lets an expletive fly before pulling me with him as he trades his gun for his phone and begins shouting into it. "We've got a man down just north of the lake, about ten paces up from the picnic tables and into the woods. Run in until you find us."

"*Noah,*" I pant. "I shot them. It was me. I heard them threatening to kill you, to kill—"

Noah drops to the ground, and then I see him.

"*No,*" I expel the word in less than a whisper.

Everett lies motionless with his eyes open as he looks to the sky, his shirt soaked with crimson liquid.

I drop to my knees next to him and let out an unearthly cry.

I did this. I brought on this nightmare. I am fully culpable.

I had the power to stop it, and I didn't.

I caused it.

"*Everett,*" I call out as my body falls over his.

Oh, Everett. It was me who was a danger to you all along.

Noah says something, but my mind can't process it.

A smattering of dark stars rises from the nexus of the melee, and my mouth falls open.

"No." I shake my head as I attempt to charge that way, and Noah holds me back. "No, no, no."

Those dark stars swirl into the shape of a navy tornado as they illuminate the night, and sure enough, the ghost of Essex Everett Baxter appears fully formed.

"He's here," I pant. "His ghost. I can see him."

Everett offers a mournful smile my way. "*Lemon*."

RECIPE

From the kitchen of the Cutie Pie Bakery and Cakery
Lottie's Blueberry Muffins

Hello there! It's summer in Honey Hollow and we're celebrating the birth of our great nation. Mayor Nash requested that I bake some blueberry muffins for the event and he even requested that I frost them! Of course frosting is always optional when it comes to sweet treats. I'll leave that entirely up to you. Hope you enjoy these delicious goodies as much as I do. Have fun baking!

Ingredients

1 ½ cups all-purpose flour
    ¾ cups granulated sugar
    ½ teaspoon salt
    2 teaspoons baking powder
    1/3 cups vegetable oil
    1 egg
    1/3 cup milk
    1 ½ cups fresh blueberries

1/3 cups granulated sugar
1/3 cups all-purpose flour
¼ cup butter (cut into cubes)
2 teaspoons ground cinnamon

Directions

Preheat oven to 400°

Prepare muffin tins by buttering them up or popping in cupcake liners.

In a large bowl mix 1 ½ cups all-purpose flour, ¾ cups sugar, and baking powder. Stir in vegetable oil, egg, and milk. Add blueberries and fold into the mixture. Fill muffin tins all the way to the top.

Crumble Topping:

Combine 1/3 cups sugar, 1/3 cup all-purpose flour, cubed butter, and cinnamon. Mash with fork, and sprinkle over muffins before putting them into the oven.

Bake for 20-25 minutes until toothpick comes out dry.

*You may frost, dust with powdered sugar, or eat them plain! They are scrumptious any way you serve them.

Enjoy!

BOOKS BY ADDISON MOORE & BELLAMY BLOOM

Paranormal Women's Fiction

Hot Flash Homicides

Midlife in Glimmerspell

Cozy Mysteries

Meow for Murder

An Awful Cat-titude

A Dreadful Meow-ment

A Claw-some Affair

A Haunted Hallow-whiskers

A Candy Cane Cat-astrophe

A Purr-fect Storm

A Fur-miliar Fatality

Country Cottage Mysteries

Kittyzen's Arrest

Dog Days of Murder

Santa Claws Calamity

Bow Wow Big House

Murder Bites

Felines and Fatalities

A Killer Tail

Cat Scratch Cleaver

Just Buried

Butchered After Bark

A Frightening Fangs-giving

A Christmas to Dismember

Sealed with a Hiss

A Winter Tail of Woe

Lock, Stock, and Feral

Itching for Justice

Raining Cats and Killers

Death Takes a Holiday

Country Cottage Boxed Set 1

Country Cottage Boxed Set 2

Country Cottage Boxed Set 3

Murder in the Mix Mysteries

Cutie Pies and Deadly Lies

Bobbing for Bodies

Pumpkin Spice Sacrifice

Gingerbread & Deadly Dread

Seven-Layer Slayer

Red Velvet Vengeance

Bloodbaths and Banana Cake

New York Cheesecake Chaos

Lethal Lemon Bars

Macaron Massacre

Wedding Cake Carnage

Donut Disaster

Toxic Apple Turnovers

Killer Cupcakes

Pumpkin Pie Parting

Shameless Kisses

The Social Experiment
The Social Experiment
Bitter Exes
Chemical Attraction

3:AM Kisses, Hollow Brook
Feisty Kisses
Ex-Boyfriend Kisses
Secret Kisses

Naughty By Nature

Escape to Breakers Beach
Breakers Beach
Breakers Cove
Breakers Beach Nights

Escape to Lake Loveless
Beautiful Oblivion
Beautiful Illusions
Beautiful Elixir
Beautiful Deception

A Good Year for Heartbreak

Someone to Love
Someone to Love
Someone Like You
Someone For Me

Throne of Fire

All Hail the King

Roar of the Lion

COMING UP NEXT

Thank you for reading! I hope you enjoyed Lottie's latest adventure!

Up next: The summer heat continues in Honey Hollow but not everyone lives to tell about it. Grab Honey Buns Homicide today!

See you in Honey Hollow!

ACKNOWLEDGMENTS

Big thanks to YOU the reader! I hope you had a wonderful time. I can't thank you enough for spending time in Honey Hollow with me. I hope you enjoyed this bumpy ride with Lottie and all of her Honey Hollow peeps as much as I did. The MURDER IN THE MIX mysteries are super special to me, and I hope they are to you as well. If you'd like to be in the know on upcoming releases, please be sure to follow me at **Bookbub** and **Amazon**, and sign up for my **newsletter.**

I am SUPER excited to share the next book with you! So much happens and so much changes. Thank you from the bottom of my heart for taking this wild roller coaster ride with me. I really do love you!

A very big thank you to Kaila Eileen Turingan-Ramos, and Jodie Tarleton for being awesome.

A special thank you to my sweet betas, Lisa Markson, Ashley Marie Daniels, Amy Barber, Stacie Bucholtz, and Margaret Lapointe for looking after the book with their amazing beautiful eyes. And a shout out to Lou Harper for designing the world's most beautiful cover.

A mighty BIG thank you to Paige Maroney Smith for being so amazing.

And last, but never least, thank you to Him who sits on the throne. Worthy is the Lamb! Glory and honor and power are yours. I owe you everything, Jesus.

ABOUT THE AUTHOR

Addison Moore is a *New York Times, USA Today,* and *Wall Street Journal* bestselling author who writes contemporary and paranormal romance. Her work has been featured in *Cosmopolitan* Magazine. Previously she worked as a therapist on a locked psychiatric unit for nearly a decade. She resides on the West Coast with her husband, four wonderful children, and two dogs where she eats too much chocolate and stays up way too late. When she's not writing, she's reading. Addison's Celestra Series has been optioned for film by **20th Century Fox.**

For up to the minute pre-order and new release alerts
*Be sure to **subscribe to Addison's mailing list** for sneak peeks and updates on all upcoming releases!
Or click over to the WEBSITE
AddisonMoore.com
✦Follow Addison here for the latest updates!

✦Follow Addison on **Bookbub!**
✦Like on **Facebook**

*Want to chat about the books? Hop over to Addison's Reader Corner on Facebook!

Feel free to visit her on **Instagram.**

Made in the USA
Las Vegas, NV
08 December 2022

61542175R00146